AMBUSH

ON THE STREETS OF THE PACIFIC NORTHWEST

EMERGENCE BOOK II

LISA PARSONS

CONFLUENCE ADVENTURES LLC

**In memory of
April Dehuff**

PROLOGUE

"PULL UP RIGHT THERE," Kelly said.

Brian pulled the medic unit up behind the fire truck at the entrance to Highline Community College. They grabbed their medical kits and followed Kevin, one of the firefighters.

"Hey, Kevin. What do we have?" Kelly asked.

"Just our local homeless guy who says he has chest pain. It looks like he got off the bus and found his way inside. With this rain, he's probably looking for a warm place to sit out the weather."

"It's that time of year again," Brian said.

"Did the lieutenant call an ambulance?"

Kevin nodded. "Already have one on the way."

They walked past the cafeteria and in between some campus classrooms. Kelly strained from carrying their heavy kit and the ECG machine.

"How far back is he?" Kelly asked.

"Toward the middle of the campus. I guess we should have warned you it would be a hike."

Kelly leaned her head towards the radio mic clipped to her

jacket and depressed the button. "Dispatch, have the ambulance crew bring their stretcher to the scene."

"Copy," the dispatcher replied.

After navigating a maze of buildings, they found themselves at a double glass doorway. The entrance had a plaque with "Environmental Climate Science" written on it. The building looked brand new.

They entered a large foyer surrounded on three sides with floor-to-ceiling glass windows, revealing each floor. Kelly could see people in offices and classrooms.

She turned her attention to a sitting area across from the door and saw one of their regulars, Bob. Bob was sitting in a chair, bundled up in an oversized tattered wool jacket with a dingy red down vest opened to reveal his chest. The firefighters had him on a heart monitor and oxygen.

"How are you, Bob? I'm Kelly, the paramedic who saw you a few weeks ago."

"My chest hurts. Here." He put his hand to the middle of his chest.

The firefighter started to give his short report. "Sixty-year-old male complaining of chest pain. Vitals BP 200/120, pulse 120. RR 16..."

Kelly noticed Bob was sweating profusely and fidgeting with a hole in his wool pants. His dull blue eyes darted from his black canvas backpack to the doorway, and then he looked up at Kelly.

Something seemed different. His clothes were dirty, but he'd recently showered. His usual long greasy strands of gray hair had been cut short, and his face looked like he'd shaved the day before. Kelly noted that the backpack appeared new too.

"Bob, we haven't seen you for a while. What have you been up to?" Kelly asked.

"I've been around. Stayin' with friends."

"How did you find yourself here?" she asked, curious why he would be deep in the college campus. Usually, he was at the bus stop at the entrance to campus or at the local 7-11 up on Pac Highway.

He leaned forward with his head tilted slightly downward. His cloudy blue eyes looking up at her from the side. "I was just walking when this chest pain started, so I came here. It's real bad."

"Are you taking your blood pressure medicines?"

Kelly looked back at Bob's backpack sitting on the table next to him. "Can you check to see if his meds are in his pack?" Kelly asked the firefighter.

Bob blurted, "Can we just go!" His raspy voice had an edge of fear as he tore at the patches on his chest. "I feel like I'm going to throw up."

He vomited a large undigested meal onto the ECG machine at his feet. Looking up at Kelly, vomit dribbling down his chin, he said, "I'm sorry."

The last thing that Kelly saw was Bob reaching up to wipe away the vomit from his chin. From his backpack came a powerful explosion, disintegrating the building and everyone in it. As the yellow and red flame erupted outward, the intensity turned the pouring rain to steam before it hit the rubble and body parts left in its wake. The attack could be felt miles away.

CHAPTER ONE

NICK AND MAYA sat on the back gate of her SUV. Maya leaned her head on Nick's strong shoulders, grateful for his presence. She couldn't imagine being alone in that moment. Nick was not only her fiancé and best friend; he was her anchor against the harsh winds blasting her from all directions.

Kali, Maya's Belgian Malinois, sat on the ground before her, looking directly up at her, watching to make sure her person was okay. Maya could tell she was worried about her. Kali always seemed to know every nuance of Maya's mood.

As the sun set, Maya leaned her head on Nick's shoulder and dug her hands into the soft fur of her other dog, a white German shepherd, Rio.

"I still can't believe they're gone."

Maya was still reeling from everything that had happened in Tahoe when she received the phone call from Jeff. She was devastated; Kelly and Brian had only been on the job a few years.

Maya cried all afternoon. Emotional exhaustion finally

overwhelmed her as they drove to the top of Winnemucca Peak in Nevada to camp.

The next morning, they made their way home to Seattle, trying to stick to their original plan to take their time and see some of the sights. Along the way, they tried to enjoy the drive, but Maya hadn't slept well. Every irritation seemed like knife edges cutting across her mind. When an oncoming car drifted slightly towards the center line of the highway she shouted, "Look out!" afraid the car would crash into them. When they stopped at a gas station, a loud bang from a truck backfiring caused her heart to pound as her vision narrowed. She was under fire again. She tried to push down the panic, but it coursed through her body.

Just past Sun Valley, they hiked through tawny meadows and green aspen groves, past flocks of sheep guarded by big white Great Pyrenees, whose warning barks told them to stay away from their flock. Rio and Kali quietly dropped in next to her and Nick. The dogs knew they were no match for these fierce protectors. Maya preferred the predators that attacked sheep to those awaiting her at home.

As they drove over the pass between Ketchum and Stanley, the rugged peaks were like mighty fortresses against time. Here her time felt so fleeting and temporary compared to the stone that had been there for millions of years.

Kelly and Brian were just doing their job when the bomb went off. A bomb that killed everyone in that building at Highline Community College. Why there? It was a question she kept asking herself.

That evening she broke down again. "Nick, we need to go straight home. I need to be there for my coworkers."

He looked at her with his deep brown eyes that said, *I've got your back.*

She didn't mention the panic attacks and hopelessness she

was feeling. She'd been ready to work on her mental health, but now she just wanted to put it all behind her. Processing her feelings about the murdered police officer and the attempts on her life in Tahoe would have to wait. She just needed to get back to work. There would be time later. If she could just hold it together.

The following morning, they drove directly home. Maya looked out the window and planned how to get back on shift.

The first step started with a call to her chief.

"Chief, hi, this is Maya."

"Maya, hello. How are you doing?" asked Chief Anderson with an edge of concern in his voice.

"I'm okay. I'm calling to follow up with you about coming back to work."

"Maya, I'm not so sure. You've had a lot of stressors, and now you've got the loss of Kelly and Brian to contend with. Why don't you take more time?"

"Chief, I can't sit on the sidelines with something like this going on. Just let me come back. If I feel it's too much, I'll let you know. I promise."

"Here's what I want you to do. Make an appointment with our psychologist. If she thinks you're ready to return to work, I'll consider it."

Maya wondered if she could convince their psychologist that she was okay. She'd been able to handle everything before the ambush. If she could convince everyone else...and herself she was ready, she could return to the medic unit.

"You really aren't considering going back to work when we return, are you?" Nick asked.

"Like I said, I need to be there for my coworkers."

"Maya, you were nearly murdered when the police officer was executed. That call drove you to take time off from work to recover but you didn't get that. Tahoe was worse. We just left

Tahoe where Don tried to strangle you and now you want to jump right back into a volatile work situation. Think about it. Is that a good idea?"

Maya looked away from Nick, out the passenger window, tears threatening to spill from her eyes. "Look, I know you're concerned, but my mind's made up. You don't understand. You don't work in our profession. We rush in when others rush out. It's our job!"

Our profession—did she just say that? Would Nick, like her previous boyfriends, start to feel he'd never be able to compete with Maya's coworkers, whose bonds were forged by the knowledge that their lives depended on each other?

CHAPTER TWO

MAYA SAT in the waiting room, thinking about her next steps. She had to convince the psychologist that she was okay to return to work.

The door opened, and Dr. Julie Harrington waved her in. "Maya, it's good to see you again."

Maya knew Dr. Harrington. She had given presentations on mental health resilience for first responders at their monthly continuing education meetings. Maya had heard that Dr. Harrington understood the challenges that first responders faced.

As Maya sat down, she suddenly felt extremely nervous and exposed. She leaned back against the chair, trying to give the impression this was a social visit and not an interview to establish whether she was fit for duty.

After taking in some details, Dr. Harrington sat quietly for a minute. She seemed to read through Maya's calm exterior.

"So, my understanding is you want to go back to work, and I'm your gatekeeper."

That caught Maya off guard. "Well, yes. I need to get your

sign-off to return to office duty. I, I really want to help because of everything that's going on. As you know, we are down two paramedics."

"I get that. But first, let's talk about what has happened. Chief Anderson gave me some background on what you've been through, but I want to hear it from you."

Maya gave a brief, detached recollection of the events, starting with the police officer shooting, the events in Tahoe, the ambush of Kelly and Brian, and ending with the upcoming funeral. "I know it's a lot, but I feel I'm processing it well. I've discussed it with Nick, my fiancé, and some of my coworkers. I know I've been through a lot, but I'm tough. It's part of the job."

"Maya, I know you're tough, but no one is invincible. How many of your coworkers could have gone through what you've been through and still be okay? Wouldn't you tell them to take it easy and get some help?"

She paused, looking down at her feet. "It's just that I can't sit on the sidelines. I want to be back at work. I *need* to be there to support my coworkers. For me, helping is therapy."

"Yes, paramedics are great at taking care of others but not good at taking care of themselves. If you don't take care of your-self, you won't be as focused and able to take care of others. I want you to think about what you would want for your coworkers if they were in the same position."

Maya knew she was basically asking her to admit she needed help. Maya cut to the chase.

"Look, I get it. If you release me to light duty, I'll agree to come in every week and dig deep to work through everything that has happened. Just give me a chance."

Dr. Harrington looked at her. Her eyes softened. "Maya, while I don't agree with this, what I hear you saying is that if I allow you to go back to light duty, maybe you'd be willing to open up a little?"

"Yes, absolutely!" Maya replied.

"Okay, I'll release you back to light duty, but I want you to come in two times a week to start with. Then we'll see how things are going and figure out the next steps."

Dr. Harrington knew them well. She knew that if she stuck to a strict plan and enforcement, her strong-willed medics would just shut her out and refuse to cooperate. Maya felt relieved. Little steps. As soon as her sprained arm healed, she'd push to get back on the trucks.

Maya started back to work as if nothing had happened. She set up a desk in the office and met with Chief Anderson to set out a plan for her to work on implementing the details of their new domestic terrorism directive. She attended meetings with Homeland Security (HS) trainers and their regional training consortium. As she reviewed the plans, she drew on her personal experience when she and her coworkers were ambushed during the police officer's execution.

Maya also helped integrate the training that would launch the following month. Training that would raise their situational awareness and give them tactics for staging and retreating if necessary. She organized their new, more protective, bullet-proof vests. They added ballistic helmets that they could comfortably wear on every call. She inventoried the antidotes for chemical weapons intervention. Her goal was to ensure that she and her coworkers were covered while working on the streets.

CHAPTER THREE

THE FUNERAL DETAILS were taken care of by management in coordination with different agencies. It was essential to honor the fallen paramedics and firefighters and show solidarity. Maya had participated in the process to ensure that the funeral itself wasn't targeted by the people who had lured them into the police officer's execution and the bombing at the college.

Maya looked out at the hundreds of firefighters, paramedics, police, and others who stood at attention as the Puget Sound Pipes and Drums entered the stadium. A single bagpipe echoed throughout a sea of black Class A uniforms. They turned in solidarity to watch the procession. The entire band of pipes and drums joined the lone bagpipe and filled the stadium with a haunting chorus.

She'd never had to attend a funeral for one of her coworkers. Now she stood in her starched Class As with her family of paramedics, mourning the loss of her two paramedic coworkers and three firefighters.

The air was heavy with grief...and anger.

Maya was seated at a table with her coworkers. Half-empty pitchers of beer sat on the table. She looked around. Others were here, the Class As traded in for street clothes. The local bar served as an unofficial meeting place for paramedics, police, and firefighters who had attended the funeral.

"Did you hear they shut down I-5 yesterday for eight hours because someone called 911, threatening to detonate a bomb on the freeway during rush hour?"

Daniel's grip on his beer mug was the only tell that he was on edge. He was the most laid back of Maya's coworkers. She liked Daniel. His demeanor was always calm, even during total chaos in some of their most challenging situations.

"Turned out it was just some dirtbag capitalizing on the fear. I think things will get worse before they get better," Jeff said. His jaw clenched as his eyes hardened around the edges.

"This is crazy!" Daniel exclaimed, the edge in his voice a sudden departure from his previous detached explanation of the I-5 call. He took a drink.

He faced more stress on the job than most. He was the first African American hired by their agency. He always wore a smile at work and never let on that some of the comments from a few of his coworkers bothered him. She wondered how he felt when the right-wing militia executed the Black man walking down Pacific Highway. She'd touch base with him.

Randy looked down at three shots of Tequila sitting before him. His rough meaty hands grabbing each shot glass as he drank one after the other. Straight, no lemon or salt. "I can tell you: I'm bringing my gun to work. I don't want to be caught without protection."

"How's that going to stop a bomb?" piped in Emily.

"It won't," Maya said.

"But it will help if I'm caught in the same situation as Maya," replied Randy.

"Our job is to save lives, not return fire," Emily replied. "Besides, that's what the police are for. We need to focus on treating the patient and getting them to the hospital. Maya and Jeff were trying to save that police officer's life when they were shot at."

"He died," Randy doubled down on his position. "Just saying. I want to protect myself and not end up like him."

Maya sat quietly with a glass of soda. She was trying not to drink her grief away. She'd spent too much time on that already.

Randy Croften, his solution was always to lock and load. Why was it always about taking up arms? One side, insanely armed, and he wanted to bring a handgun to the fight?

Most of the old-timers she worked with were old-school white men. Great men who made you simultaneously love them and hate them. From what she could tell, the attacks were orchestrated by a right-wing militia composed primarily of white men with many grievances. The kind of grievances that made it harder for women and minorities to be accepted in their line of work. Were any of her coworkers sympathizers? What side would they be on if there was a civil war? Would all her coworkers be on the same side? The thoughts were unsettling.

Which side was Randy on? Here they were caught in an emerging civil war because men wanted to get richer selling weapons and, as an incentive, war. But Randy knew that. Technically, he was an international arms dealer selling the weapons. *But ahh, shucks,* he'd say. *I'm just trying to make a few extra bucks on the side.*

He'd signed up for the Navy Seals after 911. Then when that stint ended, he used his connections to sell the weapons of war. It was lucrative. She had no idea why he became a paramedic. Penance or a twisted sense of irony. She didn't know.

She was always curious whether he was for real or playing a role. He seemed grounded until he went off on Antifa. At times she loved their quick back-and-forth banter of opposing ideas, but other times...he scared her.

"Maya, what do you think?" Emily said, looking for an ally.

"I think we're in for a wild ride."

With that, Maya waved over the bartender and ordered three shots of Tequila and a beer. *Fuck sobriety*, she rationalized. *This could be my last day on Earth.*

Chief Anderson walked over to their table and sat down across from Maya. "How are you guys doing?"

"Just fucking great," Randy thundered.

Maya noted that Randy was already smashed.

"Chief, I really miss Kelly and Brian," Emily said. "We're all a little worried. It's been quiet the past two weeks, but who knows, right? They have yet to catch any of the men who did this. They don't even know who this 'White Dawn Militia' group is."

"Is that why they delayed the funeral. For our safety?" Maya asked.

Maya watched as the chief paused before answering, then carefully chose his words. Probably because he knew what he said to his paramedics would affect how they perceived his ability to keep them safe. *Will he be able to keep us safe?* she wondered.

"Yes, that was one reason the funeral was delayed. Kelly and Brian will be missed. I rack my brain every day to figure out how we could have avoided their deaths. I think we all thought their attacks would be bolder, like the shooting of the police officer to draw us in. We had a plan for that. No one anticipated that one of our regular homeless guys would be carrying a backpack with a bomb. Now, we know it could be any call.

"Homeland Security is working on a group profile to see if there is a connection between them and a larger, more organized coalition. They are also trying to get a profile on what, who, and how they target specific incidents and then draw us in. We seem to be a target, but why? Why the college's Environmental Climate Science building?"

Randy chimed in, "What if it isn't this 'White Dawn Militia.' You know, it could be Antifa. They could have taken the homeless guy in, fed him a meal, and then got him to agree to carry the bomb."

"You think a homeless guy would blow himself up for a free meal? A bottle of Jack Daniels, maybe," Jeff joked.

"Maybe they threatened him to get him to do it? They really should be looking at Antifa as players in this."

"Randy, geez, you need to stop watching so much Faux News," Emily admonished him.

Emily. Sweet Em. At 5"3', she was small but fierce...and sweet. She had no problem standing up to the guys when they pounded their chests. She could challenge the best of them and then disarm them with her smile.

"Mark my words. You know they're tearing this country apart," Randy shot back, his voice starting to slur as he downed another beer.

"Okay, you guys," the chief interjected. "Homeland Security has got this. We'll have a directive shortly for how to conduct our responses. In the meantime, as you know, we are sending in a standby SWAT security detail on any call to large institutions or any call that seems questionable until we have a more strategic plan."

"Good," Maya said. "I know I said I was going to take time off, but we've lost two paramedics." She let that hang.

"Maya, you don't need to come back. We've already covered your shifts."

"I can't sit on the sidelines anymore while everyone else is risking their lives. I want...I need to come back."

"Let's talk about this in a couple of days. Right now, let's mourn and remember Kelly and Brian."

The chief guided the conversation. Maya knew it was vital for them to process that Kelly and Brian were gone but not forgotten.

"Remember during driver's training, when Brian put the medic unit on two wheels out at Pacific Raceways?" Jeff said.

"Oh my god, yes. Brian had just finished paramedic training. He was so amped up on adrenaline. We thought for sure he was going to lay that medic unit on its side as he took that corner coming into the straightaway..." Daniel said, and everyone laughed.

Maya, still laughing, added, "And Kelly. You could hear her feet hit the floor when the alarm bells went off. She was always first to get to the medic unit. I asked her how she was able to get out of bed so fast. She told me she slept in her clothes. She didn't want the senior medics to think she was a slacker."

"Man, I gotta take a leak, then I'm outta here." Randy laughed as he got up and staggered toward the bathroom.

"Looks like Randy's had a bit too much to drink. I hope he isn't driving," Daniel commented.

The mood turned somber again as they watched him leave.

Maya thought of Kelly. Why Kelly? Kelly just had her first baby. She was full of enthusiasm for her new job as a paramedic and her new role as a mother. Maya had looked forward to being an adopted aunt, filling in for Kelly's sister, who lived on the East Coast. Now all that had changed. Everything had changed in such a short time. Suddenly, the loss struck Maya to her core. She looked around at her coworkers. They no longer seemed so invincible.

Maya awoke the following day, her head throbbing with an

epic hangover. She stared up as morning came into focus. She looked over to see Nick's side of the bed empty. He was already up.

She tried to recall yesterday. As the evening progressed, she remembered talking about making sure they weren't victims again. They had to ensure that no one else would die. Later, Maya, Daniel, and Jeff split off to quietly talk with each other and hatched a plan to proactively look for their attackers.

After a certain point, all she remembered was calling an Uber to get home. She'd gotten so hammered. *Why did I drink again?* She replaced her remorse with a determination to get up and get back to work. She needed to be there for her coworkers. She couldn't cave now. Everyone needed to show up. Do the job. Be there for each other!

She jumped out of bed and let a shower shake out the effects of too much alcohol and grief. She pushed down that deep abyss that threatened to swallow her every time she let her guard down. Her resolution was action. If they wanted a fight, they'd get one.

As she put the coffee on, she called Nick.

"Are you just getting up?" Nick commented with a hard edge to his voice.

"Umm, no, I just got out of the shower. Yesterday was hard. We went out together afterward and I, we drank too much. I'm still feeling the effects."

"You were barely coherent when you came in last night. I thought you weren't going to drink anymore?"

"I didn't plan on drinking. I just, well, it's tough right now with Kelly and Brian's murder and everything that is going on at work. It's going to take some time." Maya tried to downplay her lapse in abstaining from alcohol. She could hear an edge in his voice that worried her.

"And getting drunk is going to help that?"

"No, I messed up. It won't happen again. I promise. Can you just hear me out. I want to talk to you about something. It's about the group claiming responsibility for the attack, the White Dawn Militia."

"Yes?"

"Well, Jeff, Daniel, and I discussed fighting back and not becoming victims again. The organization has changed our approach to emergency responses. We thought that one way we could stop them is to track down their online presence. That's where I thought you might be able to help."

"What did you have in mind?"

"Well, we talked about Reddit, 8Kun, Discord, and other online forums where these people might hang out. Jeff and Daniel said they'd be willing to sign on to some of the forums under aliases and see if any talk might reveal individuals behind the attacks. Other than that, do you have some ideas?"

"Possibly. Let me think about it, and we'll talk tonight. On another note, about the drinking, have you thought any more about the treatment program you checked out, the IAFF Center for Excellence? Maybe you should take some more time to take care of yourself."

"Let's talk about that tonight."

"Okay." There was a tense pause, then Nick let out a long sigh and said with some concern in his voice. "I'll be home around seven. We can talk then."

CHAPTER FOUR

———————

WITH THE FUNERAL BEHIND THEM, their work continued. As part of her duties working in the office, Maya was responsible for organizing the new training sessions. She laid out the notebooks containing the new procedures for responding to calls as part of the new domestic terrorism directive. She knew what had happened to her and what followed would forever change how they looked at and responded to calls. Gone were the days when they arrived on the scene for a "routine" chest pain. Now they looked at every call with suspicion and...apprehension. The only way to alleviate those feelings was to change the rules and regain as much control and safety as possible. She knew that first responders were aggressive and would do everything they could to ensure they were safe while taking care of the public. They didn't have the option of not responding, so they had to change their approach.

Em and Jake arrived first, having just finished their shift at one of their busiest stations. Em handed a mocha to Maya. "I thought you might need this to start the day."

"Em, I'm already wired, but I never pass up a Starbucks' mocha. Thanks."

"So, what's the plan?" Jake asked.

"You'll find out. It's not a huge overhaul, but there are some significant changes. Alden and Homeland Security instructors will present the new directives and training. Go ahead and grab your new flack vest and helmet from the tables over there. Your name will be attached to them."

Maya had set them out earlier. Just looking at them took her back to the event that had set the tone for this training.

"I'll feel a little safer with the new gear," Em commented.

"As safe as you can be under fire," Jake added.

"It's better than nothing," Maya said. "The training and new directives will hopefully lower our risk and the need for them."

Jake was such a rookie, but a really smart one. He'd discovered paramedicine via a fire science degree. When he saw what the medics did daily, he decided he'd rather be on the frontlines instead of in the fire investigators' office. She loved working with and mentoring him. If she could just get over the fact that he looked like, well, a twelve-year-old kid.

First responders started trickling in. The familiar faces of Randy, Daniel, Jeff, and Lou intermixed with new faces from police, fire, and the local ambulance companies. With the ambulance company's high turnover rate, transfers, and inexperience, she wondered if they could consistently follow the procedures put in place.

Alden came in with the two homeland security trainers, Steve and Marcy. Maya had gotten to know them through their many meetings during the lead-up to the training.

Two hundred personnel filled the chairs of the new training building. They'd expanded their training facility to include a large auditorium, as all training was consolidated under one roof. Now, more than ever, everyone needed to be on the same page in their zone and region.

When everyone was seated, Alden opened the training. He stood before them in his perfectly pressed white shirt with two gold lapel pins on his collar and a gold badge. His black pants were perfectly starched. His head clean shaven. He had the polish of a military sergeant. He was all business, and his business was ensuring they were trained to meet the unfolding crisis.

"For those who don't know, I'm Alden Bancroft, the consortium training chief and paramedic. All of you know why we are here. Many of you know Maya, and her partner Jeff, who were involved in the event in June where we lost officer Petrov." Alden acknowledged the police that were present. "It was followed by the second, more deadly event at the college, where we lost two paramedics, three firefighters, and civilians in a bomb explosion. These two events have elevated our threat level and made it imperative that we are operationally ready to recognize those threats, adapt to them, and respond safely to all the calls in our zone.

"This is the first of multiple trainings. The training will take place over several days under the training consortium umbrella. All the fire departments, police departments, ambulance companies, and the paramedic service will attend training so that every agency is on the same page, and we can implement the changes throughout the region. Each service will also conduct its own agency-specific training that addresses specific guidelines around day-to-day operations for police, fire, and medical responses.

"There will be small field training exercises with our tactical teams so that we can coordinate our responses in all circumstances. The last piece will be zone-wide mass casualty incident training, where all agencies will participate.

"Today, we are covering the new directive from Homeland Security and how we've integrated it into our daily operations. I thank Maya for working in the office and lending real-world experience to the decision-making process."

Maya suddenly felt nervous. She hated being singled out. She operated better as a team member than the focus of attention.

"Here to present to us today are Steve Goden and Marcy Taylor. They are trainers from the Homeland Security Task Force assigned to this area."

Marcy walked up to the microphone as Steve ensured the computer was projecting their slideshow. Beaming from the projector was the Homeland Security emblem.

"Thanks for the introduction. Thank you for your service and dedication to your profession. Teamwork like this will make the difference between success and failure in meeting these new terrorism threats.

"First, I want to take care of some rules for this training. As you know, there have been some police, ex-military, and other first responders that have ties to some of these militias that we will be addressing today. What you see and hear here stays here. Leaking information on how we conduct operations could lead to someone you know being killed. Here, we are all in this together.

"On that note. Everyone attending this training has been the subject of an extensive background check. Those who have 'issues' have been notified and interviewed to ensure we are all on the same page."

The room grew quiet as people looked around, wondering if anyone they knew had been pulled in. You never knew. Maya shuddered to think that someone she worked with could have been complicit in what had happened to them.

Marcy continued, "Domestic Terrorism is now considered

the number one threat in the United States today. The threat is predominantly from white nationalists and right-wing militias with several connecting ideologies. Many of these groups are mainly operating as small, disconnected cells, but there has been outreach by two more prominent militias to organize these groups nationally.

"Currently, our assessment is that the two local incidents have been perpetrated by a small, localized militia. However, they seem very well organized; so far, we haven't identified their base of operations.

"Our job is to help your agencies respond safely, regardless of who perpetrates the attacks. In most situations, awareness and operational procedures can lessen the risk, but not completely. What happened on Pacific Highway and at the college were two different tactics. It's the latter that has us the most concerned. A routine call that doesn't elicit our concern can now turn out to be deadly. We need to be ready for anything."

Marcy pointed at the computer screen to a slide outlining the task force's coordination between agencies. "We have been working with your leadership to recruit and train new SWAT rapid response teams made up of experts in tactical weapons, bomb squad technicians, and tactical medics that are ready to respond to calls in each response area. They will be staged at central locations that can be deployed as needed."

When Marcy and Steve were finished, Chief Bancroft continued to outline specifics.

"From Monday on, dispatch will notify incoming agencies to stage at facilities that have been identified as potential targets and that have the potential for mass casualties, even if the call is for something as routine as "shortness of breath." Dispatch may request that the patient be brought out to the responding units.

"We'll use dispatch criteria and your situational awareness

to guide our responses. We can send in the SWAT tactical team to do extractions, render initial medical care, and do sweeps of the area. Local law enforcement will be used for additional manpower, and we'll call in more resources should we deem it necessary.

"You are the eyes and ears on the ground. Together, let's keep everyone safe and take care of our citizens."

While Maya was cleaning up after the training, two police officers walked over to her.

"Hey, we just wanted to thank you for what you did for James. If you ever need anything, let us know. We've got your back."

"Thank you. We've got yours too," Maya replied.

They left her as she finished up. She walked to Chief Anderson's office to check in before leaving. "Hey, Chief, I just wanted to let you know I'm heading out for the day. A few of us are meeting at Airways Brewing."

"Have fun. I'll be here working late again. All these changes make for long days. Hey, great job on helping to put this together today. Things went really well."

Maya was surprised by his compliment. Usually, she only received feedback about what she did wrong, not right. That was because, in this job, it was expected that you would do everything right. People's lives depended on it. So, if someone made a mistake, it needed to be dealt with, and in a profession designed around crisis, it was crisis that caught everyone's attention. Whether it was on the scene or in a lack of perfor-mance. She knew the key to survival in this profession was to keep her own scorecard of what she knew to be her accom-plishments.

Maya looked around as she walked through the door. Airways Brewing was already getting crowded. It had become a favored meetup place after training events. The high ceilings, crisscrossed with ductwork and soundproofing material, dampened the laughter and conversation throughout, while dim overhead lighting illuminated the open industrial room. A contingent from their training event had taken over the space. There were also the usual after-work groups and individuals taking a break before crawling home in gridlock traffic. She grabbed a beer at the bar and headed to the back, where her people congregated.

Maya approached Em first. "Hey, Em, guess what?"

"What?"

"The chief complimented me on the way out today."

"No way. Are you sure it was him?"

"Oh, it was him, working into the evening."

"Of course. At least you managed to get out of there before being enlisted to work on another project."

"Hey, I've missed you guys. I've been stuck in that office for way too long. It's good to see you outside of the office scene."

Em motioned for Maya to sit next to her. Maya quickly joined in the conversation, which was, of course, about the presentation by Homeland Security.

"The training was thorough," Jake said. "Thanks for working on this, Maya. I'm glad these guidelines are out. We've been in a gray area since the events. Now at least we're all on the same page."

"We've been in similar scenarios before," Lou said, drawing their attention. As an old timer, he'd seen just about everything. "This isn't new. Just different. We used to have a police escort at the apartment complex up on Kent's east hill when the occupants threatened to shoot any police or firefighters who came in. The key is to use good judgment. Be proactive."

"Good judgment. How do you anticipate being ambushed?" Maya asked.

Lou looked at Maya with his warm, friendly eyes. "Okay, I

know. Sorry, Maya. No guidelines will keep us safe a hundred percent of the time. That's when that 'gut feel' comes into play."

"And armed medics," chimed in Randy.

Em gave him a sour look. "Geez, Randy, don't get started on that again."

"I'm just sayin'," Randy replied.

Everyone joined in at once. "The only way to stop a bad guy with a gun is a good guy with a gun." They all laughed.

"Right, we've seen how well that works," Maya said. "All those police officers at our scene were armed. Didn't stop the ambush."

Randy slammed down his beer. "Whatever. You younger medics just don't get it. They know we're weak. If we show strength and don't back down, they'll think twice! I gotta bug out here. I have a meeting to go to. Go back to your peace, love, and understanding, and let the real men take care of things."

Jake looked on in disbelief as Randy stormed out of the brewery. "What's gotten into him? That was way over the top, even for him. Besides, I joined the tactical medic team. I know what the stakes are."

"But are you a 'real man'?" Daniel joked.

"As real as they come."

"Coming from the guy whose girlfriend refers to him as her SNAG," Jeff said.

"SNAG?" Lou asked.

"Sensitive new age guy," Em replied.

"I've never heard that before, but I'd have to agree, Jake's a SNAG."

Jake looked down nervously until Lou reached over and gave him a light punch in the arm. "It's okay. I'll still work with you, rookie."

"True, but will I work with you? That's the real question."

"You better be careful. I'm still your senior," Lou replied.

"Senior citizen," Jake retorted.

"Hey, boys." Maya gave them a serious look. "Senior or otherwise, the point we were making is that we need firm guidelines in place we can use. I had input into our training. Jeff and I looked for any signs we missed in the days leading up to the ambush call. That area has always had issues. When the African American man was shot walking down Pac Highway, we thought it was another gang retaliation, not a hate crime."

Daniel leaned in. "Was anyone here aware that these right-wing groups were beginning to launch attacks in our community? As a Black man, I'm hyperaware these right-wing groups are dangerous, but even I couldn't have anticipated that they would detonate a bomb at the college. That's crazy!"

Jeff added, "You know, we've seen the flags flying and the growing hostility out where we live. I didn't think it would lead to these deadly attacks. I thought it was a bunch of hot air. The most vocal guys I've met look like they couldn't survive a day of military training, let alone launch a terrorist attack from their armchair."

"You would know with your combat experience. Is that why you signed on as a SWAT medic?" Jake asked.

"Absolutely, it makes sense to have those of us who've been in firefights on the front lines with SWAT. It's important to put that experience to good use."

"I don't have the combat experience, but I want to help on the front lines. I hate standby. I want to be where the action is!" Jake said.

"Jake, we need you young guys to step up. I'd consider it, but those days are behind me. Besides, my wife would never let me," Lou said.

"For our day-to-day operations, we need to be aware and augment our approach to responding, especially if we feel dispatch or the firefighters may be missing something." Maya sighed. "I've done that on dispatches that just don't sound right. Like Lou said, I'm going to listen to my gut feeling more closely. Maybe I'll catch something, maybe I won't. At least I did my best.

"Bottom line. I want to be able to keep my focus on saving a life while SWAT and PD do their jobs. Hopefully, these new guidelines will bring in enough of a deterrent that anyone considering another ambush will think twice. If they see SWAT showing up at one of their targets, maybe they'll back off."

"I guess it will depend on what their goals are. At this point, we don't really know," Jeff said.

Maya realized Jeff and Daniel knew more than they were letting on. They had been looking deep into the dark channels of white supremacy and right-wing groups. From what they'd told her so far, it sounded like more bravado than concrete plans.

"Here's the good and bad news. It's been more than two months since we've had any incidents," Lou said. "The bad news is, it's easy to fall into a false sense of safety. We need to make sure we stay vigilant. Who knows if or when it will happen again."

Em nodded. "That's the terrorism part. Not knowing if and when."

"Just stay focused on your job, practice the new training, and try to stay vigilant," Lou said. "We've had threats before. We've lost people in the past. We'll get through this and be better prepared because of the training."

"My band's playing here on the last weekend of the month. Are you guys going to come out to see your favorite medic?" Daniel asked.

"Sure, I'm in. I'm not sure Nick can make it. He's been working a lot." Maya took a sip of her beer.

"Melissa and I will be here," Jeff said.

Everyone nodded, except Lou.

He shook his head and said, "I'd love to come, but we have the grandkids on weekends. Too bad. I haven't had a chance to hear you play yet."

"You're missing out. Daniel and the DTs are the best blues band north of Tacoma," Jeff said.

"North of Tacoma. Who's your competition down there?" Lou asked.

"My uncle. He recently relocated up here from our old stomping grounds in LA. Something about missing his favorite nephew. You guys will meet him. He's going to come and hear us play, maybe even sit in for a set."

"What does the DTs stand for?" Jake asked.

"Delirium Tremens, my friend."

"Of course, I should have known. Right out of the annals of paramedic student life at Harborview," Jake said.

CHAPTER FIVE

THEY DROVE three thousand feet up a gravel road to the Suntop Trail, skipping the long climb up to the top in exchange for bringing their furry companions, Kali, Rio, and Cloe. Maya hadn't had a chance to mountain bike with Georgia since she'd returned from Tahoe. Georgia, as always, looked amazing for her age. Her new short pixie haircut perfectly complemented her sleek, muscular figure. She was in better shape than most of the guys she worked with.

"Your new haircut looks great."

"Do you like it? I just got sick of trying to keep it tied up while I was working. I'm too old for long hair now anyway. It's a lot easier to manage short like this."

"Too old, hardly, but this new haircut looks good on you."

She could go long periods without seeing Georgia, but they always stayed in touch by phone, and when they finally did get together, it was one of those friendships where it felt like no time had passed.

As they unloaded their bikes, the dogs followed up on the

scents they'd discovered with their heads out the windows on the drive up.

As Georgia and Maya pedaled to the lookout, the dogs sprinted ahead, releasing their pent-up energy from the car ride. Cloe took the lead as the youngest and the fastest. Kali was right behind, loving the chase that Cloe offered her. Rio sprinted and then settled in beside Maya, keeping pace with her rear wheel.

At the top, they took a minute to enjoy the view. "The mountain is out. I wondered if we'd see it again before summer," Maya commented.

The snow-covered giant lifted 14,400 feet over the Puget Sound basin. From their vantage, they could make out the glaciers that snaked off the summit.

"Georgia, when was the last time you climbed Mount Rainier?"

"I think it was before I met Jack. I was dating that mountain climber, remember Ed? Anyway, the last time I climbed it was with him. We did the Emmons Route."

"I'm going to have to attempt that someday. What ever happened to Ed? Is he still climbing mountains?" Maya asked.

"No, he died. A few years ago, he became a Mount Rainier National Park law enforcement officer. He was trying to intercept an attempted murder suspect who blew through a roadblock in the park. The suspect exited his vehicle and shot and killed him. He'd only been on the job for two months."

"No way. I read about that but didn't realize it was Ed. He was such a good guy. I can't believe it."

"Neither can I. The suspect was a meth dealer who shot four people outside of Yelm."

Georgia led as they descended from the lookout. The trail plummeted down the ridgeline along a narrow edge. Maya followed Georgia. The dogs sprinted in a line behind them. The recent rain meant Georgia's tires didn't kick up dust. Maya could hang back just enough and follow Georgia's line as they snaked down the mountain. The moment's focus gave her the freedom from work that she needed. The thick northwest forest blurred at the trail's edges in shades of greens, reds, and browns. She inhaled the scent of thick moss and cedar mixed with the crispness of autumn mountain air.

They climbed another rise before dropping into a descent that tumbled steeply toward the White River. Before long, they turned off onto Deer Creek Trail, a shortcut to an airstrip and the Buck Creek Camping access. They paused as the dogs, tongues hanging out, panted from their fast pace. Maya sprayed water from her camelback hose into the dog's mouths while Georgia gave them a few treats. It took a few minutes for the dogs to recover, but soon they grew restless. Their noses started hunting along the edges of the airfield. This was Maya and Georgia's cue that it was time to continue.

They crossed the airstrip towards Buck Creek Campground. As they made their way down the long airstrip, Maya noticed a collection of ATVs and stacks of giant dozer tires strategically spread out. A row of razor wire was strung between two sets of tires. They stopped and watched as a group of men in camo seemed to be running maneuvers between the tires. Maya commanded the dogs to sit next to her and Georgia. One of the men would disappear and then pop up with a rifle pointed at a hanging target farther afield. A look of concern crossed over Georgia's face. They waited to see if the men were going to fire the weapons. They hadn't heard any gunfire on their ride, but this looked like a serious exercise.

A group of men standing off to the side under a camo pop-up tent looked in their direction. Someone yelled something.

Immediately, the men running maneuvers stopped and retreated to the tent where the other men were standing.

One of the men, a tall, stocky man, waved to them and yelled out, "It's okay. We aren't shooting. You can pass through."

They got back on their bikes. Maya commanded the dogs. "With me." They trotted next to Maya and Georgia as they hesitantly made their way toward the camp. Cloe clung to Georgia's rear tire as they skirted to the right side.

One of the men called out, "Good ride today?"

The voice sounded familiar, but Maya couldn't place it. "Yes," she replied.

As they rode by, she saw the voice attached to none other than one of the volunteer firefighters she knew from calls. How could she mistake that thin, lanky build and bird-like nose? She tried to disappear under her helmet, but he recognized her too.

"Maya, is that you? It's Glenn."

They rolled to a slow stop. Maya motioned for the dogs to sit by her side. Kali and Rio ignored her and sat between Maya and the men. Both had their eyes focused on the men.

"Oh, wow, I didn't recognize you. How are you doing?"

"Great. Just out with the boys, havin' some fun."

That doesn't look like just fun, she thought. She looked at the other men standing with him. A man with a shaved head and round features looked like he was sizing her up. He had a camo flak vest over his camo T-shirt. She recognized another man from the auto repair in Enumclaw. She'd been on a chest pain call for his boss. He had long brown hair and was wearing the same green mechanic overalls. All the men had serious looks on their faces.

The air hung thick with unanswered questions as she replied, "Looks like fun. We just came down from Suntop. We're in a hurry to finish our ride but it was good to see you. Hopefully, I'll see you on a call," she lied. She'd never really liked him, which added to the feeling. Something just didn't seem right.

"Ya, we'll see you around," he replied. Some of the other men laughed under their breath.

Maya and Georgia pedaled past the men. Kali and Rio trotted between her and the men until they were on the trail. Then they dropped in behind Maya as she picked up the pace. The farther they got from the men, the safer she felt. When they could no longer hear the camp, they stopped.

"Well, that was creepy. To think that guy is a firefighter. I felt like we just rode into the middle of a militia camp," Georgia said.

"Could be. I hate to be paranoid, but I'm concerned that not only do we face threats from the outside, but we also face threats from the inside. HS said they ran background checks on all our first responders, so they should know if he is a threat, right?"

"Maybe, but what if he doesn't have a history? How do you determine if these are just a few good ole boys getting together for fun or something more serious?"

Maya took her glasses off to clean them. "I wonder if I should alert our contacts at Homeland Security. I hate the idea of turning someone in without solid evidence, though. I don't want to be that kind of person."

"Well, the problem is all the rules have changed. Now keeping quiet might be deadly. You know, it's their issue, not ours. It was hard enough being one of the original women in the fire service. Now some of these same guys are taking up arms. We need to be safe, and if some of our ranks are targeting our people, then it's better to be safe than sorry."

"Even now, they scare the hell out of me. I really want this to stop. Why, when I'm trying to get back out on the streets, do I have to run into this? I just wanted an uneventful ride."

"I know, Maya. Are you sure you want to dive back in? It might be a good time to lay low. No one's going to blame you for taking more time off. You could use it as an excuse to go on extended leave. Maybe this will blow over by the time you return."

"Right and leave everyone else covering my shifts and taking on the extra work. No, for now, I'm in. Let's ride."

"I wouldn't want to be one of those guys if they try to mess with you. They need to know what happened last time someone tried to take you out!"

"That's right. The last man who tried to take me out on the trail didn't do so well!"

Even so, Maya was afraid. Afraid if she said anything, they would come after her. She quickly pushed it from her mind and focused on the trail ahead of her. Skookum Flats demanded her full attention. It was a technical mix of rock and root obstacles. She couldn't worry about Glenn and his group. If she did, she might miss a move and launch herself over the side of a steep drop above the White River that could just as easily derail her career.

Soon, they were moving at a fast pace. Maya took the lead and picked her way through slippery roots while keeping her tire straight, so she didn't slide sideways on them. She loved northwest mountain biking. The wet roots and rocks added another level of challenge.

Western red cedar, Douglas fir, and hemlock towered above them, blocking out the sun. After pushing themselves through a rough section, they finished the ride on smooth forest duff along the river's edge.

As they rode into the parking lot, Maya noticed that someone had spray-painted "Patriot Army" on the Forest Service sign while they were gone.

"Georgia, that wasn't there when we parked here earlier."

Maya walked over and touched the paint. "The paint's still tacky."

She looked around the parking lot, but it was empty. Dark gray clouds rolled in from above as they hurried to load up.

"Let's get out of here," Georgia said.

CHAPTER SIX

SITTING on the couch in Dr. Harrington's office, Maya paused, hesitating before revealing the reality of how she felt. "I think I felt so out of control during the ambush. That was the first time I thought I might die on the job. I mean, before then, it only seemed remotely possible.

"At the same time, I pushed away any fear as I tried to save the officer's life. I did what I always do. I put my head down and focused on saving a life, but...after, it suddenly hit me, sitting there on the back bumper of the rig. I felt so utterly exhausted and powerless to change the outcome. We did everything we could to save his life, but it wasn't enough, and we were almost killed ourselves."

"So, you say you felt out of control, but from what I hear you saying, you and your coworkers made the best out of a terrible situation," Dr. Harrington stated.

"I know, but it's just that he died, and I haven't been able to put it behind me, let it go like I usually do. I'll be doing something, and suddenly I..." Maya hesitated. She didn't want Dr. Harrington to think she wasn't ready to return to work. She went on downplaying how she really felt. "Suddenly, I'll be thinking about him and what happened. It was all so meaningless. Why him? What's wrong with these people?

"I think that's the thing that's taking away my love of this job. It's all these crazy people killing each other and themselves. Now they're trying to kill us. I feel like all we see is the worst of humanity!"

"Do you really think that is all there is? Yes, you see the worst of humanity, but what about outside of work?"

"Like in Tahoe?" Maya retorted.

"Well, let's set that aside for a minute. What about the calls where you make a real difference in someone's life? We talked about the woman who had a cardiac arrest while taking a walk. You said her husband waved you down in the grocery store and thanked you for saving her life. What about those moments?"

"Yes, but they seem isolated compared to most of what we see."

"I want you to visualize putting all those calls into a place where you can leave them and focus on other things. Can you think of a place?"

"Yes."

"Okay, where is that?"

"Well, the back of the medic unit. I can put those thoughts and bad calls inside the medic unit and slam the doors shut."

"That's what I want you to do when those feelings and the images of the call with the police officer come up. Then we can talk about them and do some EMDR work when you're here. We're at the end of our session, but I want you to close your eyes and imagine putting everything in the back of the medic unit. Talk me through what that looks like."

Maya closed her eyes and visualized, feeling the sensation of being under siege and watching the police officer bleed out all over the medic unit floor. She imagined getting out of the medic unit and found herself in a sudden dome of silence as she heard the isolated sounds of the doors closing. No sirens or first responders yelling. No sound of gunfire.

Later that week, Maya found Nick working on the computer in his home office. He was sitting at his large monitors framed by the wall of windows as driving rain cascaded down the glass.

"Hey, I have some good news. I received approval to return to the trucks next week," Maya said.

Maya was feeling less under siege all the time. Talking about it during her sessions was helping her see it for what it was, enabling her to work towards managing the intrusive thoughts and physical sensations that followed. That sense of constant danger was finally receding a bit. Dr. Harrington had reluctantly agreed to let her go back to the trucks as long as Maya continued to meet with her once a week.

Nick turned around from his monitors and looked at her, his eyes tinged with worry. "Well, that's good and bad."

"Why?"

"Jeff and Daniel think they have found a chat room with some members of the White Dawn Militia. There is an uptick in activity calling for action. Nothing overt, but for those who know, there may be coded information. In one of the discussions, they said they needed to make sure that the right people turned out on Election Day. Then someone replied that maybe they needed to do something to scare those 'libs and democrats' to keep them from turning out. Someone brought up the district where Kale is running and said they needed to make sure she won by any means necessary. That's your response area, right?"

"Yes."

"Anyway, that aligns with some of the research I've been doing."

"So, what do you think it means?" Maya asked.

"I think it means you guys better be ready out there. We haven't gotten any specific details, just general conversation. As someone who loves you, I'd rather not have you working on the streets now. I want you to come home."

She was shocked. "Nick, I know you're concerned, but we have a lot of safeguards in place that we didn't have a few months ago. We still have a job to do. We're as ready as we can be. You knew when you asked me to marry you that this is the world I live in." Maya wondered if Nick could be counted on if things got worse. Asking her to stay off the streets was not what she wanted to hear right now.

"There is another thing I wanted to let you know about. I've found a couple of your coworkers in these chats. I traced some of the profiles and discovered them by accident. At this point, I haven't heard anything from them that indicates they are involved in the actions of the White Dawn, but just be careful."

"Who?"

"You know one of them, Mike. That guy you said you hate working with. Then there's a firefighter, Chris Hoffman. I think I met him, with you, at the Medic One Foundation auction last year. Recently he was asking about where to buy an untraceable AR-15. He occasionally agrees with some of the more radical talk, but he never posts his own ideas. In a recent chat, he did ask members to stand down and not target firefighters and first responders. He said many of them side with the movement and that they are not the enemy. He has spent time trying to distance the first responders from the 'libs and democrats.'

"I don't understand how anyone in your profession could support what they have been doing? Don't they know they'll be caught in the middle, even if they aren't the targets? Some of the guys you work with... Well, let's just say, I'm surprised they passed the HS background checks."

"Nick, what we see on the streets can lead some first responders to see the world as a dark place that needs saving. That makes them easier to recruit. It makes it more understandable, but that's not a defensible excuse.

"I didn't want to know that I have coworkers involved in a local militia chat room. It's hard enough doing my job without worrying about being undermined by some of them. Don't they know this could impact them as well? We're all in this together. I don't know how much longer I can do this if I can't trust some of the people I work with. God, it's crazy making. On the one hand, I want to be there on the front lines with everyone, you know, to support them. On the other hand, I have to watch my back. How am I supposed to function in an environment like that and watch out for terrorist attacks too? Just tell me?"

Nick leaned toward her. His look was more reserved than she'd seen for a while. Was he distancing himself from her? Or from what was happening?

"I think that's something you need to figure out. I can't tell you how to navigate that environment. I couldn't work in your profession. You know I prefer a little less direct front-line work, like cybersecurity. I'm here to support you in any way I can. Just let me know."

She felt conflicted. Would he really be there for her? She didn't want to lose him, not now when her world was falling apart. If only he could hang on until this insanity was over.

She walked over, looked directly into his eyes, and kissed him with a playful passion. "I know. I'm lucky to have the most amazing person watching my back. I say *person* because Kali and Rio are the most amazing dogs, also watching out for me."

Hearing their names, Kali and Rio came trotting over to take advantage of Maya's attention. She knelt and gave both dogs a big hug. "You guys are my heroes too!"

She hoped that lightening up the mood would shift Nick's perspective.

"Maybe you should be able to take them to work with you."

"You know, that might not be such a bad idea. Maybe I can get Dr. Harrington to write me a prescription that says I need to have my emotional support dogs at the station with me when I work."

"I think you're on to something," Nick said.

CHAPTER SEVEN

MAYA WALKED INTO THE STATION. She felt like she had been gone forever, yet she'd only been off the trucks for just over two months. The familiar aroma of freshly brewed coffee filled the room, making her realize that nothing and everything had changed.

"Maya, I heard you were coming back to the trucks," Mike said as he typed on the office computer. "How are you doing?"

Her heart sank. Of all the people she had to follow on her first day back. Mike and Dag. Two of the most negative medics she'd ever worked with. They were good medics, but absolutely heartless toward their coworkers. She knew that "How are you doing?" was a loaded question, especially now that she knew Mike frequented the right-wing chat rooms.

"I'm doing great. I had a good break. Well, almost, minus a few more attempts on my life." She laughed with an edge of casual sarcasm.

"I heard. Did you just say a few attempts? Who was it that tried to kill you? I heard about the one attempt where that guy drugged your dogs and tried to shoot you."

"Well, it was a little more than that, but yes, that incident. Before that, the same guy hit me over the head and threw me into a river near Tahoe. Then just to top it off, the husband of the dead woman I found tried to strangle me after running me off a mountain bike trail."

"No shit. That all really happened?"

Maya knew he was just trying to get her to give up more information. She realized the rumor mill had circulated long ago about what happened. She guessed he wanted more info to share at gossip time during the next shift change when she wasn't present to tell the story.

"Yes, I almost drowned, but I saved myself using my skills. I think I would have drowned if it weren't for my training as a whitewater boater and swiftwater technician—and a bit of luck."

"Wow," Dag commented from the kitchen. He was grabbing the trash from the can to take it out.

"Did you guys just get back from a late call?" she asked.

"Yes, shortness of breath at Carrington Care. The usual report of 'The patient was fine five minutes ago.' It's always the same, just in time for shift change."

"Ya, right," Mike said. "She was up to her lips in yellow pus. I couldn't believe she was still alive. Her oxygen sats were in the seventies, with a temp of hundred and three. Of course, she was a full code."

Maya felt a sinking feeling settle into her mind. More ugliness. *Just give me a quiet first day back.* With that thought, their pagers went off.

Mike held out his pager, and she grabbed it, thinking, *There goes my chance of just easing back into things.*

She grabbed her gear and rushed out toward the medic unit. Her partner, Jeff, had just pulled into the parking area. She waved and motioned that they had a call.

He parked and jumped into action. After stowing their gear, they hopped into the rig. Maya drove while Jeff sat in the officer's seat. At least she wasn't the officer on her first call back since...that night.

They were responding to a report of chest pain. Was it really chest pain or were they walking into another trap? Her mind reeled from the thought that even something this routine could be luring them to their deaths. She pushed it out of her mind. She had a job to do. If it felt wrong, they could always retreat and call for backup.

Maya felt relieved as she walked in and saw an older woman sitting in her recliner in front of the television. Her gut told her it was just a routine chest pain, but even so, she felt on edge and searched for anything that looked out of place.

The firefighters were talking to her over the sound of Faux News on the TV. Maya walked over and turned it down. The drone of anger withered, becoming background noise. Probably got the old lady wound up with fear, and now she was having chest pain.

Jeff got the run down from the firefighter standing next to the woman.

"Hey, Jeff, this is Helen. She's a sixty-five-year-old female complaining of chest pain for about an hour. She said she was just watching TV and drinking her morning coffee when it came on. She thought it was indigestion, but then it got worse, and she started to feel short of breath."

Jeff introduced himself and Maya. "Maya is going to put some ECG patches on your chest so we can look at what's going on with your heart."

Maya knelt down, laid her hand gently on Helen's arm, and smiled. "I'll need to open up your robe and lift that night shirt to apply these patches."

She applied a line of patches across Helen's chest, one on each arm and leg that attached to cables leading back to their ECG machine. Then she added the patient info onto the touch screen.

"Hold real still," Jeff said.

Helen sat still and stared off at the TV as sweat spilled from her forehead, down her cheeks. They waited as the machine registered Helen's heart rhythm. Then a printout rolled out of the device. Jeff picked it up and studied it. "Well, Helen, changes on your ECG are consistent with a heart attack. We are going to take good care of you. We will start an IV to give you some medicine to help with the pain. Then we'll put you on our stretcher and transport you to the hospital."

The firefighters were already heading out to get the stretcher. Their well-orchestrated intervention progressed as Jeff, Maya, and the firefighters saved another life.

Helen looked up at Maya with eyes full of fear. "Thank you," she whispered.

Maya opened the door of the medic unit. There she reacquainted herself with the layout. The stretcher lay between the two red bench seats. The drawers, full of stock, framed the pass-through from the patient compartment to the driver's compartment. She'd been so busy on the last call that it hadn't fully registered yet that she was back at work.

She jumped into the back of the medic unit with Jeff and helped him check the stock and clean up from the last call. The routine felt familiar, grounding her in the moment as she made sure that everything was in its place and could be grabbed at a moment's notice.

That familiarity was offset by the fact that she'd forgotten to wear her bulletproof vest on the last call. Just like AIDS in the nineties had made wearing gloves a requirement on all calls, now armed ambushes made wearing a bulletproof vest mandatory. It just added to the gear she needed to have ready. Mental checklist: bullet proof vest, helmet, HEPA mask, bunker gear, gloves, digital tablet, pager, radio. Her mind raced down that rabbit hole. They'd added more medical equipment and protocols while she was off the trucks that she had to become familiar with and memorize. Typically, all these changes wouldn't faze her but returning to work after being off for so long made her feel overwhelmed. The addition of the bulletproof vest was just a reminder of how much things had changed in a short time.

Her mind was suddenly jolted back to the here and now. Her pager beeped with yet another dispatch. *Well, it's going to be one of those days*, she thought.

"Respond to northbound highway 169 at mile marker ten for car versus motorcycle."

They put away the medical kits, closed the doors to the medic unit and put on their bulletproof vests. Maya jumped into the driver's seat, while Jeff got into the officer's seat.

"So soon, you and your tendency to attract shit, Maya. Couldn't you just give me a break? I've been working so much overtime since we lost..." He rolled his eyes and half smiled at her.

"I thought the same thing. I just wanted to ease back into the chaos, but that doesn't look like it's going to happen. I'm going to hate wearing this vest on every call."

They entered the highway on the northbound ramp. Traffic was already backed up past the onramp. Their sirens blared as they made their way across the traffic to the inside lane, to get to the accident. Jeff got on their loudspeaker and reminded drivers to move to the right as Maya navigated through the congestion to make their way to the scene of the accident.

As they arrived, they saw additional police officers

standing at attention around the scene, surveying traffic on both sides of the highway. They saw the motorcycle lying across the inside traffic lane. A car was pulled over just ahead of it. PD was directing traffic to move onto the right shoulder. Maya pulled in behind the motorcycle at an angle. Behind them, the engine company blocked both lanes for their protection as they worked. Maya and Jeff jumped out and put on their helmets.

The driver was standing by his car. The motorcycle rider was lying next to his bike. She could see right away that his left leg was fractured. Jeff directed one firefighter to the driver, as another watched to ensure the scene was safe. Another engine arrived as Maya and Jeff reached the patient. Jeff radioed for the incoming engine to grab their traction splint, a backboard, and a stretcher.

"Sir, what's your name?" Jeff asked the rider.

"Dave. My leg. God, my leg hurts!"

Sweat was running down his face. Maya grabbed her trauma scissors and started to cut his leather pants.

"Don't cut my pants. These are expensive," Dave said.

"Hey, I'm sorry, but your leg is fractured. We need to cut your pants to treat your injury."

"Is there any way you can just take them off?"

"No," Maya said as she cut through the thick leather of his pant leg. The leg was literally twisted around at the femur."

"I wondered why his foot was at such an odd angle, it's rotated backward," the firefighter said.

"It's what?" Dave whimpered.

Maya looked him in the eyes. "Dave, you're going to be okay. We'll need to pull traction and then rotate your leg back around."

Maya and Jeff had been joined by three firefighters who were setting up the traction splint, c-collar, and backboard. Jeff directed one of the firefighters to cut the patient's jacket off and take his blood pressure.

"Maybe we should start an IV and give him some sedation first. Then I'll remove his boot, and we'll pull his leg into place," Maya said.

"Let's do it. I'll start the IV while you two get the leg ready for traction," Jeff directed the firefighters as he started to cut the opposite sleeve and prepare an IV.

"No, don't tell me you're cutting my jacket too!" Dave said, before yelling and screaming in pain. "God, my leg, okay, just give me something for the pain!"

Maya unlatched the straps of the traction splint as Jeff gave him morphine and Valium to ease the pain and dim his memory of what they were about to do. Maya reminded herself that femur fractures were very painful. Pulling a leg with all its muscles contracted and bones jammed up against each other had caused more than a few patients to scream in agony or pass out from the pain. Afterward, the relief they felt was worth the minutes of excruciating pain.

Jeff told the patient what they were going to do.

"On the count of three. 1, 2, 3."

Maya removed the boot and directed the firefighter to pull traction as they untwisted his leg into the normal position. Although he was sedated, he still screamed from the pain. Jeff gave him a couple more milligrams of morphine. Then they placed the long metal traction splint on his leg, secured straps around his ankle and hooked it to a ratchet on the bar below. They ratcheted the tension until his leg extended to its normal length and the femur bone was realigned. Maya reached down to check his foot for a pulse. She was relieved that he had good blood flow to his leg below the fracture.

"He has a strong pulse," she said, vocalizing for Jeff to acknowledge it.

Maya looked up to see the tension in the patient's face dissolve as the traction along with the medication relieved some of his pain.

They placed the patient carefully onto the backboard, loaded him onto the stretcher, and wheeled him to the medic unit. As they did, she heard wheels skidding to a stop followed by a loud impact. Maya's first reaction was to dive for safety inside the medic unit. Everyone turned toward the sound and saw a car, going the other direction, had rear-ended another vehicle.

"Looky loos. Great. Now we have two accidents." Maya shook her head and turned back to the patient. He was oblivious in his medicated state.

"At least it was just looky-loos," echoed one of the firefighters.

She looked at Jeff and the firefighters and could see concern in their eyes. They were all on edge as they quickly loaded the patient into the medic unit and shut the doors.

Jeff asked one of the firefighters to drive. It was only ten in the morning, and they were on their way to Harborview again. *Another long shift,* Maya thought as she started another IV.

With Dave's helmet off, she could see that he was in his early twenties. It was going to be a long recovery for him. At least for now, he was blissfully unaware of what awaited him once he hit the ED doors.

They made it back in time to get lunch. They quickly made their lunches and sat down to eat them. Maya got one bite in before their pagers went off again. They ran out the doors, leaving their lunches stored in the refrigerator for later, off to another "shortness of breath" at Carrington Care.

The next morning, Maya sat in front of Dr. Harrington, a tall cup of coffee in hand and dark circles under her eyes.

"So, I take it your first shift was a busy one?" Dr. Harrington asked.

"An understatement. We had twelve calls, transported seven, and were canceled on five. It was quite the welcome back."

"Sounds like it. How did it feel being back?"

"Like everything is normal and yet everything isn't normal. Wearing my vest on every call constantly reminds me how things have changed. Not to mention dispatch putting SWAT on standby for a call at the Renton City Hall. I don't like this new normal."

"Did you feel good on the calls, like you were ready?"

"I did. The routine is familiar. We still take care of our patients. Having the SWAT on rapid standby and then the extra police on an accident we were on did help make me feel safer. I didn't have to look around, constantly gauging where the threat would come from. On a chest pain call for an elderly woman, I worried that someone would come barging through the front door with a gun. It's doubtful, but now it is a possibility."

"So, you felt unsafe on that call?"

"Not unsafe, just aware that any call could be a trap. It's terrorism, right? They want us to feel vulnerable and defeated by putting us on constant high alert. They've accomplished that. It just makes every shift harder. It's much harder to focus on the patients and the details when I constantly feel under siege."

"So, do you think you are ready to be back?"

"Of course. You know, it's just different. I'm adjusting. Right now, I'm exhausted. I'm back to sleepless shifts and constant fatigue. Just part of the job!" Maya minimized how she was feeling. She just had to get back to finding her edge. It was there, she just felt that being on her 'A game' was elusive.

What would it take to feel that sense of command that she'd had before everything changed? Before she changed.

She left her appointment with Dr. Harrington feeling drained. As she headed home, she knew she wouldn't accomplish much. Maybe she'd go for a mountain bike ride. If she could release some of the tension in her mind and body, she could take the rest of the day to relax and, more than likely, drown out her feelings with alcohol.

CHAPTER EIGHT

MAYA THOUGHT a short getaway with Nick and the dogs outside the city would be a great way to fill her first row of days off after working. Working Monday through Friday in the "office" was not for her. She preferred to have a string of days off where she could really disconnect, and she felt she'd really earned them after all her work on the new training.

Through her side gig on the Search and Rescue canine team, she'd made friends with a local couple, the Gunthers, who lived along the Green River Gorge. They had a house perched on a cliff overlooking a beautiful, deep emerald-green pool surrounded by sandstone cliffs draped in maidenhair ferns. She'd become familiar with the area because their house had the first accessible access point in a very remote section of the Green River Gorge. It was there, scared and soaking wet, inner tubers crawled up the first trail they found, looking for a way out of the gorge. Maya had been on a few paramedic calls for hypothermia, and even a few broken bones at the Gunthers' house.

When someone didn't show up at the other end of the

gorge, that's when she showed up with Kali and the Search and Rescue team. They'd get a call out for a missing boater or inner tuber in the gorge. Usually, it was in the summer when the water was low, and they couldn't take a raft down to search for the person or people. One of the first stops out on a search was from the Gunthers' house. Kali was given a scent, and then hopefully, she could catch on to a scent path to follow. The water made it more challenging but not impossible. At low water, no one could just float down the river without having to hop over protruding rocks or skirt their way along the shore.

So, Maya had gotten to know the Gunthers quite well. Now they had moved into town and occasionally visited their cliffside home. They offered Maya and Kali a place to stay when Maya came out to whitewater kayak the river.

Since Maya had met Nick, she hadn't done as much kayaking. They'd mostly run a few river expeditions and a couple of day trips on international travels. She figured it would be an excellent time to jump back in the kayak since the water was up from all the rain. They'd take an easier lower gorge run from the house and then run the upper section the following day.

As they passed Maple Valley and entered Black Diamond, she noticed a giant "Don't Tread on Me" flag billowing above the old auto shop on the highway. She didn't remember when she'd last worked out in the area. Also, several houses they passed had thin blue line flags associated with support of the police. Something that infuriated her as she remembered the police officer dying in her medic unit. Did they really know what that meant?

A big black pickup truck pulled out of the gas station as they turned towards the gorge. Two American flags whipped in the wind as it sped off toward Enumclaw. She felt like these towns she'd worked in for years were changing before her eyes. Once again, the sound of a vehicle backfiring sent her mind into a panic. She used her new training to calm her breath and redirect her focus to her body. She was safe. Nick was in the SUV with her. Rio suddenly licked her on the face. He knew that she needed to be brought back to a safe place.

"What a show. What's going on out here?" Nick looked out the window at the fast-disappearing pickup truck. "Are these the same people chatting online about dismantling the government and taking up arms? You should hear some of the talk on the encrypted websites. The number of weapons some of these guys have is surreal. I guess we'll be safe out here. No one wants to break into a house if they think the occupants are heavily armed."

"It's a crazy place but mostly, they tend to shoot each other...in the foot or in some cases, the balls." She shook her head.

"Really, in the balls? You've seen that?"

"You bet. I went on a call up the road for a guy who was cleaning his gun and accidentally discharged the only bullet left in the chamber and shot his nut off. Just the kind of guy you want packing a concealed weapon in a crowded room."

"You're kidding, right?"

Maya sighed. "I wish I was. That's what makes this whole gun culture thing so scary. Lots of weekend warriors out there with an arsenal. Then there are the serious ones that are training for the downfall of civilization. I don't know which is worse."

"Let's just hope that the downfall doesn't happen today. We'll be in paradise in no time."

They headed up the hill and turned onto a narrow private road. They punched in the code at a gate, and it slowly opened into a little piece of paradise.

The Gunthers' place was at the end of a road at the river's edge. The road ended at a garage tucked into the sidehill above the house. Steps led them down to the front door, which opened to a large wall of windows revealing a forested landscape across the river from the cliff where the house was perched.

Nick unloaded the SUV, leaving Maya to meditate on one of her favorite places, the Green River Gorge.

Maya opened the French doors to the deck. The sound of the tumbling water below filtered through the branches of towering cedar trees on either side of the house. Across the river was a sandstone cliff with a skirt of undulating maidenhair ferns hanging over a deep green pool. The sounds of the river, the green of the forest, and timelessness of the sandstone cliff calmed her mind. For a moment, she felt like her old self, calm, confident, strong.

Kali started barking and looking toward the river as an otter dove off a rock island and disappeared into the emerald-green water. A few moments later, an otter head emerged and looked up at them before disappearing again. Kali wagged her tail and waited expectantly for another sighting. Maya left her on watch and sat in a chair where she could look at the wildness around her. She watched as a giant golden maple leaf twirled through the airspace above the river, heralding the approach of winter. If they were lucky, they'd see salmon returning to the river's upper reaches.

In the morning, Maya and Nick walked down to the river's edge. Rio had his canine life jacket on, ready to go for a swim. Nick tossed a stick across the slower current in the green pool. Rio launched into the air, splashing into the water. Then he swam vigorously toward the stick as it floated downstream. His ferry was perfect, and before long, Rio angled in, grabbed the stick, and swam to a sandstone ledge on the other side of the river. He dropped the stick and shook before picking it up again, then he plunged back into the river, and ferried back to

Nick and Maya. They repeated the exercise until Rio exited the river and stood with his eyes locked onto the stick as his body shivered uncontrollably.

"He'll keep going until he can't walk. Enough, Rio. You're done." Rio looked at the stick as if he hadn't heard a word she said. "No more." Maya's final command meant they were done.

Kali heard the command and returned from her exploration of the shoreline. Maya was sure she had been searching for the otter she'd seen the day before.

"Let's get our gear ready and head out for a paddle. Jeff and Melissa said they'd be around today to pick us up at Flaming Geyser when we're done. I'll text him with an ETA."

"Got it. Gear bags are already on the deck. Kayaks are in the driveway."

They walked back up and put on their drysuits, helmets, lifejackets, and river shoes before putting the dogs inside for the day.

"If only they could ride in the kayaks. We could take them along," Maya commented.

Nick grabbed his kayak, hoisting it up on his shoulder. "Rio could just swim the river with us. Kali would probably try to run along the entire shoreline instead of swimming."

"She's been on more than a few rescues out here. She'll swim if she has to, but yes, she'd rather be on shore."

They carried their kayaks and paddles down the mossy trail to the river. Maya stretched her spray skirt over her cockpit, seal-launched off the shoreline into slack water, and then crossed the river into the eddy behind the maidenhair fern wall on the other side of the river. Nick slid in behind her and caught the current. She dropped in just above him at the top of the eddy. At the higher level, the water moved quickly, carrying them downstream. A few larger sandstone blocks, otter lounges, still protruded out of the water at this higher water. Under the surface of the current were boulder gardens and sandstone shelves that she and Kali had hiked down on their low-water search missions. The shoreline of ferns, cliffs, and cedar trees rose steeply from the water's edge, leaving very little room for shoreline navigation.

The rare presence of the sunlight created a green glow in the water that seemed to originate from below instead of above them. They played their way downstream as the late morning light flickered through golden autumn leaves. The chill of the early morning faded, except in the deeper shadows along the river corridor. The river spread across shallow sandstone shelves framed in narrow bands of forest below cliff walls. As the river curved to the left, they passed the head of Jellum Peninsula, a protrusion of land that stuck out like a thumb on a map. Maya had been on a rescue for a fisherman who'd fractured his leg after falling on some of the slippery rocks along the shoreline. It was one of the easier hikes to the river, but as they had found, it was a long drive on old logging roads. Now two older fishermen stood along the shoreline, waving as Maya and Nick passed by. She apologized for disrupting their fishing.

Maya gazed down into the shadows cast across the water and, to her surprise, realized they were passing over schools of returning salmon. As she placed her paddle in the water, they quickly darted away from the invader to quieter realms. Maybe her passage would send the salmon in the direction of the fishermen, making their presence less disruptive.

The deeper pool gave way to a series of shelves as the lower forest fell away, revealing a tall, dark cliff face and evidence of trees that had been unearthed by higher water lying along its base.

An island separated the current of the river. Big waves hugged the left cliff wall, and a shallower path spread to the right over a rocky channel. Maya and Nick chose the bigger waves along the cliff wall before dropping down into the pool below Paradise Falls. Here the water was a light emerald green created by sunlight catching the water dancing below the falls.

Maya paddled over to the falls. Nick parked in the eddy across from the falls and took photos of her as she gazed upward into the light spray of the water cascading over the sandstone and into the water next to her.

They continued through the green tunnel, a narrow channel where all the water was corralled between two sandstone shelves. Ferns clung to the walls, and the overhanging forest created a green canopy. Here the water was steeped in dark jade-green shadow. Sunlight broke through tree branches in diamond-shaped prisms and played across the undercut sandstone alcoves.

They exited the channel and eddied out on the left above Paradise Ledge, a surf wave that was one of their favorite play spots. Finding a perch above the ledge, they enjoyed a snack. Then they hiked upstream along a sandstone trail lined with moss as cedars clung to impossible perches on the stone. The sandstone sloped closer to the river upstream of the green channel. Water-carved sandstone depressions framed in bright green moss were filled with rainwater.

At the end of the shelf, the trail turned through an arch formed by two large sandstone blocks. Ivy hung down along the entry like a curtain into a magic realm. On the other side, giant cedars parted and revealed a long, narrow waterfall cascading off a two-hundred-foot white sandstone cliff.

"I can't believe we've never stopped here before. This is incredible," Nick said.

"Well, until recently, it was closed to the public. The property is owned by a family who didn't want the liability. Too many people jumped off those cliffs we paddled under and got injured. I've been on calls for people who've ended up paralyzed or worse. She pointed to steep wooden stairs that led up from the river. "We had to carry them up those stairs to the old Green River Gorge Resort."

"Of course. Hopefully, they weren't too heavy."

"No comment."

They followed the trail to a split. One way went up toward the stairs. The stairs looked new liked they'd been rebuilt for the reopening. The other led to a rock alcove to the side of the falls. Maya felt a tingle in her spine as they passed the alcove. To the side of the stairs, a trail led under a sandstone ledge behind the falls. Carved into the floor of the undercut were soaking pools with a view through the curtain of whitewater cascading across the opening from above. The edge of the ledge had a cable railing to keep people from falling into the river rocks below.

Wax spilled around an old candle anchoring it into the stone near one of the pools, while water dripped from the ceiling.

"This is amazing. Is this natural?" Nick asked.

"I think so. I love this place. One of the benefits of doing search and rescue is discovering places like this. Although, often not in the best circumstances. However, I get to come back later and bring you." She smiled and looked over at him.

"Well, I'm the lucky one, seeing this place without the chaos of an emergency."

"Very true," Maya said as she gazed out at the river and the specter from so many calls. A deep sensation of nausea overwhelmed her; for a moment everything turned dark like night. She kept talking through the feeling, trying to push it down. She heard herself saying, "We should get out of here."

"Out of where, here? You sound strange."

Maya suddenly returned to herself and her surroundings. "Oh, I just meant we should leave and head down the river," she said and quickly skirted past Nick and back to the trail they had come in on.

"Are you okay?"

"I'm fine. I just felt a little odd right before you said something. It's gone now." She walked quickly back to their kayaks, leaving Nick wondering what had just happened.

They surfed Paradise Ledge, dropping into the reversal that formed the beautiful surf wave. They took turns dancing from side to side with their kayaks. Nick effortlessly executed some cartwheels as he found his rhythm. Maya side-surfed, bracing against the downstream wave. She flipped over but quickly rolled her kayak up again.

"Brrr, this water is so cold!" Still, she slid back into the wave again and again for another dance of body, kayak, and moving water, reconnecting her mind and body to the present.

She was so glad that her swim and near-drowning in Troublemaker on the South Fork of the American River hadn't dampened her love of whitewater kayaking.

They continued downstream, catching eddies and navigating the frothy whitewater. Towering maples released brilliant orange and yellow leaves that floated down onto the deep jade green of the deeper pools. At a place called Icy Creek, they saw salmon swimming madly up the shallow entrance of the creek. Their backs were exposed as their bodies writhed wildly, pushing up into the stream to return to their home.

Farther down, the sandstone changed again. Honeycomb formations peeked out from behind the branches of evergreens. The river dropped over small boulders into pools draped with maple branches. A giant mudslide encroached into the river just before they crossed under the highway 169 bridge. She'd driven over that bridge many times on her way to emergency calls.

They caught an eddy on the right and paddled into a small

cave carved into white sandstone. She always felt like an explorer when she entered this cave hidden in the downstream side of the rounded cliff face.

As they continued, the river relaxed as the gorge widened on its final stretch before Flaming Geyser State Park. Paddling into the eddy at the takeout, they saw the local ranger talking with some fishermen along the shore. They stopped talking and looked at Maya and Nick.

Justin immediately recognized Maya and waved. The fishermen stomped off as he turned his attention to Maya.

"Hey, Justin, great to see you," Maya said.

"You too. Did you guys paddle down from Kanaskat?"

Maya and Nick peeled back their spray skirts and stepped out of their kayaks as Maya caught up with Justin. "No, we're staying up at the Gunthers' place. Enjoying some relaxing time off and a couple days of paddling."

"Ahh, the Gunthers. How are they? They moved into town recently, didn't they?"

"They did. It's great, though; they invited Nick and me to use the place anytime. To keep an eye on it and make it feel lived in."

"Aren't you lucky! If I had the money, I'd buy that place in a minute."

"Ya, it's pretty special. How's the ranger business going?"

"It's been a pain lately. Like those fishermen you saw me talking to. They were complaining about having to buy fishing licenses and started to bully me right before you showed up. They seemed to be looking for a fight...over a fishing license! I've had a lot of argumentative visitors lately, especially locals. I just don't get it. How hard can it be to follow the rules? People."

"More awful people than usual? That's saying a lot. You have your hands full."

"Don't get me started. Recently we've had some night-ops dudes out flying drones and moving along the trails in the dark near Kanaskat. We got a call about the activity because the local neighbor saw these guys driving their ATVs into a closed area. They had access to the gate. These guys were all dressed in black, carrying rifles, and wearing night vision goggles.

"I guess they didn't realize that one of us lives in the park full time. We intercepted them at the boundary. They weren't too happy to have us shining a spotlight onto their night vision goggles. They turned and fled. We chased them down the old roads, but they just disappeared. Followed up with local law enforcement. Made me think of that call you were on a couple of years ago, in the gorge."

A jolt went through Maya as she remembered the woman lying on the ground up the river in the Green River Gorge, her eyes frozen open. She was able to shake it off, but an uneasiness settled into her. "That's not good. Did local law enforcement give you any indication on whether they were able to track them or not?"

"No, didn't hear a word from them. We are just keeping our eyes on the park. If we see them again, we'll be more aggressive in tracking them down."

"Well, just stay safe. If it's the same guys that executed that woman, they mean business. I don't know if they are the same militia types that have targeted us, but it seems more than a coincidence." That sense of uneasiness that Maya felt deepened. Again, she shook it off.

"Or the Russians. Been a lot of rumors lately about illegal compounds owned by Russian organized crime out in Ravensdale."

"Could be," Maya replied. "We've had a few calls in questionable living situations out in some of those more remote houses. Nothing that leads me to suspect roving militias of black-clad men, though."

"Be careful. I've heard about a couple of rafters getting harassed by some guys near the Gorge Resort recently."

"We just stopped there. No one bothered us."

"That's good to hear. Keeping our good visitors in the area helps deter the bad ones."

They said goodbye. As Maya and Nick carried their kayaks up to the parking lot, Maya was suddenly struck by a sense of déjà vu. "Nick, I know why I was so off-kilter when we stopped along the river at Paradise."

Nick laid the kayak down and turned to look at Maya with that worried expression of his. "Why?"

"That's where the execution of the woman was two years ago, in the alcove below the falls. You know, when those guys executed her right in front of me. God, I'd completely forgotten about that. I just didn't think about it. How come that call didn't affect me, but the ambush did? I was in as much danger then as during the ambush."

Nick paused. Maya noticed that detached look in his eyes again. As if he was stepping back from what she was saying. Maybe it was too much for him to hear from his future wife. "I don't know, Maya. Maybe you should bring that up in your next session with Dr. Harrington."

Maya looked back towards the river, hesitating before replying. "You're right, I should. It's so crazy. Nothing about how I'm feeling seems predictable. I'm fine one minute and then the next... I just need to figure out what is going to set me off. I'm dealing with the ambush, but maybe there is more I need to address." She turned back to look at Nick with her disarming smile. "I'll bring it up next time I see her."

As she said it, she felt like the words were meant to appease him. She wasn't sure if she should bring it up with Dr. Harrington.

"I know danger is just part of the job, but it has to take its toll after a while, especially after these recent events," Nick said.

Maya could see it in his eyes. She needed to be more guarded in what she shared with him. For most people, her life would be inconceivable. Even Nick wasn't immune from wanting to have things be uncomplicated and predictable. Right now, she was anything but those things. She was on top of things before the ambush. Now that she'd opened the door, maybe other calls affected her in ways she wasn't consciously aware of. That feeling that had overwhelmed her seemed to appear out of nowhere. It's not like she was thinking about witnessing an execution when she and Nick were admiring the waterfall and sandstone oasis. She'd focused on the near-drownings and injuries from jumping off the cliffs. She hadn't thought about the execution for a long time.

Well, just add it to the list, she thought.

Maya texted Jeff that they were ready to be picked up at Flaming Geyser takeout. He texted her back that they were already in the park hiking down the Bubbling Geyser Trail and would be down in about ten minutes.

Maya and Nick peeled off their drysuits. Underneath their clothes were dry. They sat on their kayaks, waiting for Jeff and Melissa. They appeared along the trail near the Wolf Bauer Lodge. They looked relaxed as they made their way over to their truck. Maya hadn't seen it parked under the cedar trees. Jeff drove it over to where Maya and Nick had their kayaks, and they loaded them in the back.

"Thanks for the lift, Jeff," Nick said.

"No problem. It got us out of the house and out for a hike. Ever since we bought the property up here, we spend all our time doing yard work and house projects. Feels good to get out and enjoy the reason we moved here."

"I'm glad we could help," Maya said. "You'll love the Gunthers' place. It's a piece of paradise."

As they drove across the bridge out of the park. Maya saw the two fishermen down along the shoreline with their lines cast in the river.

"Jeff, have you noticed more of those 'Don't Tread on Me' flags lately? Driving in yesterday, we saw businesses and trucks flying those flags. I don't remember seeing those last time I worked out here."

"They are all over now," Melissa replied. "Our neighbors have them at the entrances to their properties. It's been mostly in the last year. Maybe it's an election thing. We have the election coming up for the area's position on the County Council. We noticed the Republican challenger, Titus, launched a fierce campaign against his Republican incumbent in the primaries. They called the incumbent a 'RINO,' you know, Republican in name only. After he won, Titus shifted to a ruthless campaign against the Democratic challenger."

"Okay, so they don't like the Republican they elected anymore?" Maya asked.

Melissa continued, "No, he disappointed them last year. Titus, the new candidate, is a local guy who wants to cut taxes, arm teachers and put prayer back in schools. I thought they never allowed prayer in schools anyway. You know, separation of church and state."

"The guy has the support of a local mega-church, so it makes sense that he's pro-religion in schools," Jeff said, and as he spoke Maya could see his jaw harden. "Leave religion in the church where it belongs. We moved out here to have some space and a quieter lifestyle. We're planning on having kids. I want my kids to be able to choose whether they want to partici-

pate in any religion. In school, they need to learn, not be indoc-
trinated."

"You guys are planning on having kids? Soon? Don't tell me
we're going to lose our DINK friends," Maya said.

"DINK?" Melissa looked at Maya inquisitively.

"'Dual income, no kids.' Basically, friends that we can go
out and do things with. Once you have kids, it's all over. We'll
be coming over for birthdays. We'd love that, but we're slowly
losing our footloose friends. Everyone is having kids."

Jeff laughed. "Hey, just because we're going to have kids
doesn't mean we won't be able to do things with you guys.
Besides, there's no turning back now. Melissa is three months'
pregnant. We were going to tell you guys tonight at dinner, but
now is just as good."

"Wow, congrats. We're happy for you. Even though we'll
miss out on doing things with you for the next eighteen years,"
Nick said.

"Hey, we'll make the time. Besides, once our kids are
teenagers, they won't want to do anything with us anyway!" Jeff
replied.

Maya laughed. "True enough. I can't believe you're having
a baby. Congratulations!"

They turned down the road to the Gunthers' gate. It started
to rain, so Jeff switched on the windshield wipers.

"Good thing you guys finished up when you did. You
lucked out today. It's been raining so much this fall. I just hope
it doesn't start flooding again," Jeff said.

Nick nodded. "You seem to get a lot more rain out here
than we do in Seattle."

They pulled into the driveway. Maya could hear the dogs
barking at their arrival. Once they were in the house, Maya let
the dogs out, and they immediately headed for the river.

"I'm just going to follow the dogs down to the river. Rio

might as well swim. With this rain, he'll already be wet. Do you guys want to join me?"

"We'll pass. Maybe it will stop in a while, and then we can go down," Jeff said.

Maya followed the trail down to the river. The dogs were already there. She heard a big splash as Rio dove into the river. Maya hunkered down under her raincoat. She could feel big drops falling from overhead trees. As she stood there, it started to rain harder.

She was awash with the sound of rain and whitewater as she watched Rio swimming in circles waiting for her to throw a stick. She reached down, picked up a large branch that had fallen off an overhanging maple, and swung it across the river as far as she could. Rio took off in pursuit.

Maya thought about the execution she'd pushed out of her mind. In light of what had happened with the ambush, it seemed odd that she would have completely brushed off a call where she watched as a woman was executed right next to her. *How did I feel after that?* She tried to remember. Nothing. She'd attended the debriefing and, like almost everyone she worked with, felt it was a waste of time. She'd already moved on. Talking about it just seemed like an arduous task of rehashing the details. *Better left in the past,* she had thought without a hint of, well, any emotion.

Rio barked at her, drawing her attention back to the sole reason she was there, to throw the stick for him. She chuckled. "Rio, you keep it real!"

Kali grabbed the branch from the water's edge and brought it to Maya. "Thanks, Kali," she said as Kali dropped it at her feet. Maya heaved the branch across the river, promptly followed by Rio diving in again to chase after it. His large paws surged through the green current.

"Okay, Rio, that's the last one. I'm getting soaked out here."

She turned to start walking back up, knowing that he'd only follow her if he was sure she couldn't be guilted into another round. Pretty soon both dogs joined her on the walk back. Inside, she spent another ten minutes drying the dogs.

Nick, Jeff, and Melissa were sitting in the living room. Looking out the tall windows as the rain pelted the glass, she was thankful for the warmth of the fireplace as she grabbed a glass of wine and joined them.

Nick looked up as Maya walked in. "We were just discussing what Jeff and Daniel have been following in one of the right-wing forums."

Maya sat down next to Nick. "Nick has told me some of what you guys have uncovered to date, but fill me in."

"We were talking about an uptick in chatter from an encrypted web forum Jeff located," Nick said. "Lots of, well, it sounds like a lot of code words and talk that is meant to give instructions and information. It has a more serious tone to it than some of the other sites we've come across. I geolocated it to a place just outside North Bend near the old Mailbox Peak Trail we hiked last summer."

Maya took a sip of her wine. "Maybe we should go up there and check it out?"

"Maybe. Jeff, would you be interested in going?" Nick asked.

"You bet. If we can track down some of these guys, we can give HS more information to build on. I have a hard time believing they don't have their eyes on these guys already now that they are blowing up buildings and shooting first responders. They have to have their investigators tracking the movement of these groups."

"It would certainly be a change in course. Not too long ago these groups were given a free pass to do pretty much whatever they wanted. Remember those militia members who occupied that government building down in Oregon?" Maya asked.

Jeff rolled his eyes. "I do. Aren't they the ones who called for someone to bring them food and supplies to tide them over during their occupation?"

Nick nodded. "That was them. From the look of things, these guys seem to be a little more organized than the group down in Oregon."

"Sounds like a good excuse for a little recon, and we'll get a good workout in," Maya said.

Melissa looked worried. "Are you guys sure? It could be risky. What if they find out you're there to investigate their location?"

"How would they know? There are a ton of hikers on those trails in the Middle Fork on weekends. We'll blend in with everyone else." Maya smiled at Melissa in an attempt to alleviate some of her fear.

"I guess you're right." Maya caught Melissa looking at Jeff, her eyes asking him not to do it.

"I know this seems trivial, given what's been going on at work, but be careful," Melissa said.

"You know we will, but remember, we won't be any safer until these groups are neutralized." Jeff's previous military experience was showing through. "These groups are not only a danger to us personally, but also to our communities. If unchecked, the stability of the country could unravel. I've done my time in third world countries whose governments toppled. It's not something I'm willing to stand around and watch happen here."

Maya saw the edge of fear in Melissa's eyes as she realized that Jeff wasn't going to avoid the danger of a recon. She should've known him by now. Jeff thrived on risk and danger.

"I agree," Nick said. "Too much of what we've been finding

leads to local and national movements. Anything we can give HS that provides them with information on this movement is one way we can help. Besides, I will not be able to sleep well, knowing that at any time another bomb could go off or you could be ambushed again."

"Me too," echoed Melissa. "I never used to worry, but since the ambush, I've been stressed out every time Jeff goes to work. It makes me realize what it must be like to be a cop's wife."

"I know how hard it is on you two. Jeff and I, at least, can break it down into solutions and tasks to keep from being over-whelmed by what could happen. But, even for us, everything has changed and made it harder to just do our job."

Fear gnawed at the edges of Maya's mind. She redirected her attention. "Let's plan on going next Saturday. Do you have the GPS location we can use to navigate ourselves as close as possible to get a view of the place?"

"We do. I'll overlay the location with the Mailbox trails and see if we can't get close or at least find a few vantage points where we can see the site," Nick said. "Jeff, let's do more research and see if there are any links from that group on some of the other channels you and Daniel are on. Then maybe we can locate some of the other players."

Maya felt relieved. Nick seemed genuinely engaged in making sure she was safe. Maybe he just needed to feel more in control of what was happening to her at work.

"Daniel and I will work on it this week. It might give us more information on the ground," Jeff said.

"On another note, Nick and I were talking to the ranger at the park today. The rangers stumbled on a militia-type night ops maneuver near Kanaskat State Park. The description sounds similar to the group that showed up the night they executed the woman at the Green River Gorge Resort."

"I remember that. You were working with Doug, a probie at the time," Jeff said.

"Anyway, I will follow up with HS about what the rangers intercepted. He said he hadn't received any information from local law enforcement after the event was reported. You would think the local sheriff's office would have followed up with the rangers."

"You should definitely let them know. I sometimes wonder how information gets shared in some of these rural areas," Jeff said. "They are a lot more connected out here. People know each other, and law enforcement often lives in these same communities. That reminds me. You know the husband of that woman executed at the gorge? Jay and Doug responded to a call at the Gorge Resort. He committed suicide. Blew his brains out. They said it was a mess inside his trailer. Brains everywhere."

"Hey, TMI, Jeff. I'm nauseated enough as it is without that description," Melissa said.

"Sorry, sorry. I know you hate when I bring up the gory details of the job, especially around food." He smiled at Melissa as he grabbed a handful of tortilla chips from the bowl on the coffee table.

Melissa shot him a scorching look.

"They're sure it was a suicide?" Maya asked.

"From what Jay said, it all pointed to a suicide. Single gunshot to the head. No note, but that doesn't mean anything. I'm sure the medical examiner did an autopsy. I don't think Jay followed up on the outcome, and nothing was on the news."

"Hmmm, could be," Maya said. "I'll ask Jay more about it when I see him." Maya reached for the bottle of red wine on the coffee table and poured herself another glass.

Melissa stood up. "Jeff and I brought lasagna and a salad. We knew you guys would be on the river most of the day. Let's get dinner going and talk about something a little more light-hearted, like Kali pushing Rio off his dog bed. I guess Kali likes it as much as he does."

They all looked over at the dogs. Kali was sprawled out on her side, with her legs strategically pushing Rio slowly off the side of the bed. His head hung down over the edge and they could see that he was trying to resist by digging in with his front legs while his back legs were making an exit.

They laughed. "Who do you think is going to win?" Jeff asked.

"Rio, definitely Rio. He's letting her feel like she's winning, but in the end, he always gets the bed," Maya said.

They left the dogs to battle for the bed and moved to the kitchen to get dinner started. Before long, they were feasting on lasagna and salad. Maya's attention was diverted by good conversation and a mild buzz from a couple of glasses of wine. So far, she'd done pretty well, backing off on the drinking, not quitting, but cutting back. She knew drinking more tonight wouldn't help her get her head straight, but right now, she wanted to ease into an easy banter with her good friends. Even so she couldn't quite shake the feeling that Nick was looking at her with displeasure. She was drinking again when she told him she wouldn't.

CHAPTER NINE

AS MAYA SAT BUNDLED up in a blanket drinking her coffee on the deck overlooking the river, soaking in the early morning sun, she tried to remember the details of the woman's execution.

The call came in as a domestic disturbance on Green Valley Road. Above the beauty of the Green River Gorge was a place that Maya knew from various calls. The Green River Gorge Resort hadn't been a "resort" in years. Inside its walls were the echoes of a different time. Outside a few old timers sat on a dusty porch with an occasional lazy dog. Resident peacocks strutted across the road or perched on the resort rooftop.

Beyond the building was a hodgepodge of travel trailers, fifth wheels, and RVs. Some had been there so long they were covered in moss with fern-covered roofs. From what she could tell, it was a mix of eccentric characters, old hippies, ragged locals, traveling full-time RVers, and maybe even some outlaws living on the edge of Green River Gorge.

Apparently, the couple had gotten into a raucous argument. Both had been drinking all day. The woman ran, half-clothed, from their trailer to the stairway leading down to the river. The man was heard yelling, "I'm going to kill you, you bitch" as he stumbled after her. One bystander said they heard the clang of the gate to the stairway. Then they heard a scream and the sound of something tumbling down the stairs, another scream, and the sound of something hitting the rocks below.

They were called for an assault and fall. Maya's medic unit and the city of Enumclaw firefighters joined the local volunteer fire department. The sheriff's deputies had arrived first and had subdued the drunk pursuer, yarding him up the steps before he became another fall victim.

At three in the morning, the only light illuminating the gate to the stairway was from a streetlamp that illuminated the road near the entrance to a one-lane bridge that spanned the river gorge. Beyond that, the lights from the emergency vehicles flashed against the dark shadows of thick forest, barely cutting through it.

The firefighters grabbed their rescue gear, litter, and large flashlights to illuminate their descent into the gorge. Maya and her partner, Doug, put on their rescue helmets with headlamps and life jackets. They grabbed their backcountry medical kits, and flashlights, then followed the firefighters down the rickety stairs. Maya heard a loud creak as one of the bigger firefighters stepped onto the landing. He almost slid across the moss-covered landing toward what remained of a broken railing. Everyone stopped moving.

"We're going to set up ropes from above," the fire captain said. He motioned to the volunteer next to him. "Glenn, I want you and Chris to carefully go down and see if you can get to the patient and quickly assess what we need to treat her. Take the Stokes litter with you."

They could periodically hear the woman moaning and

whimpering from below the broken railing. Maya called out, "I'm Maya, a paramedic. We'll be down to help you. Hold on a little longer." The woman didn't answer back.

Maya turned to the captain and stated, "I'm going to go down with them and see if I can start treatment."

"Absolutely not! It's too dangerous. We need to get protection set first."

"I understand, but I've been here many times before. I know what to expect down there, and it's going to take a while for you to get set up."

"Look, I can't let you go down there," he replied.

"Then don't," Maya said.

She turned to Doug and instructed him to go up and set up treatments in the medic unit for when they brought the patient up. With that, she turned and headed down the stairs as the captain looked at her in disbelief.

She walked carefully down the stairs using her lights to inspect the treads. She placed each foot firmly before proceeding down the next step. Before long, she was squeezing between two rocks into an alcove. The woman was lying in a couple of inches of water with the two firefighters crouched next to her.

Maya asked, "How's she doing?"

"She's in and out of consciousness," Glenn replied. "She has a weak pulse. We haven't taken a BP yet. She's freezing. It looks like her right femur and right arm are fractured. I can't tell yet what other injuries she has."

"Let's see if we can get her in a C-collar, backboard, and into the litter to get her out of the water and up to a place where we can work on her. This is not the place to try and do that," Maya stated.

As they worked, they heard a commotion from above, loud yelling over the sound of the river and waterfall. Then the gate slammed, followed by multiple footsteps pounding down the rickety stairs, and a cracking sound. A male voice yelled, "Fuck, goddamn stairs."

"You idiot. Pull yourself out of there. Let's get this done!" came another voice.

The footsteps grew louder. Three men appeared from the entrance of the alcove. As Maya's light illuminated them, she saw they were dressed in all black with ski masks hiding their faces. She also saw their AR-15s pointed at her and the two firefighters.

The firefighters immediately stood up and backed away from the woman. Almost as though they had been expecting something like this to happen.

"Miss, you need to step over there," said a more prominent man who seemed to be in charge. It was the same voice she'd heard yelling at the man who fell through the stairs.

"I need to start care of..." Maya suddenly realized that something else was going on here. She stood and backed up.

She watched helplessly as the man pulled out a handgun, pointing it at the woman lying on the ground. A flash erupted as he fired a bullet into the woman's head. The moaning stopped. Maya shuddered in fear as she realized what had just happened.

Just as quickly as the men had appeared, they receded through the alcove and into the darkness of the night.

Maya reached down to feel for the woman's pulse, but she already knew there was nothing she could do.

She heard more commotion above. Then someone called down on a loudspeaker. "Stay where you are. We'll be down to get you."

Maya looked over at the firefighters. They were unusually reserved, considering what had just happened.

"Do you guys know who those guys were?"

"Couldn't tell. They were wearing those masks. Just knew they weren't here to help," Glenn said.

"Sure looks like they didn't want her to leave here alive," said the other firefighter as he stared down at the dead woman.

Maya looked down at her again. Under the illumination of their flashlights, they could see blood oozing out of the entrance wound on her temple, mixing with the pool of blood and brain matter from the exit wound.

"I wonder why they wanted her dead," Maya said as she looked back toward the alcove entrance.

"I guess she knew too much," the second firefighter said.

Glenn gave him a stern look, and he didn't say anything else.

"I think her husband must have had some friends help finish what he started. Domestic turned deadly," Glenn said.

Maya felt that he knew more. Something was off here. She could feel it.

Four deputies came into the alcove. "Are you guys all right?" one of them asked.

Maya could hear more incoming sirens, lots of them.

"Yes, we're okay. The men seemed to have come here specifically to murder our patient. They shot her in the head." Maya pointed her light towards the dead woman's entrance wound.

The lead deputy pointed his flashlight at the woman. "So that's why they showed up."

"Who?" Maya asked.

"Not sure exactly. All we know is that the woman and her husband are known members of a local militia. She must have pissed them off."

He looked at Maya and the firefighters. "Let's get you guys out of here and back up top. We'll take it from here."

Maya picked up her pack and followed two of the deputies

up the stairs. She was followed by the two firefighters. The other deputies stayed behind to secure the scene and any evidence left by the executioners.

As they walked up the stairs, Maya saw where one of the men had fallen through the rotted stair tread. She could see some blood along the right edge. She ran her flashlight up and down the stairs and noted the blood drops going down the stairs but none going back up.

"Looks like one of them was injured when he fell through the stair tread. There's a blood trail leading down the stairs. You might want to flag this to preserve the evidence trail," Maya said to the deputies.

"We'll get on that. Thanks for the heads up." The deputy radioed up for more flagging.

"No problem. I heard a man swearing as he fell through."

When they got to the top, there were more sheriff's deputy cars and fire department vehicles. Their medical shift supervisor, Greg, had arrived and stood next to the fire chief and sheriff's sergeant at the command center behind the chief's vehicle. Lights blazed in every direction illuminating a wide swath of roadway and penetrating the edges of the surrounding forest. Police were spread out around the perimeter of the command area.

Just then, a County tactical SWAT vehicle rolled in. Its size and black paint commanded attention. The SWAT team members filed out of the personnel carrier. One of their members walked towards the command center. Maya watched as SWAT command tied in with the sheriff's sergeant.

Maya walked over to Greg and the fire chief. "What happened? One minute this was a domestic, and then the next minute, three shadowy goons showed up and executed our patient."

"Maya, there were twenty of them," the chief replied.

"They just appeared out of the woods and held all of us at gunpoint while three of them went down to where you were treating the patient. Once they heard the gunshot, they disappeared back into the forest."

"Same thing down there. The men shot her and then disappeared into the dark," Maya replied.

They all looked up as they heard a helicopter approaching from the west. They watched as a spotlight started scanning the forest. Maya wondered how well the executioners knew the gorge.

"Look, you guys are on standby while SWAT tracks these guys. We also have more deputies with dogs to search in and out of the gorge," Greg said. "They want us here in case anyone gets injured."

"Good luck to them," Maya said. "That is rugged country down there. I hope no one falls into the river, or we'll be doing a body recovery."

She watched as a small SWAT team headed down into the gorge. The rest fanned out into the trailer park and surrounding forest.

"They're securing the trailer area to ensure no one is hiding there," the chief said. "They'll interview the residents to gather information. They are being staged in the house above us."

Maya's partner joined them from the medic unit, where he'd hunkered down during the ambush.

"What a start to your career, Doug."

"That was intense! I wasn't sure what was going on at first. Then I saw a guy under the streetlamp, all dressed in black, with a black mask and what looked like a rifle. I ducked between the cab and the box, hoping I wouldn't be seen. Then I radioed that we were under attack."

"That explains the quick response of additional resources," Maya replied.

"Good move," Greg said.

Maya saw the look of satisfaction as Doug received praise from Greg. It was rare to receive recognition in their line of work.

"All right, rookie, don't get too big of a head. We've got a long night of standby ahead of us," Maya said.

Maya feared for him. Times were changing fast, and the danger had grown exponentially with the rise of the right-wing militias destabilizing communities. She feared this was the rise of something worse than a few isolated local events.

"How are you doing?" Maya asked.

"I'm great. I'm just glad everyone is okay...well, except the patient."

She could see the mix of fear and excitement in his expression that accompanied those first calls as a new paramedic. This was a call he'd never forget.

CHAPTER TEN

NICK SPENT the week researching the compound using the most recent aerial photos and correlating that with his GPS signal location. After mapping the compound, they devised a strategy to take a closer look.

Maya and Nick met up with Jeff at the Starbucks just off the freeway in North Bend. Maya and Nick were surprised to see Melissa with Jeff.

"Why do you look so surprised? I decided that if he was risking his life off duty, I was going with him. If I stayed home, I'd have worried about him," Melissa said, giving Maya a hug.

Maya laughed. "I'm glad you're coming. It will give me someone to talk with about other things besides spy craft. They're taking the lead on this operation. I'm just a follower."

They walked out with their coffee. "Hey, where are Kali and Rio?" Jeff asked.

"I thought it might be good to leave them at home today. If we were intercepted and they thought I was threatened... Well, you know how Kali took out Xavier in Tahoe. No need to put them through that kind of stress."

They rode together in Jeff's truck. At the trailhead, Nick pulled out his iPad so they could see their recon map.

"I ran the coordinates and have a good plan. The property is southwest of Mailbox. You can see it here on the map. It sits on the top of a slight rise. The property is cleared at the top, close to I-90. There is an old road along the property that joins the main access road to the site. This trail down from the old Mailbox Peak intersects that road. We can start up the main trail and divert onto this trail that leads to the road. Then we can walk the road up to the property.

"See, this fenced area? The fence emerges from these trees, then hugs the edge of the clearing and slopes toward the freeway and main access road."

Nick pointed to the road and how it intersected the clearing before continuing down towards I-90 and the road that paralleled it. Maya could see what he was talking about. Easy access except for the section that crossed the clearing.

"We can get a look on the ground and then turn around, hike up to the top of Mailbox, and use our binoculars and your camera to get an overhead view of the area. I'd use a drone, but that might be too obvious."

"I'm sure they wouldn't be too happy to see a drone flying overhead. Although now that everyone's buying them, it's probably happened once or twice," Jeff commented.

"Well, does this all sound good to you guys?" Nick asked.

Maya, Jeff, and Melissa nodded.

"Also, Jeff and I discussed this ahead of time. Here is mace for you and Melissa." He reached in his pack and started to hand a small can of mace to each of them.

Maya shook her head. "I've already got mine."

Melissa looked at her and then took the can of mace from Nick. "I didn't realize this was quite so dangerous."

"Jeff is going to carry on this one."

Jeff lifted his loose sport shirt to reveal a holster with his gun.

"You didn't tell me you were bringing a gun. Do you think we need that?" Melissa asked, a look of disapproval on her face.

"Look, I wanted to have it just in case. Especially since you decided to come. I want to be able to protect us if we're intercepted near the property. I should have told you."

"You know you should have," Melissa replied.

"Hopefully, we won't need it, but I didn't want to leave it to chance." Jeff looked at her with a protective stoicism that she knew too well.

They arrived at the busy trailhead and snagged the last spot in the parking lot. "It's only 7 a.m.," Maya commented.

"It's a popular area. Mountains to Sound Greenway conserved these areas along I-90. One of the reasons I love living here, but it does get a bit crowded on weekends," Melissa said.

Maya looked around at all the cars. "I wish there weren't so many of us out enjoying the trails. It's hard to commune with nature when surrounded by a city's worth of people."

"Well, this is one of the busiest day hikes in the Greenway, but that will be perfect for today if we're spotted," Melissa said.

Nick nodded. "I agree. However, let's discuss our cover story, so if we get discovered along that fence line, we can talk our way out of any confrontation."

As they walked, they discussed strategy. "If we're seen, let's play dumb," Nick said. "We just took a wrong turn. If we take photos, let's do it under the guise of taking photos of each other. Jeff, I'll put you on that. You probably have a better idea of what we might be looking for."

"Will do."

The approach to the Mailbox climb was straightforward.

Before arriving at the steep climb, Nick pointed out the side trail. "This is our turn-off. We take this to the old road."

They turned onto the overgrown trail through tight stands of young trees. In places, it was rutted with what looked like motorcycle tires. Maya observed that it was probably an established motorcycle trail.

"The old timers at work told me the Middle Fork drainage used to be the wild west," Melissa said. "Wild camps and off-road vehicles. People used to dump their garbage or leave it when they were done camping."

Melissa, always the exuberant talker, turned to her recent yoga retreat in Costa Rica. Maya just listened. She thought it might be a good idea for her at some point. A way to get more centered after they got through this crisis. If they ever got through it. Again, she wondered if this was just the beginning of a new civil war.

"Maya, you should come with me next time," Melissa said, breaking through Maya's diversion to darker thoughts.

"I was also thinking about that. Once we get through this crazy time, I'll do it as a reset. It certainly wouldn't hurt me to meditate and connect with my body. Sometimes I feel a disconnect between my body and my mind. The stress of the job throws everything out of balance. Then throw in those sleepless nights..."

"Jeff has started doing yoga with me."

"At first, I wasn't interested in it, but she talked me into it," Jeff said.

Maya smiled. "Imagine that."

"I quiet my mind and stretch those muscles that always seem to be in knots from our kits. When will they design something that works for the human body? Forty years of tradition unimpeded by progress. The old guard is happy with the status quo."

"Jeff, you'll be the next generation of leadership in no time. Then you can make changes. For now, we just adapt. Right?" Maya said.

"Adapt. Right. Don't change what's wrong. Just ask your people to suck it up and deal with it."

"Jeff, we were talking about the benefits of yoga, not what's wrong at work," Melissa said.

"You're right. I don't know where that came from."

Maya knew where Jeff was coming from. Change was coming but at a generational pace. Luckily for her, there was a growing acknowledgment of the mental health challenges inherent in the job, but why couldn't things change more quickly?

"It came from the frustration of living with the decisions of those above us. Like I said, just wait. You'll get your turn. I can see you want to make leadership decisions to improve operations. We will change things if we can just hold on."

Soon enough, they reached the road. A well-worn gravel road that headed both east and west. They turned to the west.

"We're getting close to the open area. We'll take the right side of the loop. That will let us stay in the forest so we can get closer to the area with the most buildings.

"We have some time before we access the area. I'll let you know when we're getting closer," Nick said.

As they approached the clearing, they encountered a cargo container just inside the fence.

They looked for cameras or any sign of movement. Jeff motioned for Nick to stand in front of the container and quickly took some photos of it. As they reached the end, they saw a series of haybales, stacked logs, and a carved-out hillside of dirt and rock. Against it were targets set up at various heights. On the ground were rectangular blocks and sandbags.

On the opposite side, they could see a long open shelter that faced the hillside.

"Jackpot. Looks like we got what we came for," Jeff whispered. He quickly shot a few photos on his cell phone. "Hey, girls, how about a couple of photos? You know, for our friends back at the station."

Maya and Melissa mocked like they were holding guns with the compound in the back. Jeff used this as a way to zoom in on various details.

"Let's keep moving. We want to get as much intel while we can," Nick said.

The road turned back into the woods, away from the clearing. As they followed it, they heard motors, like ATVs.

"That was quick. Looks like the compound has cameras," Jeff said.

Jeff stashed his cell phone. Maya placed her mace in her side pants pocket, just in case.

As the roar of the engines grew louder, they prepared themselves for the confrontation. Two rock crawlers appeared from around the corner in front of them, stopping fifteen feet away. The rock crawlers were painted camouflage, and the two occupants wore camo. They had helmets and buffs with skull faces pulled up over their noses.

They exited the rock crawlers. A tall, imposing man with a fit physique and tattoo-lined arms stepped toward them, his hand on a gun at his side. He kept his buff over his lower face. He was wearing sunglasses, so Maya couldn't read his eyes. Maya noticed they were wearing bulletproof vests.

"You're trespassing. You know this is private land, right? What are you doing here?"

Nick stepped forward. Maya watched as he took a non-threatening posture. "No, we weren't aware. We're out for a hike. We saw this connection up Mailbox and thought we'd take advantage of the extra mileage."

"This area isn't open to the public. Turn around and go back the way you came."

"We'd be happy to do that, and we're sorry for the intrusion," Nick replied.

The other man stepped up to join the first man. "Why were you taking photos back there?"

He scowled at them as his stocky frame stood at rigid attention with one hand resting on his gun. "Hand over your phone!"

Jeff came forward. "Look, we were admiring your facility. We had no idea this was here until now. I know, it's stupid. We just got caught up in the moment. It's not worth losing my phone over this. I'll delete the photos if that will make a difference."

"Delete those photos. I'll watch you do it."

"Got it." Jeff slowly walked over to the shorter man. He pulled out his phone and faced him. He showed the man the photos and then selected and deleted them.

"Empty your trash," the man commanded.

Jeff went to his recently deleted folder on his phone and deleted the images. "Okay, they're deleted. Are we good?"

"I suppose so. You're lucky. We could have shot you for trespassing, and we'd be within our right to do so."

"Hey, Rick, relax. These people aren't here to cause trouble. Just let them go back the way they came. We're good," the tall man said.

"Thank you, sir. We'll be on our way," Maya said.

"Just a minute," the shorter man said. "Show me your driver's licenses. I want your names. That way, if you decide to come back here, we'll have a record that you were here before. Next time, we might not be so nice."

Maya tensed. Déjà vu overwhelmed her. She didn't want to be a target if they decided they were a threat.

"Hey, we'll be on our way. We don't carry our licenses when we're hiking. As you can see, we are traveling light," Jeff said.

"Don't give me that bullshit! Pull them out now."

"Jesus, Rick. Don't make this into more than it is."

The man ignored the taller man. "Slowly get them for me."

Maya, Melissa, Jeff, and Nick looked at each other. Then Melissa interceded, "Sir, this was a misunderstanding. We thought it was part of the Washington State Fire Academy. Jeff, here, is a firefighter, and they've run trails out of the facility. We just thought this was part of that trail system. Didn't Weyerhaeuser used to own this land?"

The taller man looked at Jeff. "You're a firefighter?"

"Was, now I'm a paramedic and ex-military. Like I said, we were hiking. Gotta stay fit."

"Where do you work?"

"In South County. I can give you my badge number."

"No, that won't be necessary. Rick, let's go. You guys have a good day. Enjoy your hike."

Rick was just about to say something when the taller man cut him short. "Forget it. Let's go. We'll talk later."

The men stood and watched as they turned around and hurried off in the direction they had come from. They could feel the eyes following them from behind. They were done with their 'on the ground' recon. This place was obviously outfitted with surveillance cameras. Who knew how many?

When they were back on the Mailbox Peak trail, they stopped to catch their breath.

"Well, that was interesting," Nick said.

"Good call, Melissa. You disarmed them with that firefighter pass," Maya said.

"Well, I thought it was worth a try. Like getting pulled over for speeding, and the cop sees your IAFF sticker. Besides, everyone likes firefighters!"

"I'm not sure I would have complied with their request for our licenses. I don't want people running around in camo with guns having our addresses," Nick said. "Next time, if there is a next time, we'll make sure to come without identification."

"I agree. Too bad the smaller guy made you delete the photos, Jeff," Maya said.

"Well, luckily, I uploaded them to the cloud right after I took them. Just in case we were intercepted."

"That sounds like something Nick would do. Smart," Maya said.

"Who does own that land now?" Melissa asked.

"When I pulled up the ownership, it was an LLC, Gunmount Land Excavation," Nick replied. "From what I could see from the satellite, it looked like it had grading equipment parked at the front of the property. Interestingly, much of what we saw wasn't obvious on the sat image."

"Since they are a land excavation company, I'll see what I can pull up in the County's permitting database," Melissa said.

"I forgot you work for the environmental consulting agency and can access that information," Nick said. "That might lead to more details on the land use and ownership. See if we can get behind who owns the LLC."

"Now we can get our workout in and see what we can from the top of Mailbox," Maya said.

Melissa started to run, calling over her shoulder, "Last one to the top has to buy dinner!"

Nick quickly overtook her and sprinted upward. Soon all their attention was on the precariously steep footholds. It was less a trail than a steep ladder of earth, roots, and rocks.

"I forgot how steep this trail is," Jeff commented.

"It's definitely a challenge," Maya said.

The adrenaline she still felt from the encounter with the men pulsed through her body, and she easily pushed her pace. Luckily the encounter turned out okay. She wondered what would have happened if they had shot them as trespassers on their property. Would it be legal for them to do that? Maya realized they might have literally dodged a bullet. *God*, she thought, *I have to quit doing this on my days off.* But if this is what it took to make her workdays a little less dangerous, then she guessed it was worth the risk.

Trees crowded around the well-worn path. Chunks of rocks protruded in awkward angles as snaking roots created trip hazards. They passed hikers going at a slower pace. As they emerged from the forest onto an open scree field, they could see rocks and more rocks paving the way up the false summit before the last pitch.

Maya kicked into high gear to try and keep up with Jeff and Nick. Melissa was breathing down her neck. Sweat streamed down her back as she pushed harder to the summit. The last section of steep dirt wove between mountain shrubs and small trees. They topped out at the famous Mailbox sticking out of its rocky perch atop the mountain. Before them, the views spread out in all directions, and so did all the people. Every rocky perch was taken up by hikers.

"What were you saying earlier about the crowded parking lot?" Jeff commented.

"I know. Everyone is up here," Maya replied.

Maya searched around and found an area just off the top where they could sit and see the compound. "I noticed that the view from the lower scree field is better, but let's take a break. We can look from here and take another look lower down."

Dripping with sweat from the challenging push up the mountain, Maya was now cooling down. She reached for a jacket before pulling out her camera with its 600-zoom lens. She zoomed in for a closer look at the compound but couldn't make out details. They might have a better view if they went down to the lower scree field.

Maya turned her attention to the views surrounding her. From their perch, she could see the I-90 corridor and hear the distant hum of traffic. Farther to the south, beyond the forested ridgelines, she could see Mount Rainier. The clear day meant the "mountain was out." To the west, she could see North Bend and Lake Sammamish. Surprisingly it was clear all the way to the distant Olympic Mountains on the other side of Puget Sound. To the north, she could just make out Mount Baker. A spectacular payoff for getting to the top.

"I love this view," Melissa said.

They sat in silence, even Melissa, while they enjoyed the view and snacked, fueling up for the hike down. Maya looked at Jeff. "Jeff, did you bring it?"

"Of course, I did."

"What?" Nick asked.

"I asked Jeff to bring a copy of a photo of Kelly and Brian we all signed at the funeral memorial. I wanted to leave it in the mailbox. To honor them and let them know we're looking for the people who murdered them," Maya said.

"Oh, I didn't know."

"I didn't mention it. The mailbox is just a place where people leave mementos and like now, tributes for those who are no longer with us. It's just a little thing to remember them by. It seemed a good place, considering we are here to try and find their killers." Maya almost started to cry but quickly pushed the emotions down. *I've never been this emotional in public. What's wrong with me?*

"Are you okay?" Nick asked.

"I'm sad and frustrated that we still haven't found out who

murdered them." She got up and motioned to Jeff to head up to the mailbox. "We better get this done while I still can."

They all walked up to the mailbox. On the outside of it were colorful stickers, mostly outdoor gear emblems. Maya opened the lid. Inside were an assortment of handwritten notes, photographs, painted rocks, charms, and other odd offerings to the mountain gods. Jeff pulled out the photo. He placed it in the mailbox as people around them looked on. How many had brought their own offerings to this special mailbox?

"To Kelly and Brian," Jeff said quietly.

They all stood silently for a moment. A chill ran through Maya's body. Whether from the memory or the light breeze swirling around her.

Without saying another word, they all started back down the trail. When they arrived at the lower scree field, they found an excellent location to set up surveillance. With their focus on the compound, Maya felt her emotions settle into resolve instead of sadness.

From their new perch, they had a much better view of the compound. Nick and Jeff had high-powered binoculars that could magnify more details. Her job with the camera was to take photos they could take a closer look at later.

She scanned the interior of the clearing and zoomed in on the shooting range. From above, the hillside behind the clearing was covered with trees. She could see the roof of the covered area was painted with the same color as the earth surrounding it.

"Look, another area has buildings and more structures behind the hillside. The rock crawlers are parked near one of the structures. There is a large area draped with camouflage at the edge of some trees. I can't see anything underneath it. I guess they don't want anyone to see it from the air."

Jeff moved his binoculars to the area Maya was referring to.

"Look, there's a group coming out from underneath the camou-flaged area. It's a group dressed like the guys we met down there. They're getting into the rock crawlers. One guy is returning under the cover. The others are driving toward the shooting area."

"Wait, look, two black pickup trucks are leaving through the main gate. There's a guard at the gate. He's got a gun slung over his shoulder, and he's waving them through."

"I'm taking photos of them right now along with that guard. Their turning towards North Bend."

I'll take a few of the camo area, too," Maya said.

Just then, Maya could hear the distant pops of gunfire down in the valley. The sound echoed off the hills.

"Well, that explains why they can shoot there without too much exposure. I guess, unless you are close to them, the sound could be coming from anywhere," Jeff said

"Hey, I know you guys are doing recon, but could I get a look through one of your binoculars just so I feel included?" Melissa asked.

"Sure, anything for you, darling," Jeff said and handed the binoculars to Melissa.

Maya zoomed in on the shooting area and tried to capture as much as possible. As she focused on the targets, something caught her eye. "Nick, Melissa, can you guys get a closer look at those targets? They look like real people, not paper targets."

"I'm looking. It looks like dummies on a stake. Bullets hit one of them, and the stake lurched backward and righted itself. You're not going to believe this, but one of the dummies is a Resusci-Ken."

"No way!" Melissa said. "Yep, your right. I recognize that from my CPR class."

"Ahh, they're killing Ken. Too bad he's already dead," Maya joked.

They all laughed, relieving the tension they'd been holding while trying to get an idea of what was happening.

"Stop, you guys. I can't stop laughing. It's not funny. Ken is a CPR doll, not a trauma doll," chirped Melissa.

That sent them into fits of laughter again.

"Well, that's not good. The other dummy resembles our eastern County councilmember, the Democrat running against Titus," Jeff said.

"Doesn't the council district include this area too?" Melissa asked.

"It does," Maya replied.

Their laughter abruptly ceased, and their seriousness returned. They knew that targeting people was no laughing matter.

"Maya, get a photo of that. Not that it's a direct threat, but it's worth documenting. Titus's followers have been vocal about their hatred of the Democrat challenger. How far would they go?" Jeff asked.

Maya zoomed in and was able to get a photo. If they enlarged it on the computer later, it might show more detail.

The gunfire continued. They sat and watched for any changes.

"Don't they have anything better to do?" Melissa asked. "My environmental consulting firm recently worked on a plan to clean up a contaminated site with the County. They had to clean up shell casings, lead bullet contamination, and all sorts of dumping out on some old logging roads south of here. The locals, for years, were using the area as an unofficial shooting range. The cost to clean it up was over nine million dollars."

"That's a lot of money," Maya said. "What exactly does your firm do?"

"We consult with governments, businesses, and nonprofits to come up with a cleanup plan based on input from multiple stakeholders that meets all the regulatory requirements, and then we draft a plan. It's a pretty complex process to get everyone lined up and on the same page."

"I bet. I know how hard it is to get the different agencies on the same page with our new domestic terrorism training program."

"I know, and that is just one site. There are many more out here like that."

Thirty minutes later, the gunfire stopped. The people returned to their rock crawlers and drove to one of the buildings, disappearing inside.

"Hey, it's getting late. How long do you guys want to stick around?" Melissa asked.

"I'm ready to go," Maya said.

"How about fifteen more minutes, and then, if nothing happens, we'll head down?" Jeff asked.

"Hey, Jeff, didn't you mention that they moved the Washington State Fire Academy a few years ago?" Nick asked.

"They did. I found out first from Melissa."

"My firm worked with the Department of Ecology to find a suitable replacement. The air quality up here can get bad from inversions. The smoke just sits in this corridor, and with all the new development up here, it was time for them to move. The air quality was putting a stop to their live fire training. Eastern Washington is a little more smoke friendly. I figured those men would at least know that it used to be the training academy."

"I wonder what it is being used for now?" Maya asked.

"I'll check when we get back," Nick said.

The minutes passed without any more movement below them, their cue to start heading down.

Let's take the new trail instead of the climber's trail," Melissa said.

As they descended through the thick evergreen rainforest.

Maya noted the tangle of ferns, salal, and Oregon grape. The longer trail was already well-worn and easier to hike. The contour had a gentler grade up to the summit.

"I love Mailbox specifically because it's such a tough climb," Melissa said. "I'm going to continue using the old trail to go up and this one to descend."

They arrived at their truck to find that their windows and many of the windows of the surrounding vehicles had been smashed. Piles of auto glass littered the ground. At the entrance to the parking area was a deputy's vehicle, with a group of people standing around talking with him.

"I'll go," Jeff said. He left them and walked over to the deputy.

Melissa took photos of the interior of the truck. She walked around to the back. The tailgate was open. "I can't believe it. They stole Jeff's bunker gear and his bulletproof vest."

Melissa left and walked over to where Jeff was talking with the deputy.

Maya looked on dispassionately. "Probably the local meth heads looking for something to pawn," she said. "Just another day in paradise."

Melissa returned. "Apparently, this is not the first time this has happened. They haven't been able to catch the thieves because it occurs so randomly. We're going to have a breezy ride back to North Bend. Maybe we can drop it off at an auto glass place and get a ride home with you guys?"

"Sure," Nick said.

Jeff returned with unsurprising news. "It's doubtful that they'll catch whoever did it. I'll let the chief know about my gear. Let's get back to North Bend and figure out what's next."

CHAPTER ELEVEN

JEFF AND MAYA sat at a traffic light in downtown Kent, discussing where to get lunch before their shift, when Maya noticed a large black truck coming down Central Avenue with flags billowing in the draft created by its forward momentum. Two large American flags overpowered a "Don't Tread on Me" flag, a Confederate flag, and a flag with the name "TITUS," the Republican running for the County Council office.

As it passed through the intersection, Maya noticed the man driving was wearing a black cap and a skull buff over his lower face, concealing his identity.

Following behind the truck were others, all with flags billowing off the beds or sides of the trucks. Several had slogans painted on the sides that read, "Freedom from Tyranny," "God Bless America," and "Christians for TITUS."

They watched as ten trucks roared through the intersection. Maya was struck by the similarities to images she'd seen on TV of black-masked ISIS members with weapons of war, driving their Hilux trucks through the desert with black flags proclaiming their allegiance to Islam. Maya had never thought about it before, how the only difference between these displays and ISIS was that there weren't men in the back of the trucks with machine guns and rifles poised for battle. *Yet*, she thought.

But some of these right-wing adherents had tried to murder them on the streets and had assassinated a police officer and a Black man walking down the road. Maya's mind reeled from a sense of impending doom as she remembered the ambush threatening her life and the lives of the other first responders. It was a fear so deeply etched into her psyche that adrenaline coursed through her limbs, her heart pulsed with fight or flight. Those displays—the flags, the trucks, and the slogans—were meant to elicit fear and intimidation, and the fear she felt shook her to her core. She felt her vision narrow as she took a deep breath and told herself that they were only posturing, that she was safe...at that moment. *Breathe,* she thought.

The light turned green, as one more truck ran the red light. "What the fuck?" Jeff said.

His voice brought her back. "Jeff, give me a minute. I'm trying to work through some anxiety right now. Seeing those guys just sent me into a full-on panic attack."

"Well, I just about pulled out in front of that one. He nearly caused an accident. I'm sorry, Maya, are you okay? Do you want to go home? What can I do to help?"

"I'll be fine in a minute. I'm learning to work through these attacks. I'm just afraid it's going to get worse. When I became a paramedic, I never imagined that I would be targeted by militant groups of Americans. I thought the threats would be from outside, not from within."

Jeff proceeded through the intersection as he replied, "It's been coming for a long time. These Titus supporters are pretty fired up. I won't vote for him, but I have neighbors who will. They think if he wins, they will be able to control their property rights, which is a big issue out where we live.

"My neighbor said his family was all set to subdivide their farm, then the government changed the zoning making his property ineligible for development. That was their retirement gone. Now his parents live on the property with him, and he supports them by working at Boeing. I guess I'd be angry too. We'll never be able to subdivide our property and make a profit someday when we are ready to sell. It's a tough balance between environmental protection and property rights."

"Angry is one thing. Killing people is entirely something worse." Maya shuddered again. Along with the ambush, she wondered, again about the execution of the woman in the gorge. What had made them ambush the first responders, execute that woman, and set off a manhunt. How could the perpetrators just disappear into the blackness of the night, and to this day, still not be caught?

They pulled into the station. As they backed up, Maya could see the station mechanic standing in his shop. When they exited the medic unit, she could hear the familiar rant of the talk show radio host railing against the "dems" and "libtards." She hated that constant drone of hate filling the garage. She'd often pull the medic unit out and close the garage door, so she could do her rig check in silence.

Maya sat in front of the computer focused on her work on the online training she had helped develop for their upcoming mass casualty terrorism incident training. One of the biggest changes was moving patients sooner and quicker from the site of the disaster. They would do that by using colored ribbons to mark patients based on severity of injury. Red was immediate threat to life. Yellow was serious but the patient could wait. Green was walking wounded. Black was dead. She shuddered to think that they had to make a choice between saving the one or saving the many. Getting bogged down on each patient they encountered might save that one person, but ten more might be lost. That and moving patients from the treatment area to transport sooner, would hopefully, save more lives.

She pushed her chair away from the computer, stretching away the tension she felt. This would be their biggest event related to terrorism training. Just thinking about it was exhausting. Time for a break. She got up to get a drink when their pagers fired.

"Units respond to Green River Community College student union building. Shots fired. Stage at Parking area B."

Jeff and Maya looked at each other. Maya felt that deep sense of foreboding as she remembered Kelly and Brian. "Do you think?"

"Anything's possible. Let's get our gear on and be ready."

They made their way to the trucks. Each footstep felt leaden. She resisted the urge to flee but knew she wouldn't. It was her job to run toward chaos, not from it. Time felt like it was moving in slow motion and, at the same time, too fast.

Maya and Jeff put on their bulletproof vests and Kevlar helmets before jumping into their seats. Maya pushed the computer button, which indicated they were responding.

Dispatch was silent as information was shared only over the dispatch computer. "Units responding. Shots fired. Unknown if the shooter is still in the vicinity. SWAT and PD are responding to secure the scene. Staging changed to SE 314th Street and 124th Ave SE. Change to channel three for the incident."

Maya changed the channels on their portable radios and the main rig radio. She watched as the number of units grew exponentially on the computer as more reports of possible multiple shooters evolved.

"It's just getting worse. Do we have an army up there?" Maya questioned.

She looked at Jeff and said what they had both been thinking. "After this, we'll just take the rest of the day off, a mental health day."

It was something they said to release some of the tension on calls that sounded like the worst call of their careers. Given that this sounded like the worst call yet, they needed something to give them hope that they'd make it through this one too.

They drove, with just their lights and no sirens, to the staging area. Maya ran through her mental checklist, everything that would happen as their response teams geared up for a possible terrorism incident. She knew that they were in a much better position than before the last two incidents. They'd get through this. Everyone knew what to do. Now, they just had to hope they weren't driving into something they hadn't anticipated.

Three police cars sped around them on their way to the call.

The computer was scrolling with updates. "Student said they heard shooting off in the woods."

"Unable to locate shooters. Searching south side of college, where gunfire was heard."

Maya and Jeff arrived at the fire station and staged with the firefighters as they waited to be brought in behind SWAT.

The tactical SWAT vehicle drove past the station toward the college.

They waited, talking through their response for a mass casualty incident.

How many students might be lying there dying? Sometimes the big picture was just too much to comprehend. That is when Maya broke it down into individual tasks. Manageable parts in a bigger event. Each responder tasked with handling different aspects that the event threw at them.

"All units. Cancel all units. All units, code green," the dispatcher said over the radio.

"What? A few minutes ago, it was multiple shooters, and SWAT was responding. What happened?" Maya took in a deep breath and a longer exhale.

"Hey, I'm just relieved that it wasn't another ambush," Jeff said as he pulled out of the fire station parking area to head back.

"Me too."

They returned to the station. Jeff called the MSO. When he finished talking to him, he relayed his conversation.

"He's up at the fire station where we staged. Apparently, some men were hunting below the college on Department of Natural Resources land where hunting is allowed. They got their buck. Luckily, an off-duty security guard heard the call come in and notified the college that his friends were down there hunting.

"I think hunting next to schools and businesses shouldn't be allowed now. How are we supposed to know the difference between the sound of gunshots aimed at game animals and those aimed at college students?"

Maya looked up from her laptop. "Loose ends. Things we didn't think about when we wrote our new directives. I'm unsure how we will coordinate things like that with state and federal agencies. I'll send a note to the chief. It's not likely to change anything at the moment, but maybe down the road. Besides, closing areas to hunting right now might make things worse."

Their pagers fired again.

"Units respond to unconscious unresponsive."

They headed for the door again. *What now?* Maya thought with some irritation.

They walked into a ranch-style house in a nice neighborhood. In the back bedroom was a woman lying on her bed. The firefighters were pushing air into her lungs with a bag-valve-mask.

"Kathleen here was last seen an hour ago by her son. He found her unconscious when he went to get her up to eat. She has a history of narcotics use. Son said she had been clean for six months. Then this," said the firefighter, nodding in the woman's direction.

Maya flashed her penlight in the woman's eyes. "Pinpoint pupils. Jeff, start an IV, and I'll draw up some Narcan."

She gave a dose in the woman's left upper arm while Jeff started the IV. Then they gave her the medication through the IV. They watched as her eyes suddenly fluttered open, and she groaned and attempted to turn on her side.

"Kathleen, you need to stay on your back. We have an IV in your right arm. We had to give you some Narcan. You overdosed," Maya said.

"Leave me the fuck alone."

Kathleen reached for the IV with her left arm. A firefighter grabbed her arm and kept her from tearing it out.

She started screaming at them. "Let me go. Get out of my house."

Her teenage son appeared in the doorway. "She's always like that when you guys show up and give her Narcan."

The indifferent look on his face told Maya he'd been here many times before.

"Mom, let them take you to the hospital. They're only trying to help. I thought you weren't going to do this again."

"I'm sorry, I know, I'm sorry. Everything has been so stressful..." Then she started crying.

"Mom, please just cooperate. Don't fight them on this."

"Okay, I'll go. Love you."

The ambulance crew arrived. The crew had the woman

stand up and walk over to their stretcher. The son walked back to the living room.

Maya hated to see him so resigned to his mom's addiction. He was cooking for her while she lay unconscious on narcotics. How many times had that happened in this house? How many houses hid lives of misery and addiction. More than she could count.

Their pagers fired again. Off they drove to their next call.

"Units respond, for chest pain, Muckleshoot Casino."

They responded up highway 164 and slid behind the fire department aid car, heading to the same call.

"Chest pain at the casino. Let me guess, someone just lost their paycheck at the tables," Jeff said.

"Don't be so cynical, Jeff. It's probably just 'all you can eat' indigestion."

"Look who is cynical now."

"If our patients ate a better diet, we'd be out of business."

They pulled into the side service entrance and followed one of the employees through corridors that led out to a room that didn't have a buffet or the gambling tables, just row after row of slot machines. In front of a slot machine, an elderly gentleman sat clutching his chest with his eyes closed. A messy T-shirt stretched thin by his belly hung over his dirty blue jeans.

Maya watched as the firefighter put the ECG patches on him and got a blood pressure. In the background, she could hear an employee telling Jeff what had happened.

"He just started yelling at our server to get the hell away from him. He didn't want an Indian serving him. He asked for a white server. He was mad because she cut off his alcohol because he was increasingly hostile, yelling at the machine and banging on it. When we asked him to leave, he started complaining of chest pain. So, we called 911."

Maya then turned to the patient. "So, what's your name?"

"Jerry. Jerry Adams." His voice slurred out the words as his eyes remained closed.

"What's going on today?"

"They gave me chest pain. I was just minding my own business, my own business playing this slot machine, and they asked me to leave." His voice slurred the words together. Luckily Maya had gotten pretty good at translating drunk speak.

"Okay, Mister Adams. Where does it hurt?"

He pointed to the middle of his chest. "Here."

Maya told him she was going to press on his chest. When she applied pressure to his chest, he winced.

"Ow, you tryin' to hurt me too?"

"No, I'm just trying to figure out what's wrong with you."

"They're what's wrong! Takin' my money, those injuns. Gettin' rich, takin' my money."

The employee standing behind Jeff just rolled his eyes. "He comes in here every two weeks. Plays the slots and complains about the service and the food. This is new, though. He's never complained about chest pain before."

"Hmm," Maya said.

"Mister Adams. I'm going to put some patches across your chest and do an ECG. That will give us a better idea of whether or not you are having a heart attack."

She lifted his shirt and found a hairy chest and enlarged stomach to navigate around. A few razor shaves and the patches were on.

"Hold still while we take a picture of your heart," Maya commanded. Mister Adams sat still while Maya pushed the button to initiate the ECG.

What the printout revealed was different from what she expected. There, in all caps, was "ACUTE MI."

"Well, Mister Adams, it looks like you are having a heart attack. I'll give you some baby aspirin, and we'll take you to the hospital."

His eyes flashed open, and a look of surprise erupted on his face. He'd probably been having chest pain all afternoon, but after a few drinks that got him agitated, he thought it was all the result of the casino staff, not his heart.

"What?"—his voice was less slurred now—"I thought it was just indigestion from their terrible food."

"No, it's not just indigestion."

The employee came up to Mister Adams. "Sir, we'll call your wife and let her know that you are going to the hospital. Please take care of yourself."

Wow, Maya thought. *After all the abuse, that employee still found enough empathy to call his wife.*

"Thank you," he said begrudgingly, suddenly humbled by the one thing he couldn't control: his heart.

Back at the station, Jeff said "I'm heading to bed. This has been a crazy shift so far. I hope it doesn't stay this busy all night."

"Go ahead and try. I'm just going to finish up this report and lie down, too," Maya replied.

The pagers fired, and the lights came on. Maya looked up at the ceiling of her bedroom, the bright lights momentarily blinding her. Her heart pounded out of her chest. *God, couldn't they wake us up a little more gently?* She felt like she was having a heart attack every time the pagers fired and woke her up.

Dispatch information came over the house speakers. "Units respond. Two-car MVA. Multiple patients. One vehicle is on fire. Highway 18 at SE Green Valley Road."

Jeff followed Maya out the door to the medic unit. "That's

it. I'm requesting a new partner. I will have PTSD if we continue to have shifts like this."

"Come on, you love it. All the excitement I generate. You'd be bored working with someone else." Maya laughed.

"Ha, nobody sleeps anymore. We just get busier and busier."

They headed out the door again. This time Maya drove eastbound on highway 18. As they came around the curve towards Green Valley Road, they could see the flames leaping into the air from a pickup truck engulfed in fire. Unless the occupants had gotten out of the truck before it caught fire, there wouldn't be any survivors. The fire engine was stopped up ahead of them, and the firefighters were pulling a hose to put out the fire.

Another engine came up behind the medic unit blocking traffic from crashing into the scene. Police started arriving and shutting down traffic in both directions. As the firefighters put out the fire, the battalion chief requested that their unit come past the truck. They had a vehicle with a missing patient.

They carefully made their way around the truck. Up ahead, they passed the crumpled front end of the vehicle. There wasn't a back end to it. Two hundred feet further up the road was the back end of the car.

They pulled past it and were met by one of the firefighters from an aid car.

"The seat is missing. The patient may have been ejected out of the vehicle. We're conducting a search of the roadside between here and the front end."

The radio came to life. "We've found the occupant still strapped into the seat. He's DOA."

"Well, it looks like you guys are canceled. The other two are DOA. Looks like the truck exploded on impact," the firefighter said.

"I don't think I've ever seen a car break in two before," Jeff said.

They stared at the car's back end in the middle of the highway. It was an old vintage Chevy Camaro.

"Wow, that's an oldy," Jeff commented.

"Sure is." A police officer had just walked up to them. "We know this guy well. DUI is just one of the many things he's known for around here. We've busted him again and again over the years. Possession, domestic battery, DUI, weapons. We know his dad. Good man. Too bad his son didn't turn out the same way."

"Who's his dad?" Maya asked.

"He owns Bing's Trucking that operates near here. I mean, operated. They just went out of business after fifty years."

"You think this had anything to do with that? Possibly a suicide?" Maya asked.

"No, I doubt it. We've busted him again and again over the years. This was probably just another night of drunk driving for him. He always seemed to get a get-out-of-jail-free card."

"Why's that?" Maya asked.

"Probably his dad. He's lived in this area all his life. We figured he must have connections to get his son out of all the trouble he caused."

"What about his business? What happened?" Maya was suddenly curious. The emergent part of the call was over, and now she wondered about the lives of those who had perished.

"Hell, it was a damn shame. An environmental cleanup bankrupted his business. Just closed his doors and retired. At least, that's what I read in the local paper. Probably didn't want to leave it to his son, Rick, anyway. Who knows what he would have done to it."

"I'm sorry to hear that. What about the other occupants?"

"Don't know yet. The truck is unrecognizable," the

policeman said. "I will probably know more once the investigation is finished. They were most likely drunk as well. It is 2:30 in the morning. At least we hope they weren't innocently driving home. That would be very unfortunate."

"That would. I hate it when people are killed by drunk drivers!" Maya's voice had an edge to it as she thought of the many calls she'd been on where the drunk driver came out unscathed and the people they hit, well, they didn't fare so well.

"Just another day in south County," Jeff said.

"Unfortunately," the firefighter said.

"Well, we'll get going. You guys have a safe night."

"I gotta get Jeff back to the station. He gets kind of cranky if he doesn't get some sleep."

"Sleep. I don't sleep when I work with you," Jeff replied.

Everyone laughed, and everyone knew. Sleep was an elusive luxury in their line of work.

CHAPTER TWELVE

MAYA LOOKED around at the bright lights of shops and restaurants along Kent Station. Lou commented as they walked, "Kent used to be a Boeing town full of smoke-filled diners and even smokier bars."

Jeff, Melissa, Maya, and Nick had joined Lou and his wife Cathy for dinner before heading to Airways Brewery to hear Daniel play.

"I remember when the Boeing employees would get their paychecks, and then we'd be busy running calls for bar fights, motor vehicle accidents, and domestics," Lou continued. "It's hard to even recognize this place anymore. Kent's become gentrified."

"And more diverse," Maya added. "Do you know that Kent is one of the most ethnically diverse cities in the County now?"

"I didn't," Jeff said.

"You probably haven't been here long enough to notice the change. I remember when the only minorities were African Americans living in specific areas. No cross-over. No, this was a white working-class town. It was even wilder than when you started, Maya. I remember running calls from one end of our area to the other. It was the lawless south. One minute we'd be landing a helicopter on highway 18 for an MVA, and the next, we were giving Narcan to a heroin overdose in White Center. Some of the working stiffs around here were pretty rowdy. Add the gangs, bikers, and good old boys shooting each other, and we kept busy. It kept it interesting, though. A different time."

"Now I'm lucky if I even get enough intubations to recertify every year," Jeff said.

"Things have quieted down over the years. Before the ambush and the bombing, things were getting kind of routine, but I'll take routine over this new normal," Maya said.

"I used to worry about Lou getting run over by a drunk driver on car accidents on the freeway, but now I worry more about him getting shot at or blown up. I've been telling him it's time to retire," Cathy said.

"Not ready for that yet. I still love the job. What would I do if I retired?"

"Well, I can think of a couple of things, like grandkids and traveling," Cathy said.

"Well, we're knee-deep in grandkids already."

"So, how'd you get out of babysitting tonight?" Maya asked.

"Well, I think my daughter, Joanne, felt sorry for us. She thought the old folks should enjoy an evening out on the weekend every once in a while."

They walked into a packed house. Luckily Em and Jake had commandeered a table to the left of the stage so they could all sit together.

Maya looked around the table.

"Where's Doug?" she asked.

Jake replied, "He's coming a little late because Kristen is getting off work later."

"Kristen's a dispatcher," Maya told Nick.

"You must be Daniel's uncle?" Maya asked. It was hard to miss that he was the only other African American, besides Daniel, in the brewery.

"I am, how'd you guess?" he said slyly. "And you must be Maya?" he added with an approving glance.

"Well, it's, let's just say, pretty white in here, and yes, I'm Maya," she replied.

"I'm Charles. Nice to finally meet you."

"You too. This is my fiancé, Nick."

"Nice to meet you too, young man."

"I'm hardly young."

"Well, younger than me. I'm Daniel's older uncle. His mother was fifteen years younger than me. That makes me almost his grandpa."

"Well, you don't look like a grandpa, and from what Daniel tells me about you, you definitely don't act like one," Maya said

"And exactly what did he tell you about me?" Charles asked.

Maya suddenly felt speechless. Daniel had told her that Charles was quite the player. Never settled down and got married. She decided to reveal the other exploits that Daniel had told her about.

"Just that you and your musician friends ride motorcycles to Mardi Gras every year."

"I like you already," Charles said with a low, smooth laugh.

"Well, that's good because you're probably going to see a lot of me if you spend time with Daniel."

Lou introduced him and Cathy. "Good to see another old timer here tonight."

"As well," Charles said.

They all sat down at the table.

"I've heard so much about you, Charles. Daniel talks about

you all the time. It's good to finally meet you," Melissa said with warm enthusiasm.

"Thank you, young lady."

Daniel was on stage doing sound checks. When he saw them, he hopped off the stage, walked up to Maya, and gave her a hug.

"I see you already met my uncle."

"We did," Maya said.

"Lou?" Daniel looked surprised. "I thought you had to babysit the grandkids."

"Well, they gave us a reprieve so we could come hear you play. I've heard a lot about how good your band is. I wanted to hear it for myself."

"Hey, thanks. I hope you aren't disappointed. I'm really stoked you could make it."

Charles commented, "You won't be disappointed. I taught this young man everything I know. He's a solid musician."

Daniel glowed at this and then quickly tried to play it cool. You could tell he was impressed by his Uncle Charles. His approval seemed to lift his feet off the ground.

"Well, I have to get back to it. Thanks, everyone, for coming."

"Wouldn't miss it," Jeff said.

When Daniel left. Jeff looked at Maya and asked, "Where's Jill?"

"Don't know, maybe she's past history. I'm not sure she was the right one for him anyway. A little too wild," Maya replied.

"From what I heard, she was a lot of fun. They broke up two days ago. Sounds like she was done with Seattle rain and was moving back to New York," Charles said.

"Usually, we know more about our coworkers than their family does, but you seem to be in the know about Daniel."

"Yes, and I know he's working with you on the guys targeting you," Charles said.

Maya gave him a look that he understood.

"You know, the training," he said and left it at that.

Maya didn't want Em, Jake, Lou, or Cathy to be part of that discussion. She trusted them, but she knew medics, and they could not be trusted with secrets. They had a saying in their work: "Telephone or tell a medic." If one of their coworkers found out, they'd all know soon enough.

Given that she couldn't be a hundred percent sure there weren't sympathizers in their ranks, they'd decided to keep their investigation to themselves. She didn't think any of their coworkers would plan attacks on their own people, but if they knew about Daniel and Jeff's infiltration into the right-wing forums, they might warn their buddies.

Daniel spoke into the microphone. "Hello, how's everyone tonight?"

The patrons cheered and toasted with each other, the most enthusiastic being Daniel's table of friends.

"We have a great evening of music for you tonight, starting with this one. One, two, three."

With that, the band began to play. Daniel belted out the lyrics of "The Ballad of John Henry." Maya watched as the patrons grew quiet, and their focus turned to Daniel and the DTs. He had them transfixed right from the start. She turned to see Charles watching and smiling.

"He is such a great musician," Maya said.

Charles leaned in so that she could hear him, "That's my nephew."

From Maya's perspective, Daniel had it all dialed in. He was not only a great paramedic but an accomplished musician. Whenever they'd heard him play, he always surprised them with something new.

At the end of their set, Daniel and his band came down and sat with the group. Maya had met their bass guitar player, sax player, and keyboard player, but the drummer was a new guy. Daniel introduced everyone.

"Hey, Uncle. What'd you think about our new lineup of songs?"

"Pretty good, son. Pretty good."

Maya admired how cool Charles was. He had already connected with everyone at the table. She felt a natural deference to him. He just seemed to have a world of life experience in his eyes and etched in his face. There was more to his story than music. She could just feel it.

"Just pretty good, huh. Well, wait until the next set! We're just getting warmed up.

I'm going to go get a drink."

"How about grabbing your uncle a seltzer while you're up there."

"Sure. Anyone else want me to grab them a drink?"

"How about another pitcher of beer," Jeff said.

Daniel left them. As Maya followed him with her eyes to the bar, she was surprised to see Randy and one of his firefighter friends walking up to them.

"I thought we'd check out all this talk about Daniel and his band. Hey, Lou, good to see you here," Randy said.

"What are you doing all the way up from Olympia?"

"I'm working an overtime shift up in Covington. I thought I'd stop in and hear Daniel and his band play before I head up."

Maya thought it was interesting that they'd come. They never seemed interested in Daniel's band before. Although there had been a lot of shift-change talk about how good his band was. She guessed the word was getting around.

Daniel wasn't the first musician that had worked for the department. Everyone always had some side gig they put energy into on their days off. Maya often heard Daniel practicing on his acoustic guitar in his bedroom when they worked together.

Daniel walked back to their table and handed Charles his seltzer water, then slid the pitcher of beer along the table before sitting at the end.

Everyone talked back and forth. Randy had struck up a conversation with Charles, asking about his recent move to Tacoma. Out of all the people Maya worked with, she felt he was probably the most likely to hold racist beliefs, but she could be wrong. She'd never heard him overtly say anything. It was just his politics. She hated feeling this way. Before the attacks, there was tension, but not like this.

"Okay, I gotta head back up. I'll see you after the next set." Daniel leaned down to his uncle's ear. Maya saw Charles shake his head no.

Daniel got up on stage. "Friends, I've got someone special here tonight that I want you to meet. This is my Uncle Charles," he said and pointed towards his uncle. His uncle gave a cool shake of his head.

"My uncle taught me everything I know about the blues and playing guitar. He recently moved up here from the sunny state. If you're lucky, you'll find him playing down in his new home of Tacoma. But tonight, I'm inviting him up here to play a few songs with me."

Charles shook his head, but like the stage man he was, he acquiesced and stepped up on stage. Daniel reached from behind the keyboards and pulled out his uncle's electric guitar. Charles smiled and gave it a couple of test riffs.

"Okay, we're going to get you on the dance floor for this one." Daniel began to play a John Lee Hooker song, "Bang, Bang, Bang, Bang." Charles waited a minute and then dropped in with him as Daniel sang the lyrics. Charles stood with his eyes closed as his fingers danced along his guitar strings.

Maya and Nick started dancing and were joined by others. The song was infectious. She could hear people singing along in the background. Nick was enjoying it too. She'd had to drag him away from his work, but now she could tell he didn't regret it. He never did once he committed to stepping away from the never-ending job of running a startup business. For her, stepping away from work was the only thing that kept her mind in check. With that, she just let the rhythm carry her away. Music and dancing always melted away her tension.

Em grabbed Jake. Melissa and Jeff joined in. Lou and Cathy even got up to dance. They could move. Lou's long, tall body carried the rhythm as Cathy moved her hips side to side with the beat.

Daniel and his uncle jumped into the next song, a lively Eric Clapton tune that Maya didn't recognize. Everyone continued to dance except Lou and Cathy, who sat down. Cathy quickly pulled Randy up for a dance. He was much stiffer, but Cathy had him laughing in no time.

After another song, they transitioned into a slow-moving song called "Gunsmoke Blues." It was a duet by Charles and Daniel. Charles's guitar crooned through the hangar as the keyboard played in the background. Maya sat down and listened. The haunting lyrics hung in the air between the two men. She could feel the weight of it bear down on her shoulders. Instantly, she knew why Charles had moved up here. He was worried. Worried about his nephew. She understood. The reality bearing down on them just seemed to lurk at the perimeter, threatening them at every turn, on every call, and in the distrust she and her coworkers felt about those around them.

She could only imagine what an African American mother living hundreds of miles away would feel about her son living up north during this time. Maybe she had sent Charles to look out for Daniel.

As always, a sudden turn could send her spiraling into darker thoughts. Luckily, Daniel and Charles changed tempo with "Got My Mojo Working," by Muddy Waters. They followed that up with Daniel on the harmonica and Charles on the lead guitar. A cool instrumental that put the spotlight on Charles. Charles leaned into the mic and let the room know he was "Messin' with the blues."

After the extended set, they stepped off the stage to take a break. As they were catching their breath, Charles confessed, "You wore me out, son, and as much as I'd like to stay, I got a date later tonight."

"I figured. Didn't take you long, Uncle," Daniel said. He looked disappointed but resigned.

"I enjoyed meeting all of you. Daniel, I'll see you next week for our gig down in Tacoma. You guys are all invited too."

"Thanks, Uncle. I'll walk you out."

"I'm cool. You stay here with your friends."

Charles put on his jacket and left them.

"Your uncle was amazing. What a show!" Lou said.

"Did he play down in LA?" Nick asked.

"Play, he was well known down there. Made a small living teaching, but music was his passion. He taught me to give back to the community. He's got a big heart. Taught music in one of the toughest schools down there. He always believed it was worth his time if he could reach one kid. He reached many."

"Wow, that explains you. He must have made a big impression on you," Maya said.

"He's the reason I'm doing what I'm doing today. Music and paramedicine. The best of all worlds."

"I thought there was more to his story," Maya commented.

"Oh, there's a whole lot more, but that's for another day. I gotta get back to playing. Break's over."

Daniel got up on stage, and Maya saw him nod to a group of firefighters standing at the bar ordering beer.

"Well, I see I have some more friends here tonight. Straight off the fire engines of our local fire department, this one's for you guys. Get yourself a beer and come join my table up here."

The firefighters sat at the table. Maya smiled and acknowledged them. Daniel was getting quite the reputation.

As the riffs floated up from Daniel's harmonica, they heard the faint sound of sirens growing on the edges of the music. Everyone at the table who heard them took note. Just another weekend night on 212th in Kent. The sounds passed by the brewery and suddenly came to an abrupt halt.

"Must be a call down the road," Maya said.

Soon more sirens erupted from different directions. Maya noted they were police sirens. Then she heard another one coming from the west. *The medics,* she thought. *Car accident, probably.*

Daniel continued to bring John Fogerty to life as he sang, "Better run through the jungle."

Maya got up to get some water and saw two police officers come through the front door. She froze and watched as they walked over and talked to the bartender. He pointed towards Daniel. The police officers made their way toward the stage and motioned to Daniel. Suddenly the band stopped playing. Daniel jumped down. Maya could hear the officers. "Your uncle's been injured. He told us to come get you. Come with us."

Maya walked over to him. "Daniel, I'll go with you."

"Let's go."

They followed the police out the door. Lou told everyone to hang tight and came with them. They turned down the parking area along the front of the brewery as it paralleled 212th. There was an aid car to the west of them. An engine was parked off to the side. Three police cars were spread out around the scene, and Maya could hear more heading in their direction, sirens blaring. They turned around the end of the long building just in time to see Charles being loaded into the medic unit. Daniel jumped inside the side door as Maya stood at the back and acknowledged Mike and Dag, who were busily handing IV bags to a firefighter and starting to examine Charles.

Maya saw Daniel looking down at his uncle, whose face was bleeding profusely as Mike applied pressure with more 4 x 4s to a large gash that ran from his forehead to the side of his ear. His left eye was swollen shut.

"Here, Daniel, hold this while I start an IV."

Daniel reached down and applied pressure. His uncle reached up and grabbed his arm.

"Son, they came out of nowhere and just started beating me. They said Daniel better be careful, or they wouldn't be so nice next time. Do you think it has anything to do with...?"

"Hey, shhh, not here. We'll talk about this later. Right now, just let us do our job and get you to Harborview, the trauma center I told you about. Unfortunately, it looks like you'll see it in person," Daniel said.

Charles started to laugh, stopped, and winced in pain. "Don't do that, son. I think they broke some of my ribs."

"His BP is 160/100."

"Damn, my high blood pressure," Charles said.

Mike looked up at Daniel. They both knew his high blood pressure might be a sign that he had a more significant head injury.

Dag had drawn up some morphine and handed it to Mike.

"Okay, Charles, this should help with the pain while we get things done and get you on the road."

"Uncle, just do everything they tell you. They'll take great care of you. I'll meet you down at HMC." Daniel turned to Mike. "Take good care of him. I'll get out of your way and let you work."

"We will. You know we will."

Daniel came around to Maya standing at the back. She stepped away from the doors as a firefighter closed them.

"You know what he told me? He said that they warned him, I'd better be careful or next time they wouldn't be so nice. What did they mean by that?"

"Let's talk on the way." Maya turned around and found Nick standing behind a police officer. "Nick, Charles has been attacked. Daniel is going to the hospital. I'll drive him in his car. Can you tell everyone what's going on and come get me later?"

"Sure. Go. I'll take care of everything here."

"Thanks." She quickly kissed him and followed Daniel to his car.

"Daniel, you heard me. I'm driving."

"I know I'm not in a good place to be driving right now. I don't want to be one of those family members."

"No, you don't. I will!" Maya said.

They pulled out just as the medic unit turned west on 212th and headed up the hill to I-5. Maya turned right towards highway 167. They'd take the other way and avoid chasing the medic unit to the hospital.

"I just can't believe this happened. Here, of all places. My uncle moved up from LA only to be attacked because of me. What do you think they meant? Do you think anyone at work could have tipped off the militia about us?"

"It could be that someone tipped off the militia about us, or they somehow tracked you down through the chats. We've been so careful about not letting on at work."

"Maybe not careful enough. Maya, you know we work with some racists. I honestly wouldn't put it past them to do something like this. They are nice enough to my face, but I know they resent me for taking a job away from one of their buddies, their white buddies. They'll never admit it."

Maya caught the tenseness of his muscles out of the corner of her eye. She reached over and put her hand on his shoulder. She knew what he was saying was a way to sort through the anger over what had just happened.

"Sometimes I feel like no matter what I do, it's never enough. Have you noticed that some of our coworkers are complaining a lot more about little things we forget to do? It started about the time Titus announced his plans to run for office. It's subtle and not so subtle. I'll walk in at shift change, and everyone will get quiet like they've been talking about me. Mike has been calling the shift supervisor every time I forget something.

"Recently, I forgot to put a new roll of toilet paper on the holder. It was right before shift change, and we had to run out for a call. It's that kind of stuff that just makes me so furious. If I was in the 'good old boys club,' no one would say a thing. Now, my uncle is on his way to Harborview."

"Daniel, I know it's frustrating. The rules aren't the same for you and me. It doesn't matter how well you do the job. Mistakes happen. It's just how they are handled that is different. Besides, they're all friends. Their buddies are in leadership positions. They make the rules. I hope it will change, but I'm not optimistic with everything that's going on. You have every right to be angry about that and angry about what happened to your uncle.

"This job is hard enough without having to walk on

eggshells at work, wondering what will set off a full-blown investigation...about toilet paper replacement."

They both laughed. "It was so absurd that it's actually funny. Thanks, Maya, I needed that."

"No problem. Gallows humor, workplace jokes. Survival, Daniel, survival."

They pulled into the parking garage at Harborview just as Daniel's phone rang.

"Daniel, this is Greg. How are you doing? Are you at the hospital? Please let me know if there's anything you need. I know you work in a couple of days. I can get your shift covered if you need it. Just let me know."

"Thanks, Greg. I appreciate it. We're just arriving at the hospital. Can I call you later when I know more?"

"Sure. Take care."

"You too."

"See, that's the stuff that drives me crazy. Greg is such a good old boy. He never says anything overt, but he always supports the complaints against me when they are from one of the guys. I've always felt he resents me, yet he is calling me and asking if I need anything."

"I know. It is crazy. Just know I've got your back, Daniel. Let's go see how your uncle's doing."

CHAPTER THIRTEEN

"HOW'S CHARLES?" Em asked as Maya walked into the station where Em, Randy and Jeff were drinking coffee.

Maya sat her gear down on the floor and replied, "He's as good as can be expected. I visited him in the hospital for the last two days. The doctors found three fractured ribs, bruising on his left lung, a concussion, and a large laceration that needed stitches. Whoever assaulted him was serious.

"Once they feel like he's out of danger, they'll release him. Daniel convinced Charles to stay with him while he recovers."

Em sighed. "Oh, good. That was so awful. I just can't believe that happened to him.

"We also had another incident on our shift. Parnam, the County councilmember, was attacked as she walked out her front door yesterday. Bob and Steve said she was unconscious when they arrived. Neighbors said they started shouting at the men beating her and called 911. They took off when they heard the sirens. They transported her to Harborview.

"Randy and I have been discussing whether there is a

connection between the attacks on Charles and Parnam. A Black man and a gay woman. Who else is on the list?"

"Well, the election is coming up too. Isn't Parnam running for reelection?" Maya asked.

"She is. It could be related. I wonder if she'll drop out. She was a sure thing for reelection," Randy said.

"Isn't her opponent some woman involved in that big mega-church up on the highway?" Maya asked.

"She is. She's running on stopping crime on the highway and putting guards at the schools, including Highline, where the bombing occurred. She used to be a public school teacher but felt that the current administration wasn't helping keep students and teachers safe, so she resigned to run for office, so she said."

"I agree something must be done," Randy commented. "There should be well-trained guards. I don't know about arming teachers. If you don't practice tactical weapons use, you probably won't respond quick enough to something like an active shooter in the classroom. Personally, if I was a teacher, I'd want to have my gun for protection and give my students a chance of survival. But that's me, and I've got the military training to back it up."

"Let's just hope this attack isn't politically motivated," Maya said. She felt like she couldn't take much more. Maybe returning to work wasn't a good idea. She could feel panic and nausea threatening to overwhelm her. Taking a deep breath, she tried to calm her mind. The false shooter at the college, Charles, and now this.

"Maya, are you okay?" Em asked.

"I'm fine. Just feeling a little stressed. It's been a rough few days. I really didn't want to walk into work and hear about more attacks. I mean, it's not just the bad news. I'm still trying to deal..."

"Maya, maybe you should take the day off. No one will think less of you for taking a mental health day. I'll stay over and work for you."

"No, Em. It's not going to get any better. I knew when I returned to work things could get worse. Jeff and I will just take one call at a time. I'm going to eat lots of ice cream today, though."

"Sounds good to me. I'll treat!" Jeff responded.

"My partner didn't buy ice cream for me. Em, you're slacking," Randy said.

"Well, you really shouldn't eat any. Not at your age, old man," Em shot back.

"Older and wiser, but I still love ice cream. Can you guys leave the leftovers for me? Who knows what we'll be walking into following on Maya's heels."

"Don't remind me," Jeff said.

Roy, the MSO, walked in. "Hey, I wanted to see how everyone is doing. I heard what happened to Daniel's uncle. Did you hear...?"

"About Parnam? Yes, we did," Jeff said.

"Well, that's why I'm here. Things are heating up again. HS is following up with the attacks. They are cautioning everyone to be on extra high alert. These attacks are circling too close to us, especially with this attack on a County councilwoman who's one of our strongest supporters for integrating emergency services through our community training and mentorship programs.

"I'm not sure why Daniel's uncle was targeted. It's unlikely that it was just a random hate crime, given that we've been targeted multiple times."

"Who knows, maybe it's someone who knows Daniel is a paramedic," Maya said.

"Well, if Charles had been packing, things would have been different," Randy piped in.

"Charles was packing. He's aware that being a Black man can be an invitation to be targeted. They caught him by surprise."

"Point taken. I wish I had been out there when they went after him. Not on my watch. Daniel, he's a good guy. We take care of family."

Maya was surprised to hear Randy was so passionate about defending Charles on behalf of Daniel. That was part of their culture, but she just assumed he'd rather not have minorities or women on the job. Maybe they were softening up that hard exterior after all.

"I worked alongside a lot of those colored boys in the military. They were great fighters, at least most of them. There was one guy, though. They should have court marshaled him. Lazy son of a bitch..."

Then again, maybe not, Maya thought. She felt anger rising to her mouth. She stopped short of calling him out. It was such an insidious way to disqualify minorities or women from their place at the table.

"We need to be concerned that these weren't just individual targets but rather broader attacks," Roy said. "We could be in danger on shift and when we leave to go home. Things have taken a turn, and we need to be ready. Our County Executive feels the same. He'll be giving a speech at the County Council Chambers this evening to raise awareness about what is going on and ask the public for help in identifying the people responsible for these attacks. None of us will be safe until these people are caught."

The overhead pagers went off. Maya and Jeff quickly exchanged information with Em and Randy and headed out the door. On went their bulletproof vests. They headed out for a diabetic with low blood sugar. This was followed by a response to the local dialysis center for an altered level of consciousness. Five calls later, they started back to the station. It was way past lunch, so they stopped to get teriyaki in the small restaurant in a strip mall near their station. They watched as a woman erupted when the staff delivered her food.

"I told you I wanted regular chicken, not spicy chicken, dammit. Can't you guys get anything right? I come in here every week, and you're constantly fucking up my order. Bring me the right order, is that too much to ask?"

"Ma'am, you ordered number three, that is spicy chicken, but we'll change the order. No problem."

"I know I ordered number three. It's regular chicken."

"So sorry, ma'am, no problem. We'll get you the regular chicken."

The man went back to redo the woman's order. She looked over at Maya. "Those people, they come here, start a business, and rob us blind, and their service is terrible too."

Maya calmly came to the owner's defense, "Dan, the owner, grew up here in Auburn. We've always had great food and great service. It's one of our favorite lunch spots."

The woman was stunned silent. When Dan brought her food, she asked for it to go and made a quick exit from the restaurant.

"Hey, Dan, have a good rest of your day," Maya said.

"Oh, Maya, don't worry about her. She's always like that. She can't read the menu, so she just guesses, and we try to help her. Usually, I'm the one at the register and intervene. I've got a new employee who doesn't know her yet."

"Ahhh, I see. Why do you put up with her abuse?"

"Well, we grew up together." He leaned in. "Her dad was a raging drunk. She just doesn't know any better. As long as it's directed at me, I'm fine. If she starts on my employees or patrons, then I intervene."

"Got it. Take Care."

As they walked out, Maya commented to Jeff, "Wow, that must have been tough, being one of the few Asian kids in this primarily white blue-collar town.

Later, Maya called Nick to tell him about Parnam and asked him to look for any discussion about the incident in the chats.

Then she called Daniel, but their pagers fired again before he answered.

"Units respond to a self-inflicted gunshot wound. PD also responding. Stage."

Maya and Jeff drove into the scene after the police quickly evaluated that it was a self-inflicted gunshot and nothing more.

The man lay on the floor in his boxers and white socks. Blood oozed out of a wound in his temple. His eyes were open but vacant. His chest rose and fell. His wife stood quietly, crying.

The neighbor stood at the doorway and uttered, "Help him."

Maya asked the wife what had happened.

"He was sitting down watching TV when I went to the store. When I returned, I found him lying there with the gun, the one the police have. I don't know. He's just been so depressed lately. Boeing laid him off a week ago after thirty years. Can you believe that? Just told him his job was moving to Alabama.

"Oh my god, oh my god. What have you done?"

She sobbed as she watched Maya and Jeff start IVs, sedate him, and put a breathing tube in.

"We'll take him to a landing zone where he'll fly by helicopter to Harborview Medical Center. Do you have someone that can drive you to Seattle?" Maya asked.

The neighbor volunteered. "I'll take her. Let me get my coat, and we'll head out."

Maya and Jeff wheeled the man out into the cold late afternoon. Rain hit Maya's face as she kept her eye on the monitor, watching the man's heart rate. The firefighter opened an umbrella to protect the man from the rain. *So much sadness,* she thought as they placed him in the medic unit and drove to the landing zone.

They had no sooner finished cleaning up the back of the medic unit at the landing zone when another call came in. An unconscious/unresponsive at Highlands Evangelical.

"Touched by Jesus. How many unconscious/unresponsive people have we responded to at this church?" Jeff asked.

"Quite a few, but not usually on a weekday evening. It's normally on a Sunday morning at church services."

"True."

They drove into the large parking lot, which was packed. Lights lit up the rain-drenched blacktop. The rain increased just as they got out of the medic unit. They put their raincoats on over their vests and pulled up their hoods. A man motioned toward a side door to the left.

One of the ushers rushed out the main door on a radio. A loud voice erupted out of the opening, "Raise your hands and pray for God to deliver us from this tyranny."

Maya followed the man through the side door into a small alcove with a chaise lounge along one wall. On it lay a young girl. Her body was taut, her hands bent at the wrist with her fingers splayed out. Her legs were board straight with her feet pointing downward. She was breathing rapidly. Her face was flushed. Maya reached down to feel for a pulse, and her wrist was cold to the touch. Her pulse was racing. The girl's eyelids fluttered, and she moaned. Then she arched her back and cried, "Save me, Jesus."

Next to the young girl, a woman and two men had their hands on her head. Their prayers grew louder. "Yes, save her, Jesus. Heal her and deliver her from sin," they all said in unison.

Maya had seen this before. For whatever reason, the girl was hyperventilating. The woman and two men were drawn into the drama, which just made it worse. While the firefighter took her vitals, Maya grabbed a paper bag out of her kit. She asked the woman and two men to step aside while she took care of the girl. They backed up and held hands, continuing to pray quietly. Maya crouched down next to the girl's head. "Hi, my name's Maya. I want you to do something for me. Can you breathe into this bag that I have here?"

"No, I can't breathe." She started to breathe faster, her eyes fluttering.

"You can breathe. I can see that your oxygen saturation is normal. You are actually breathing too fast, and we need to slow it down. Can you work with me? Breathe into this bag and follow my lead?"

Her eyes opened. Maya saw her look of terror. Maya just felt that something wasn't right. She asked the firefighter to bring the stretcher. She knew the girl didn't have a life-threatening emergency, but she felt having a woman care for her would help calm her down.

She held the girl's hand, monitoring her pulse and ensuring that the girl kept breathing through the paper bag. She listened as a man's voice boomed in the background. It sounded familiar. The tone was angry and forceful. She listened as he spoke.

"There is an evil growing in our land that only God can fix. He's asking you to stand up and protect those who can't protect themselves."

"Praise Jesus," echoed a chorus of voices.

"The Church needs to be on the offensive. Be in attack mode. We need to take back our families, take back our nation. Take back our churches. Take back our schools.

Amen."

"Amen," the voices echoed again.

The stretcher arrived as a band started to play in the background. They loaded the girl onto the stretcher. As they started toward the giant doors, a familiar face greeted them. It was the fire department chaplain, Pastor Richter.

"Good, I caught you before you left. I want to pray for Tamara before she leaves."

"We really need to get her to the hospital," Maya said forcefully.

"Maya, surely you can let me pray over her." Without waiting for her to reply, he laid his hand on her head. "Jesus, we ask that you give us the power to heal this young woman. A beautiful child of God. Amen."

"You can go now," Pastor Richter said.

"Why thank you, Pastor. We'll take good care of her from here." Maya's voice hid her disbelief that he had hindered the young woman's care.

"God appreciates your service. Maya, we'd love to see you here some Sunday. God wants me to let you know he's waiting for you."

A shiver of dread went through Maya. The words felt like a snare meant to suck the life right out of her. She suddenly didn't like him very much.

He smiled and raised his hands. "Amen."

They left him with his congregation as the doors closed. Rain pelted them again as they rushed to the medic unit. Maya's gut feeling told her again that something wasn't right.

When they got Tamara into the medic unit, Maya asked

Jeff to drive quietly towards the hospital. As they left, she poked her head up front and whispered, "Take your time."

She sat back down on the bench. Looking with concern at Tamara, she asked, "So, what's really going on?"

Tamara, startled by Maya's question, responded, "Nothing."

Her breathing was normal, and her taut limbs had relaxed. She lay on the stretcher looking up at Maya with big brown eyes. They suddenly filled with tears that trickled down her face. Then the sobbing started. Great rolling waves of sobs. Maya handed her a tissue.

"You promise you won't tell anyone?" Tamara asked.

"I promise. You know, I knew something was wrong. I just want to help you."

Tamara blurted out, "I'm pregnant!"

"I take it this wasn't planned?"

"No, I didn't..." She paused. "I didn't want to have sex, but..."

She trembled. "Everything used to be normal. Then my mom and dad started making us go to this church. I've never liked going there. My parents are so different now. I don't even know who they are anymore. Today I needed to get out of there. I need help to get away from all of them," she said with such forcefulness that it took Maya by surprise.

"You know you are seventeen. It sounds like you want to avoid following your parents' path. I wish I could help, but as a paramedic, I can only offer you mental health follow-up at the emergency department. Someone to talk to that may be able to guide you."

"What if, what if I told you there is more?"

"Like what?" Maya asked.

"That the youth pastor, Brent, is the father," she whispered. "He asked me to pray with him...in private, in the chapel. I said

I needed to go home, but he wouldn't take no and convinced me to come with him."

"What do you mean pray with him in private?"

"When we got to the chapel," Tamara twisted her fingers and looked up at Maya, "he locked the door. I didn't even know it had a lock. Then he said, let us pray at the altar. As I stood at the altar, he grabbed me and pushed me across it and..."

Now she was visibly shaking as she recalled what had happened. "When he was done. He pulled up his pants. Then he told me to pull myself together and continue to pray because I was wicked for tempting him, and I needed to repent for my wickedness. He told me that if I said anything, he'd deny it." Her sobbing stopped. She continued, "I was a virgin. I've never even been on a date. My parents won't let me." She looked up at Maya with a sadness that filled her brown eyes with more tears.

Maya's heart sank. This was not what she wanted to hear. She knew firsthand how some religious figures used their position and power to sexually abuse women and children. She wished she could forget what had just been said.

"Tamara, I need you to talk to someone in the ED. What he did was rape. If this is happening, he needs to be stopped. You need to be protected."

"No one will believe me. He's got everyone fooled, and he's the pastor's nephew."

"Tamara, I want to share this with you. When I was a teenager, I had a friend whose father was a pastor at a local church. I used to go over and hang out with her. I was part of the family. One day I came over, and she wasn't there. Her father asked me in and said she'd be back in twenty minutes. That she just went to the store. As I sat there, he told me how pretty I was and that I probably had lots of boys wanting to be with me. The way he looked at me made me uncomfortable. I got up to leave, and he grabbed my arm and said, 'You probably have a different boy every night,' and he reached over to kiss me. I twisted out of his grasp and ran from the house. I never went back after that. I never told my friend, but I always wondered if he molested her. I wish I had said something. For her and any of our other friends he might have groomed. How do you know he isn't doing this to other girls?"

"I don't, but I don't know what to do. If I talk, they'll blame me. They'll say I'm lying."

"Yes, they may say that, but, more importantly, you have to protect yourself and keep him from doing anything to anyone else."

"Hey, we're ten minutes out," Jeff yelled from the front.

"Tamara, there's no easy way to say this. You have to be strong. Get away from them. Your future depends on it. This is not healthy or normal, or okay."

"I know, but what do I do?"

"Do you have anyone in your extended family or friends you could go live with? That would understand and keep you safe?"

"My sister. She's off at college. She is four years older and left before everything changed. I could see if I could go live with her."

"That seems like a good first step. Can you call your sister and ask her to come get you?"

"Yes, but she's two hours away at Western Washington University."

"Believe me. Nothing happens in the ED quickly. Here, you can use my phone to call her before we get to the hospital." Maya handed the phone to Tamara.

"Jeff, try to slow down and give us a couple more minutes."

"Got it."

Tamara's sister answered. Maya listened as Tamara told her

where she was and what was happening. When she hung up, a look of relief spread across her face.

"She's coming right away. She said she'd help me figure things out. She told me I could come live with her."

"Good. You are so brave to stand up to this. I know how hard it is to go against your church, family, and community. But trust me, there is a safer, much kinder world out there. Just know that you may have to fight for your independence. Find more women who support and believe in you, like your sister."

"Thank you so much. You don't know how much this means to me. I have been so scared. All the time wondering what to do. I didn't choose to have sex or get pregnant. He did this to me. I have my whole life ahead of me. I want to go to college too."

As they pulled into the ramp at the ED entrance, Tamara tensed up. "Pastor Richter is here with my parents."

Maya saw them. "You're going to have to be strong. Don't let them convince you to go back with them. Wait for your sister. She's coming for you, and there's no turning back now."

As Jeff pulled Tamara out on the stretcher, Pastor Richter immediately touched Tamara's arm. "Young lady, you look so much better. God has answered my prayers."

Tamara responded with, "No, he's answered my prayers."

He looked at her, and for a minute, Maya saw fear in his eyes.

CHAPTER FOURTEEN

MAYA WAS PULLING an overtime shift at the rural medic station with Jay. As usual, they had only responded to a couple of emergency calls. They used the time to catch up on their training. Maya cooked dinner for Jay, her favorite old-timer. His philosophy was to keep learning on the job. After years, his calm demeanor never faltered, even amid total chaos. When she first started, she wanted to be more like him. Working with him always left her feeling that there was more to learn. More to aspire to.

"So, Maya, I've been meaning to ask you, how are you doing since you've been back?"

Maya looked up from her plate. "I'm settling back in. Sometimes it feels like nothing has changed and other times it feels like everything has."

"I know what you mean. These new procedures and standing orders are getting in the way of us doing our job, but we don't have a choice. I've been doing this a long time, and this is the first time I've really felt concerned for our safety."

Maya looked at him. Even now, he was so calm and level-headed. He didn't have any of the stress and worry in his eyes that most of her coworkers permanently wore. If only she could find that level of calm. How did he do it? she wondered.

The pagers fired as the lights went on over Maya's head. Dispatch chimed in. "Medics, call the shift supervisor on his cell."

"I got it," Maya called out to Jay. Maya sat up and grabbed her cell phone and called Roy.

"Maya, Roy here. We've got a SWAT operation for an arrest warrant out in Ravensdale. You guys are going to be on standby while they go in. I'll meet you at the station."

"Okay, we'll be on our way." Maya hung up the phone and got dressed. She met Jay in the hallway as they exited out the door to the medic unit.

"What do you think it is?" Jay asked.

"Don't know. Probably a meth bust. Lots of meth labs out there. Let's just hope it's a bunch of tweakers cooking meth."

"The irony isn't lost on me that you would prefer it was tweakers instead of an armed militia."

"Jay, for all we know, it could be both."

"Well, I am working with *you*, so who knows!"

"I know. Imagine getting up in the middle of the night at the vacation station. This was supposed to be some easy over-time. Roy probably regrets taking his overtime shift too."

They drove to the station and parked behind it, where the firefighters parked their cars. There was a tactical personnel carrier tucked up against the back of the station, the dark exterior blending into the shadow of the large cedar trees at the edge of the parking lot.

All was quiet as they entered, none of the glaring lights they expected if the station was on alert. Roy walked in behind them.

"They're in the training room," he said.

Roy led them down a hallway to the side beyond the engine bay. Light spilled into the dark hallway from a doorway on the right. They could hear voices talking randomly. As they entered, they saw it was packed with about ten SWAT members in their tactical gear. The fire captain and the battalion chief were sitting to the left. Two men in FBI jackets stood next to the SWAT team leader.

Maya and Jay found seats along the wall near the door and settled in. Maya noticed a fresh pot of coffee on the counter at the back of the room and got up to help herself. It looked like it was going to be a long night. She brought a cup back for Roy. He looked haggard. At sixty-seven years old, he was too old to be still working on the trucks, even as a supervisor. She wondered what kept him coming back long after he was eligible for retirement.

As she sat down, the team leader started the briefing.

"We have new information on a case from two years ago that has led us here tonight. We have some intel that the men who executed the woman in the Green River Gorge may have been part of a Russian mafia that has been discovered operating in the area.

"We also have intel that may link them to the ambush on Pacific Highway. It appears they may have specifically targeted both the woman and the police officer. They may have been in positions to expose their organized crime network.

"We've been alerted to their expanded operations. They buy houses on enough property to have privacy to conduct their business out of sight. We've had an increase in these rural compounds. We know they're involved in human trafficking. We also have reason to believe they are trafficking drugs and weapons.

"We will be conducting a raid at a compound out in Ravensdale tonight. Some background. The neighbors started noticing an increase in people coming and going. Locals said an older woman with a Russian or Eastern European accent came in and set up a P.O. Box. at the Ravensdale post office. A woman was executed at the Green River Gorge Resort two years ago. She worked at that post office. Two days before the murder, the Russian woman closed the P.O. Box. The other postal worker noted that there were words between the woman who was executed and the woman who we think may be connected to her murder.

"This is a dangerous operation. We have reason to believe that there are heavily armed guards and possibly booby traps.

"We already have snipers set up in the woods. The initial team will go in, followed by the flanking team. Medics and Fire will stand by at the staging area at the neighbor's house. We'll go in and secure the compound. If we need medics, we'll call you in."

Maya was hearing this for the first time. They were the paramedic crew on standby for the raid. Their job was to treat anyone who was injured during the operation. That included the "bad guys."

She also realized that she may have been in that house before. She tentatively raised her hand.

"Yes?" The SWAT commander responded to Maya's raised hand.

"I don't know if it's relevant, but I think I responded to a call there for an unconscious infant a year ago. The call came in at 3 a.m. We were met by two young men who escorted us into an old farmhouse. Inside, a group of young women were sitting in the living room. Late teens or early twenties. A couple of the women had babies in their arms. One older couple was sitting at the kitchen table. Everyone else seemed young.

"The young men led us into the bedroom where the infant was found. It was unfortunate, but we could tell the baby was dead; rigor had set in. It appeared to be a SIDS death. No marks of trauma. They said the baby had been sleeping the last time the mother checked.

"Sitting at the kitchen table, the older couple was stoic and uninvolved. It just seemed odd that so many young women and babies were in that house, especially in the early hours of the morning on a weekday. The whole scene was unsettling."

"Thanks...paramedic?"

"Maya, Maya Murphy."

"Thanks for being on standby. Hopefully, we won't need you."

Maya nodded.

"That brings up a good point. There may be victims of trafficking present in this house. Let's not have collateral damage. Be alert. Let's get to work and shut this operation down."

The SWAT team filed out of the briefing location and got into their personnel carrier. The medic unit and the fire department aid car followed SWAT as they drove eastward into the rural hinterlands. The narrow two-lane road was shrouded in darkness, only their headlights illuminating the edges of the forest. They drove on Kent Kangley Road in stealth mode, with no lights or sirens.

Maya suddenly caught a glimpse of a coyote. Their headlights reflected in its eyes at the edge of the road. She slowed, afraid it might run out in front of them. The eyes quickly disappeared as they passed by.

They turned down a gravel road. About a quarter of a mile down, they turned into a driveway. A house sat in the darkness. The only sound was the crunch of their tires, giving away their arrival. They'd been told the residents were cooperating and were the ones who notified the police of the unusual activity on the road. They were gone, leaving their property to be used as a staging area. Command and medical support would stage while the SWAT team went another mile down the dirt road to the compound.

They waited with their engines off in the dark. It seemed like an hour before they heard the first flash-bangs and then brief gunfire. Then it was silent. The radio came alive as the SWAT called for medics. "Man down."

Maya and the team responded. As they drove down the unmaintained dirt road, she could hear the clack as their gurney bounced against the metal that held it in place.

They drove up to a landing. Lights filled the windows of the farmhouse and spilled out the open doors. Off to the right, SWAT had two men on the ground in handcuffs. The team commander motioned to them to come with him into the house.

As Maya walked inside, she saw women, babies, and three young children clinging to each other in the familiar living room. Their fearful eyes watched as she was directed to a room behind the kitchen. In there was a young man in his twenties. He lay silently on the floor. Blood oozed out of a superficial wound on his forehead. One of the SWAT members had stopped his attack with the end of his rifle. Maya directed a fire-fighter to clean and bandage the wound and get vital signs.

Another SWAT team member yelled for medics. Maya and Jay were directed out to a barn. A line of men lay, just outside, on the ground with hands behind their heads. As Maya passed one of them, he muttered something in a foreign language.

They were directed through the door of the barn. Inside, SWAT members pointed their headlamps, illuminating a man lying on a mix of dirt and hay. He had several gunshot wounds, including one to his head. She quickly confirmed he was dead. Behind him, along the walls, were stacks of boxes that reached halfway up to the ceiling. Open boxes revealed a cache of weapons, more than Maya had ever seen. One of them looked like a rocket launcher she'd seen in movies. She'd never seen that kind of weapon anywhere in real life, but here, sitting on a box in a barn, was the weapon in their service area.

Inside an abandoned horse stall lay another man. A flashlight illuminated blood flowing out of a wound in his thigh. His eyes made Maya shiver. They were cold, heartless eyes. The eyes of a killer. Had he been there the night the woman was executed? Was he one of the men who had executed the woman in the gorge? Could these criminals be connected to her ambush on Pacific Highway? Even if this man was, it didn't matter. Her oath was to save any life, even if it was one that tried to take hers.

The firefighter grabbed his shears, cut the man's pants away from the wound, and applied direct pressure with a trauma bandage. They got to work caring for the patient. As they moved him onto the stretcher, he groaned in pain. The first sound he'd uttered since she walked into the stall. A SWAT team member cuffed his wrists to the stretcher.

"Maya." Jay caught her attention. "I'm going to take this one. I think it's important that I'm the one taking care of him. Just in case anything goes wrong."

"I've..."

"Let's talk for a second," Jay said.

They stood outside the medic unit as a SWAT officer stood guard in the back.

"Look, if anything goes wrong and it's discovered that you were on the call for the woman or the ambush, and these guys were involved, it's not going to look good and could derail the charges. You drive."

"You're right. I didn't think about my connection to this raid. I'll see you on the other side."

Maya jumped into the driver's seat while Jay, the firefighter, and the SWAT member climbed into the back

Maya was grateful. Being alone in the back of the medic

unit with a man who might have executed the woman and ambushed her challenged her ability to stay calm.

Roy signaled to her to roll down the driver's window. "I've got a helicopter landing at the Ravensdale Park sports field in ten minutes. We're going to play this one from the air. I don't want anything to happen between here and the hospital."

"Drive safe. Careful with the patient. This road is a mess."

Maya turned the medic unit around and exited down the dirt road. She drove as slowly as she could, but even then, every bump resulted in groans from their patient. At least he was still alive. On the main road, she watched as three smaller County passenger buses passed her. She guessed it was to transport the criminals and their victims from the scene.

She thought back to that night when they'd responded. As with every baby call, they were stressed. It was one of the toughest kinds of calls they faced. Babies and children not only tugged at their hearts, but they presented challenges that adults didn't.

There had been an unnatural silence as they entered the room. Then she saw the little one lying there on the bed. The absence of the rise and fall of his belly with the waxy sheen of his skin told her everything she needed to know. The rest of what they observed confirmed what they already knew; the child was dead.

She'd tried to console the young mother, but she couldn't understand why they hadn't saved him. Maya explained again and again that there wasn't anything they could do. That it was too late. When they left, she could hear the sobs of the women in the background. The image of that little one sat heavily in her thoughts as they drove away.

She'd also wondered what was going on in that house. She followed up with the medical examiner, who ruled that it was SIDS (Sudden Infant Death Syndrome), but that was just part of the story. Ultimately, she ended up calling a contact at the sheriff's office and discussed her concerns that there may be something, like prostitution, going on at the house. She didn't see anything overt. It was a gut feeling based on what she saw at the scene. She had to ensure she'd done everything possible to shed light on the situation. Something was going on in that house. Apparently, her gut had been right. There was much more going on in that house than she knew.

She pulled into the parking area near the largest of the fields. The fire department had the landing zone set for the helicopter's arrival. Maya jumped into the back with Jay and the officer.

"He's holding stable. Looks like the bullet may have missed any major blood vessels. BP is 130/palp. As you can see, he is alert.

The patient suddenly blurted out, "Pain, give me something. I don't care. I'm in pain."

"I already gave you something for the pain." Jay looked up at Maya. "Maybe we should just sedate him and intubate him. I'm worried it could endanger the crew if he becomes agitated in the helicopter."

"Intubated, what is intubated?" the patient asked.

"It's where we give you lots of pain medication, but it means we have to put a breathing tube down your throat to help you breathe," Jay replied.

"No, no, don't want!"

"Well, then, we need you to calm down. As I told you, we are going to put you in a helicopter and fly you to the hospital in Seattle."

"I don't like to fly, no fly," he replied.

"Then calm down. I'll give you a little more pain medication."

Jay drew up some more pain meds and gave him small amounts. "That should help."

"Thank you," the man said as his eyes closed. He nodded off but remained conscious.

"I hope that solves the problem." Jay looked at the officer. "Are you going to drive to HMC and meet him there?"

"No, we'll have an officer meet him at the hospital. My job was to keep you safe and make sure he makes it to the hospital."

They heard the thwack thwack of the incoming helicopter. The sound grew louder and louder until they saw the spotlight and felt the wind buffeting against the medic unit. The engine whined as it powered down, then stopped.

A few minutes later, their doors opened, and two nurses dressed in blue flight suits jumped in. Jay gave a report and outlined the situation as the crew got the patient ready to transport.

"We've sedated him. He was pretty agitated until we gave him more pain meds, so just keep an eye on him."

"Great, Jay." The male flight nurse turned to the officer. "Are you going to leave the cuffs on him? We need to transfer him to our litter."

"No, but I'll zip-tie him to the litter. Everyone will be safer."

They transferred him to their litter, wrapped him in a warm blanket like a swaddled baby, and loaded him into the helicopter.

Maya watched from a distance as the pilot started up the engine, and the blades started to rotate faster and faster. The whine of the engine ramped up as they lifted off the ground. They watched it rise and turn to the north, clearing the perimeter of Douglas firs and disappearing into the sky bound for Harborview Medical Center.

Maya hadn't noticed that the sky had grown lighter as the morning sun began to rise.

CHAPTER FIFTEEN

"HEY, my friend said you guys were on the raid that brought down our terrorists. It figures it was the Russians. I knew it couldn't be our own people," said Robert, one of the old-timers.

Maya just wanted it to be over, but she doubted that the Russians were the ones targeting them on the streets. It just didn't make sense. What did they have to gain? That operation was about making money, not terrorizing Americans.

"The only good thing about the Russians is they've pushed the Black and Mexican gangs out of the area. I'm not surprised they've moved into the rural areas too. Easy to hide illegal activity. But now that the locals know, they'll find out they don't belong there.

"If our government dealt with the increase in crime on our streets, we wouldn't have these Russian organized crime groups moving into the rural areas. They just don't get it. When Titan wins the County Council election, he'll push to hire more sheriffs, and they'll go after these criminals and shut them down."

"Sure, Robert, it will be interesting to see what happens

with this bust. Hopefully, arresting this group will stop the attacks," said Jay in his calm, measured voice.

"Looks pretty damning to me. All those weapons SWAT seized at the scene. Rocket launchers, pipe bombs, automatic weapons. At least that's what my friend in the sheriff's office said. Maya, isn't that what you saw at the scene?"

"Robert, all I saw was a bunch of scared women, girls, and children. Then I was busy caring for one of the criminals who'd been shot. You know I can't talk about this," Maya said. "The fact that your friend is mouthing off about the scene isn't very professional. How'd you find out so soon?"

"Calm down, Maya. It's all over the news. I'm just glad they caught them. Now, at least we can relax."

"Right. Now everything will go back to normal." Maya got up. "Here's the pager. Have a good shift." She grabbed her stuff and hurried out of the station. *God, he just rubs me the wrong way*, she thought.

Maya stormed into her house. The dogs walked up to her and then did a quick about-face, returning to their beds. They knew she was not in a good place. Nick was sitting in the kitchen. He looked up from his computer.

"How was your shift?" he asked.

"You sure you want to ask me that question?"

"Maybe? From the sound of your voice, it sounds like you had a bad shift?"

"Not a bad shift, just exhausting. We were up all night. Jay and I were medical backup for a raid on a Russian organized crime compound that may be responsible for the ambush of the police officer and execution of the woman in the gorge."

"I'd say that was a really bad shift. What happened?"

Maya dropped her bags in the entry. Then she recounted what had occurred, including the previous call she had been on at the same location. "What really got me was that at shift change, an old timer, Robert, was ranting about the Russians and how we can relax because the terrorists have been caught. The Faux News boys will be high fiving now that their buddies are off the hook."

As she talked, she paced around the living room. She felt so frustrated with some of her coworkers' alternate reality that she just wanted to scream. "I just have a hard time believing it was the Russians. It's been the right-wing groups that have leveled threats at the government."

"I certainly hope none of your coworkers and their friends are involved, but given what we've seen in the chats, a few, at the least, are vocal about their positions."

"When does it go from spouting off opinions to taking up arms? That's what I want to know."

"Well, that's what I'm trying to figure out. Maybe the attacks helped the Russians sell more weapons?"

Finally, Maya plopped onto the couch. Rio sat his big furry head in her lap and looked up at her with his warm brown eyes. She couldn't resist. As much as Maya wanted to be angry, the softness of his furry ears under her fingers melted away all the tension she'd carried home.

"That's a reach. Usually, our Republicans amplify our own culture wars to increase weapons sales. Why would Russian criminals draw that kind of attention? Targeting first responders in their backyard. It doesn't make sense."

Nick turned toward her, a serious look in his eyes. "Well, it's not as much of a reach as you think. There may be a connection between the Russians and our extremists.

"It's interesting that the bust happened last night. I've uncovered a possible connection I passed on to HS this morning. It looks like Randy did more than sympathize. After you told me about his arms business, I did a little digging and found that he does have quite a lucrative business.

"Looks like he supplies weapons and tactical gear to security businesses across the globe. His company took off the last two years. He was making around a hundred thousand a year. Now, it looks like he'll pull in a million by the end of this year. That's quite a jump.

"I tracked one of the significant increases to a security business, Black Vulture Group. It supplies consulting and manpower to corporations doing business in some of the most volatile countries across the globe. Randy's company, Croften International, subcontracts with them to supply expertise and weapons for some of their operations.

"The Black Vulture Group was started by a Russian-American, Sergei Volkov, which by itself doesn't raise any alarm bells. He was born here. His parents immigrated in the nineties after the fall of the Soviet Union. Interestingly, Randy and Sergei served together in the military in Iraq. That is an easy connection to understand. They both developed businesses related to their contacts through the military. What is interesting is Sergei's other businesses.

"I followed the tracks and found he owns farmland through various LLCs all over Washington State. A number of these are on the Enumclaw Plateau, Puyallup, Chehalis, Moses Lake, and Aberdeen. He also owns a contract employee business that supplies domestic employees to another corporation that runs Adult Family Homes.

"Does that sound like anything that might be tied to the farmhouse raid?"

"Possibly, there were women and children at the farmhouse, but it seemed more likely they are part of sex trafficking. Young, beautiful women. I figured the children were a result of the trade. Do you think Sergei's company is bringing in workers for their businesses? Where does Randy come into this?"

"Well, if he is supplying weapons to this company and the company is involved in organized crime, there may be a connection."

"But why would he do business with a friend who has ties to a Russian crime organization targeting us? I know he is a businessman, but he is also a medic. He genuinely seems to care about his patients. Not the kind of guy who would want to see his coworkers and patients murdered to make more profit for his arms business."

Nick sighed. "If there is anything I've learned from my business, the image people present to the world is often very different from who they really are."

"I agree with you on that point, but Randy knowingly working with someone targeting us on the streets? No way."

"Maybe he doesn't know, or maybe the Russians aren't the ones who are targeting you and your coworkers."

Maya looked down at Rio's head lying in her lap. "Thanks, buddy."

He'd brought her down to earth, but now she felt her feelings spiraling out of control again. Her vision narrowed, and she felt a tightness in her chest. She reached down and hugged Rio.

"Nick, I can't wrap my mind around the idea that some of my coworkers may be involved. How am I supposed to feel safe anywhere?"

"You're safe here. We've got your back." Nick looked up from his computer at Maya and the dogs.

"At least I'm relatively safe here, but after Daniel's uncle, I'm not so sure I'm safe anywhere."

She was exhausted, but too wired to sleep. "I'm going to go for a run along the waterfront. I need to unwind."

"I wish I could join you, but I have a meeting in an hour. New client in the Columbia Tower. He insisted we meet in person. Says he needs to make sure we are a real company. The digital age. It's good business for my company but makes it harder to know what is real."

"I'll take the dogs and text you when I return. Let me know how the meeting turns out."

Maya went upstairs to change. The dogs came with her, Kali bounded up the stairs, and Rio whined with anticipation. Maya's body vibrated with pent-up stress. A run would take the edge off. Then, she could look at the reality of where she had landed since returning home.

She held Rio and Kali's leashes as she stretched with her hands on a smooth stone bench in the shape of an eye. Oppressive gray clouds rolled in from behind the Space Needle. She closed her eyes in meditation, focusing on the sound of the fountain marking the entrance to the Elliott Bay Trail. *Reset, breathe, let go of work and focus on now.* She was trying to learn to let go. To intentionally redirect her thoughts. She'd worked with Dr. Harrington to ground herself when she felt her thoughts spiraling out of control like they had this morning. *Breathe.*

Kali stretched as well, performing her version of upward and downward dog. Rio whined with impatience, ready to hit the trail running. Maya ignored Rio. *Focus,* she thought.

They started jogging down the trail, leaving Alaskan Way behind as they ran north along the shoreline of Puget Sound. The smell of salt and the threat of rain filled her lungs as she regulated her breathing to match her pace. The sound of waves breaking in uneven tones along the shoreline distracted her thoughts. She'd spent many days running along the trail and watched as it transformed from a sea wall to salmon habitat.

Everywhere there was change for the good. She just had to focus on it.

Maya unleashed the dogs at a group of giant natural stone and concrete pedestals, allowing them to traverse the obstacles as a challenge. At the last one, they watched her intently from their perch. She tossed a couple of treats as their reward for their exuberant leaps along the obstacle course.

Towering ahead of them were the grain silos with conveyors that spanned across the waterfront to towers that unloaded grain onto waiting ships. The railroad that followed the same route as the trail delivered the grain. The silos and the railway were remnants of the industry that was now replaced by the path and edges of natural habitat.

They passed underneath the long arm of the conveyor and continued north toward Magnolia. Maya kept her pace steady, with Rio and Kali at her sides. They turned inland on the trail as it paralleled the port. Beyond, she could hear the movement of forklifts and trucks as the ships were loaded and unloaded. They ran past the Seattle Yacht Club and circled back along the shore. She stopped to look at the sailboats, their sails lowered, floating next to yachts in neat rows along the docks. Behind them, Mount Rainier was hidden by the dark clouds. A heron stood motionless on a rocky edge watching for fish in the calm water between the docks and breakwaters.

Back under the Magnolia Bridge, she glimpsed homeless camps she had ignored on her first pass. Tent cities set up under the protective concrete expanse of the bridge. A man in a long, dirty blue coat walked in circles, his arms vibrating up and down. Incoherent words emanated from his mouth. Maya had seen the number of homeless growing over the years. What used to be only found under I-5 near Harborview Medical Center was now evolving under every overpass, bridge, and freeway ramp in every corner of the city. Where were they all from? What had gotten them to this point?

She knew some of the stories. Alcoholism, mental illness, drugs, and other misfortune brought them to the doors of her medic unit. It was hard to have compassion when it seemed like so many were seeking drugs, a free ride, or acting belligerent, or worse, violent. She'd learned over her years to always treat everyone with respect, regardless of how she felt. But, even so, today she was alone, and self-preservation quickened her pace as she avoided any eye contact with the man ranting to himself. Out here alone, she felt vulnerable. Rio and Kali kept their eyes on the man and the camp until they'd passed beyond their sight. At least she knew her dogs would give their lives to keep her safe.

She sprinted at top speed around the path along the industrial buildings before curving back toward the water. After it crossed under the bridge on the opposite side and joined the shoreline again, she slowed to an even pace as her breathing relaxed. The dogs matched her slower pace, their pads softly touching the pavement.

On the opposite side of the grain silo, Maya saw a giant American flag painted on the side. A chill ran down her spine. Before now, the flag was a symbol of her country, but since the attacks and war cries she heard on the mechanic's radio, she felt like it carried danger, not against enemies outside her country but perceived enemies within her country. All those feelings spun upside her. *This is so wrong,* she thought. *We shouldn't be fighting each other.*

Her thoughts were interrupted by the first raindrops hitting her forehead.

"Well, dogs, it looks like we'll be sprinting back to the finish line," she said, looking down at them as they kept pace beside her. They looked up at her without missing a step as she picked up speed again. The sky opened up, and the November monsoon reminded her that winter was almost here.

Drenched, they exited the park and continued to sprint to her SUV, seeking refuge from the pouring rain. As she pulled out onto Alaskan Way, with her windshield wipers on high, a man stood in the pouring rain holding a soggy cardboard sign that said, "REPENT NOW, end days are comin'."

CHAPTER SIXTEEN

SHE JERKED AWAKE, a gasp escaping her mouth. Disoriented and still in the nightmare, she looked over and didn't see Nick. He'd just been there in bed with her. She shot up out of bed, sending the dogs into high alert. Nearly tripping over Kali, she ran out of the bedroom door, yelling, "Nick, Nick."

"Down here."

She found herself standing in the kitchen, looking right at Nick, who was on his computer, as usual. She felt confused by the shift from dream to reality. "I woke up, and you were gone. I thought something terrible had happened to you."

"I'm here. Were you having another nightmare?"

"Yes, but this time it was different. There was this homeless man holding a sign on the side of Alaskan Way today. Only in my dream, his sign said, 'Repent, you let him die." Then I woke up. I thought it was about the officer and then I saw that you weren't in bed and in my dream, I thought it was you I'd let you die.

Maya sat down on the stool next to Nick. Rio and Kali

huddled under their feet, getting as close as they could without actually sitting in their laps. They sensed Maya's distress.

Nick put his arm around Maya's shoulders. "You don't think it was about the officer? Didn't Dr. Harrington say you could continue to have flashbacks?"

"Yes, but not seeing you there was terrifying. My mind jumped from the officer to you, and I panicked. After what happened to Daniel's uncle, I'm scared. I'm scared that we aren't safe if they know about our research. What if Charles was just a message, and if we don't stop, we could be next?"

"That's possible. Certainly, we need to be aware of what's happening around us. We have cameras around the house. The dogs will let us know if someone is snooping around. Both of us should consider safety from here on out. Jeff said he's installed cameras around their place. Daniel's moved his uncle in with him temporarily. I'm doubling down on figuring out who is behind these events. Then there is HS. We just need to make sure that we stay safe until we can catch these unhinged lunatics!"

There was an edge of anger in Nick's voice she hadn't heard before. She could tell that his lack of progress and the growing danger were getting to him. She also knew that his anger would be turned into action. He wouldn't stop looking for the people who were targeting her and her coworkers. Maya looked across at him, glad that they were a team. She didn't feel so alone with Nick, Rio, and Kali. They had her back.

"I think I'm going to let the chief know that I'm concerned that we may have medics in our own ranks sympathetic toward those attacking us. He needs to prioritize our safety and make it clear that threats from within will not be tolerated."

"Maya, that's great, but just be careful. We are still determining who may be involved. You should lay low until we know more."

"You're right, but I feel this shouldn't be allowed to go unchecked. People have died! Those responsible need to be held accountable."

"They do, but don't let your emotions get ahead of you. You know better than me that you need to check your emotions at the door and deal with the situation rationally."

"You're right, but it's hard to detach and be patient when any day could bring more attacks."

"You've got this. We'll find them; it's just a matter of time."

"I knew I said yes to marrying you for more than just your good looks."

"I certainly hope so." Nick laughed.

Rio groaned and stuck his head on Nick's foot.

"Jealous, Rio?" Nick asked. "I wouldn't worry. I'm not as good at protecting her as you are, buddy."

Nick looked up at Maya. "I'm done for the night. I'll be asleep right beside you."

"Thanks." Maya leaned over and kissed him.

CHAPTER SEVENTEEN

MAYA WAS CLEANING up as she waited for the coffee to finish brewing. Training Chief Alden Bancroft walked through the door. He looked right at her.

"Maya, I want to talk to you about something before you leave today. Let's go to the training room. I asked Em to come in a few minutes early, so you're covered in case there's a call."

"Sure, what's up?"

"Let's talk in private."

"This sounds serious. Do I need my union rep?"

"No, I need to talk to you, off the record, about a complaint we received about a call you were on recently."

"Okay," she hesitated. "Sure, let's talk now."

They walked into the training room. Alden shut the door and sat down across from Maya at the table. Maya sat with her cup of coffee steaming between her hands. It had been another long night. Why did he just show up without notifying her ahead of time? She wondered what would bring him down here at shift change. This was different from the usual protocol.

Issues like this were usually left up to the shift supervisor to address.

"Maya, we received a complaint that you overstepped your role as a paramedic on the call for the young woman, Tamara Goldman, from the Resurrection Evangelical Church. She says you told her to leave her family, move in with her sister, and that she was in danger."

"Well, there is more to this. Most of which I can't discuss without breaking patient confidentiality. At the time, I simply offered Tamara options if she felt unsafe. She told me she could call her sister for help."

"Pastor Richter and her family said you coerced her to run. Turned her against her parents and the church. He thinks you were out of line."

"I'm not sure what you are getting at. I did my job. You know some of our job crosses over into social work."

"Maya, I want to keep this between you and me. This has yet to become an official complaint. He approached me after the church service and told me about it. He was upset and complained that paramedics shouldn't be giving out advice to underage children telling them to flee their parents and community."

"He's lucky there aren't police arresting..." She stopped. She'd said too much.

"Alden, there's more to this situation than you are probably aware of. I'm going to stick by my decision to help this young woman. If Pastor Richter or her family want to file an official complaint, then we can go through the proper channels, including union representation."

"I came here as a courtesy to you and them," Alden said. "Just be aware that Pastor Richter is well respected in the community and is one of our chaplains. This one girl is not worth your time. She's well... She's had some problems, which is one of the reasons the family joined the church. Her version of events is, well, suspect at best. I don't want to see you ruin your professional reputation because you were lied to. I know how hard it has been for you to return after what happened."

Was that a threat? Did he just invalidate what the young girl had told her and threaten her reputation?

"Does this have anything to do with Pastor Richter supporting Titus for County Council? If this becomes an issue, I'm not the one whose reputation will be in question."

Alden's eyes narrowed as he assessed her threat. He knew Maya well, and she wasn't one to back down when she felt she was protecting her patients or the people close to her.

"Maya, I'm just the messenger. There's no need to get confrontational. I wanted to make you aware of the issue. I'm sure there won't be a formal complaint. They are working to bring Tamara back to us so that we can help her renew her commitment to Jesus."

Did he just say 'we'? She suddenly saw him in a different light. She knew he was a Christian, but the fact that he was involved in this church was concerning. From what she had heard from the pulpit, the message was pretty dark. Alden had always seemed a little high-strung, but she didn't take him for a radical for Jesus. Now, she wasn't so sure she could trust him.

"Alden, what happened on that call has nothing to do with my situation. I'd have done the same before the ambush. This was patient care, and I'll stand by my decision."

She respected him as training chief, but bringing this up in a formal work setting didn't seem appropriate. It was as if they were blaming her for Tamara's reach for safety and independence. She'd just supported her in finding her way out of a horrifying situation. Tamara had begged her not to say anything or report the incident to the police. She wanted to figure out how to proceed. Maya had honored her request. She gave this young woman back power over her own life and body. She would never concede that she had made the wrong decision.

"Are we finished? I'm exhausted. After I've had some rest, I'll think more about what you said."

"Thank you, Maya, and yes, we're finished. Get some rest."

As Maya and Alden walked out, Em, Randy, and Jeff sat at the kitchen table. They stopped talking.

"Hey, Alden. What brings you down here today?" Randy asked.

"Just had something I wanted to talk to Maya about. We've got the mass casualty incident training coming up. How's business, Randy?"

"Busy, it's growing faster than I can keep up with. How's life out in Maple Valley?"

"Good, although it's that time of year again when I'm overwhelmed raking the leaves. I've got to hire someone. I'd love to talk more, but I have to get going. I've got a meeting in thirty minutes, followed by more meetings."

After he left, they turned to Maya. "So, what did he really come to talk to you about?" Em asked.

"He just wanted to go over some details about the upcoming training schedule."

"Wow, he came all the way to the station. He could have just called you," Randy commented.

"You know, Alden. He's always a little stressed out before a big training. I guess he just needed reassurance that everything was going as planned. This is a big deal. We haven't had changes to our MCI plan like this since, well, the dark ages."

Everyone laughed.

"Forty years of tradition unimpeded by progress," Randy said.

"Still true today," Jeff said.

"I gotta run. Jeff, I'll see you and Melissa tonight for dinner."

"Five thirty, right?"

"Don't you guys see enough of each other at work?" Randy asked.

"You know, we have to convince Melissa and Nick that we aren't having an affair. Besides, Jeff's a great cook on and off duty," Maya said.

Nick and Maya left early to avoid the gridlock traffic through downtown Seattle, but traffic was lighter than usual. They used the extra time to drive out along Green Valley Road through farmlands. Just off the highway, Maya saw more Titus flags sagging against their upright poles perched on the beds of pickup trucks at a popular fishing spot.

As they pulled into Green Valley Meat Market, she saw election signs lined up along the road. They stopped to pick up some of their favorite smoked salmon and treat the dogs to raw bones. It was salmon season on the river, and their fresh smoked salmon was the best around. Inside, the cashier was talking to a couple of fishermen about the election. Titus was their man. Maya would be relieved when the election was over. It was a dark cloud looming over an already dismal autumn.

Maya smiled as she paid the cashier, a woman who'd been working there since Maya discovered the place. When had everything changed? It used to be pleasantries and something familiar to both of them, like her dogs, that bridged the divide between them. But now, with the political shift, the disconnect between their worlds seemed irreversible. Maya had walked through many different communities as a paramedic, balancing her version of the world with what she saw. Sometimes it was hard to reconcile how different one person's life was from another even though they lived in the same country, state, and local area.

Maya and Nick arrived at Melissa and Jeff's. She noticed the changes right away. "Hey, you guys have done a great job remodeling this place. What made you decide to redo every-thing? It was nice before too."

Jeff looked at Melissa.

"The baby. I just wanted to have everything ready. I'll show you her bedroom."

"*Her?* So you know the sex already?"

"We just found out today."

"Wow, exciting. Everything's good?"

As they walked into the transformed office, Melissa replied, "It's great. Other than the nausea and vomiting. I just can't believe it's really happening. We've planned for this, but to have a baby finally on the way, a daughter."

"I'm so happy for you. This room is amazing," Maya exclaimed as she looked around at the light-yellow room with a bamboo crib. Above were forest creatures: a raccoon, deer, fox, an owl, and a bear surrounding the letters M O L L Y.

"Molly, is that her name?"

"Yes, we had two sets of decals. One with Molly and the other with Adam. You know, if it was a boy. I was so excited that we put it up on the wall today. We aren't finished decorat-ing, but we have time."

"You guys are amazing. So much change. You're going to be great parents."

Maya knew Jeff and Melissa planned for the baby. They were ready to welcome a child into their lives. She thought about Tamara and the rape that had changed her life forever. She hoped Tamara would stay with her sister and not return to her parents and that pastor.

"Thanks, Maya. I'm happy, but I'm nervous too."

"Understandable."

"Right, but everything will be fine. Especially with Jeff planning for every possible medical issue we might encounter.

After everything he tells me that could go wrong, I'm amazed that women ever have children."

"He actually told you?"

"Well," Melissa pulled out a drawer of medical supplies, "Jeff stocked these supplies just in case."

"That's a medic for you. Plan for the worst and hope for the best."

As they walked back into the living room, Nick and Jeff were going over some of their research.

"Nick's updating me on Randy. I also find it hard to believe he would supply weapons to a Russian crime network responsible for targeting us."

"Leaving that behind, Jeff has seen a crazy uptick in chats about the election," Nick said. "People are applauding the attack on Parnam, saying she deserved it. They say that Kale should be running things and making sure the schools are safe, and they're learning the right things. They're calling for monitoring the election centers to ensure the votes are legal. Even talking about violence if Kale and Titus don't win."

"Did you know Kale has hired guards to protect her from the left-wing nuts she says have been targeting her?" Jeff asked. "She says it is the left that's more dangerous. The radio shows and podcasters have picked up her comments and amplified them."

Maya rolled her eyes. "I wish there were guardrails on what an elected official can say. It's putting everyone in danger and makes our job much harder."

"Well, we went on the call at the college for a possible 'active shooter.' If shooting school children doesn't change people's opinions, I don't know what will?" Jeff said.

"It does, but then there are the arguments about the solution, and then we are right back where we started," Melissa said.

"At some point, someone will sue some of these podcast provocateurs for inciting violence and targeting people," Nick said. "They might change their tactics once it hits their bank accounts. They are making lots of money and getting their people elected."

"Maybe," Melissa said.

"Have you heard anyone talk about Pastor Richter? I had an odd interaction with Alden regarding him this morning."

"I knew that meeting wasn't about the training," Jeff said.

Nick raised his eyebrows. "You didn't tell me about meeting with him this morning."

"I thought I'd wait until tonight because it might tie into these right-wing groups."

Maya recounted her conversation with Alden and how it clearly felt like he was threatening her. "I understand that the pastor might be worried about exposing illegal behavior in his congregation, but to send my training chief, who is a member of his congregation, to speak to me is more than concerning. That, along with the fact that Pastor Richter is openly supporting Titus, raises more concern about the tone of what I heard him preaching about."

"Wait, a pastor sent his friend, your superior, to silence you?" Anger flashed in Nick's eyes as he took in what he had just heard.

"It sure felt like he was trying to silence me."

"What illegal behavior?" Nick asked. He leaned in to hear Maya's answer.

"If I go into the details, I'm violating patient confidentiality. Let's just say it's damning. Having it come out right before an election would hurt Titus, who is counting on the support of the pastor's followers. He commands a large congregation whose support will be key to Titus winning."

"Why wasn't I called into the meeting, too?" Jeff asked.

"I don't know. Maybe your name wasn't mentioned. Besides, you can do no wrong. War vet and obvious white guy."

Jeff gave her a scorching look. "You know how to make me feel special."

"I try."

"But seriously. You're a team, but somehow you were the only one called out?" Nick said.

"That's just how it works sometimes. Besides, I'm sure the pastor thought it was all my fault.

"You need to tell me when things like this happen. I'm concerned." Nick looked irritated with her. Jeff and Melissa looked knowingly at each other.

Jeff attempted to redirect the conversation. "The point is, we need to know if the pastor has any connections with the right-wing militia groups. His sermon was scary. It sounded like he was trying to incite a holy war from the pulpit."

"Isn't that illegal?" Nick asked.

"Apparently not." Maya gave Nick a skeptical look.

"I haven't heard anything directly about the pastor in the chats," Jeff said. "We have read about an inspirational speaker calling on Christians to fight to take America back. Calls himself a spokesman for God. We'll find out where he's located. Maybe it is Pastor Richter. Maybe you heard him speaking for God."

"Interesting how they always seem to be speaking for God," Maya said.

"Maybe we should have Melissa attend one of his events," Jeff suggested.

"Why me?" Melissa asked.

"No one would recognize you, and if they did, you're local. If it is Pastor Richter, he might recognize Maya and me if we went."

"Well, he did invite me to attend his church. I should show

up as a way of putting him at ease. Then maybe he'll quit using Alden to put pressure on me at work," Maya said.

"I'm not so sure that would be a good idea," Nick said. "If they are targeting you and your coworkers, walking into their domain might backfire. I could go. I've never met him at any of the events I've attended with Maya."

"That might work," Maya said. "Although you'll have to dress the part a little more. Sensitive new-age adventurer will give you away. Ditch Patagonia for Carhartt, and you should be fine." Maya winked at Nick.

Nick looked more annoyed; he probably thought she was making light of the situation.

Jeff chimed in, "I like to wear my Carhartts with my Patagonia too."

"Well, we've been a little worried about you since you moved out to the Plateau, and now we know we should have been," Maya said.

"I hate to break it to you guys, but I'm thinking about voting for Titus if I can openly carry my hand grenades. You never know when you'll need them stateside."

"Don't joke about that," Melissa said.

"I'll research the 'Spokesman for God' and Pastor Richter to see if there is a connection," Nick said. "Then we'll figure out if my attending an event at the church is the right course of action. It might draw the wrong attention if they find out I'm your fiancé."

"You know, it wouldn't work for you to go alone, Nick. I forgot, Alden's met you. He'll recognize you. If we go together, I could grovel like I'm trying to get back on his good side."

"Let's talk more about that later. For now, it's time for drinks and food." Melissa stood up to head to the kitchen.

"I'm sorry you're caught up in his drama," Maya said. She

felt sorry for the significant others of first responders. They signed up for more than they anticipated.

Melissa put the pizzas in the oven and returned with a glass of water for her and a couple of beers for Jeff and Nick. Then she poured a glass of wine for Maya.

"Do you think Alden could be part of the local militia?" Nick asked Maya and Jeff.

"You know Alden can be uptight, but he's dedicated to his job. I can't see him doing anything that would target us. As a member of the pastor's congregation, he's probably doing the pastor a favor," Maya replied.

"Alden's always been a professional. My bet is on the favor for the pastor," Jeff said.

Maya frowned. "Let's hope that's all it is."

CHAPTER EIGHTEEN

MAYA WALKED into work to find Doug sitting in the recliner. He looked up and acknowledged Maya.

"You're not Randy?" Maya said.

Doug looked over at Em, who was at the office desk finishing paperwork.

Em answered, "The shift supervisor and Chief Anderson came by yesterday and asked Randy to come to the office. Doug came in to cover for him."

"I got called in for OT at 8:00. I figured someone called in sick at the last minute," Doug said.

"Interesting. I received a visit from Alden, who was concerned about the upcoming training, and now Randy gets called down to the office."

"Maybe the office is feeling pressure to tighten things up. Rumor mill has it, management feels the medics are getting lax," Doug said.

"Lax? If anything, we're more disciplined because of the attacks," Maya said. "Usually, the crackdown comes with a new boss. However, it could have something to do with the Executive addressing the recent attacks."

"Just telling you what I heard," Doug said.

"Or maybe it has to do with Randy and his side business," Jeff said.

Maya felt herself jump. She hadn't even heard him come in.

"They wouldn't come to get him for something that happened with his side business unless he's been distracted lately, causing him to make a mistake on a call," Maya replied.

It had to be on an OT shift since I wasn't called in," Em said.

"Maybe." Maya was concerned that it was something else, but she didn't say anything.

Em shrugged. "I'll text him later today and ask what's up."

"Did you guys sleep last night? What are you up to today?" Maya asked.

"No, we didn't sleep. I'm just visiting Daniel and Charles later today."

"I talked to Daniel yesterday. His uncle is reluctantly settling in. Charles doesn't like being taken care of," Maya said.

"That's what he told me too. I'm going to give Daniel a break so he can go to band practice. I told Charles I'd make him a home-cooked dinner."

"Good tactic," Maya said. "Nick's going out of town next week. Would you watch my dogs while I'm on shift, Em? I could bring them and hand them off at shift change."

"Sure, I'm always up for taking care of those two. As long as you don't mind if I take them for a hike."

"Do I mind? Of course, not. Thanks, Em."

They heard the door slam shut. "Did Doug just leave? That's not like him to just take off without checking in," Jeff commented.

"He was quiet all shift," Em said.

"We're all on edge," Maya said. "Maybe he's got stuff going on at home. A lot of our families are scared right now. Melissa talked about her concerns the other day. I'm sure that other spouses are feeling the same. This is a scary time for all of us."

"Less scary now that they caught the group responsible for the attacks," Em commented.

"I wouldn't let your guard down yet," Maya said.

"Why?"

The pagers fired, and the overhead alarms went off. Another abrupt start to another shift.

CHAPTER NINETEEN

THE DOGS MADE a grand entrance into the station and immediately ran up to Em. She knelt and Rio bumped against her, knocking her off her feet with his enthusiasm.

"It's good to see you too, Rio," Em said.

Rio responded with licks and an ear nibble. Kali turned toward Doug but then veered around him and came in the back way to get Em's attention. Jeff walked in behind Maya, and the dogs diverted their attention for a moment before fawning over Em again.

"Looks like Em is taking care of the pack today," Jeff said.

"I've got the dogs for a fun day of adventure. We're going to hike Mount Peak today."

Jeff looked out the window at the steely sky. "Well, you better start early. It's supposed to rain."

"It can rain. The dogs won't care," Em replied.

Doug walked up to Rio and reached down to give him a pat on the head. Rio gave him a quick look and ducked his hand before circling around him. The head duck was his usual approach to people he didn't like.

"I guess Rio doesn't like strangers," Doug said.

Maya countered, "He's just reserved around people he doesn't know well. Em and Jeff are old friends.

"So, are you on OT again, Doug?" Maya asked.

"I am. It looks like Randy is off for a while. I'm working for him a couple more shifts this month."

"Randy's off for a while?" Maya asked.

"I called him, but he hasn't called back. I texted him twice," Em said.

"That's odd. Has anyone heard from him?"

"Nobody I've talked to. The office said they couldn't discuss it. So, I guess we'll just have to wait," Em replied.

"And gossip," Maya said.

"I'm sure there is a reason we aren't aware of... In fact, here is an email from the chief on the subject," Jeff said at the computer.

"Really? Read it," Em said.

"This is to announce the resignation of Randy Croften. Randy has been an integral part of our organization as a professional paramedic. We wish him well as he continues to build his business. His resignation is our loss. Signed Chief Anderson," Jeff read aloud.

"What? He didn't say anything to me about quitting," Em said.

Maya frowned. "You would have thought he would have discussed it, at least with you."

"Do you think it had anything to do with the Russians? I mean, he does sell weapons," Doug said.

"Randy would never sell weapons to use against us. That's completely in left field, Doug," Em replied.

"You're right, but why would he resign without telling anyone? You said yourself he hasn't returned your phone calls and texts."

"You're right, Doug; it's not like him. I don't know what's going on, but I'm going to keep trying to contact him."

"Why now? He knew we were already down two medics," Maya said.

"I just can't believe it." Jeff turned away from the computer. "Randy just up and resigned. Now we're down three medics. We're all going to be working mandatory overtime until we get some new hires trained and ready to go."

"I'll work as much OT as possible," Doug said.

Maya knew there had to be more to the story. She'd call Nick later and see if he could make any connections between Randy's business and this new development.

Maya looked up as Roy walked through the door.

Rio gave a cautious woof.

"Well, hello to you too," Roy said.

Maya directed the dogs to lie down next to her. "Wow, we were just talking about all the changes happening, Roy. Do you have any info on why Randy resigned?"

"It was conveyed to me that he decided to pursue his business full time."

"That doesn't explain why he was taken off shift last week," Em said.

"Oh, that. That was another matter. Randy had some issues on a call. We were following up on the details and decided the best way was to do it while he was on shift. I think that helped guide his decision to resign."

"What issues?" Em asked.

"Em, you know I can't discuss that," Roy said as he sat down at the table.

"Why did he resign?" she persisted.

"I guess he just thought, like a few of us, that he was stretched too thin. He needed to choose between being a paramedic and running a growing corporation. From what

I've heard, his company is taking off. He doesn't need this job."

"I guess I just thought he would have at least let me know and said goodbye." Em looked like she didn't quite believe what Roy was saying.

"I'm sure he will. We'll see him at the retirement banquet next March."

"Let us know if you hear anything more," Em said.

Doug walked over and shook Roy's hand. "Good to see you, sir."

"You too. Thanks for taking some of this overtime."

"No problem. I'll work as much as I can."

"Besides, he needs to work at the busy stations. He's been moonlighting out there in Enumclaw lately. A few sleepless shifts here, and he'll level up," Jeff said.

"Here and in Rat City. I'm back-to-back for six days."

"You definitely won't get any sleep there," Jeff replied.

"Maya, I'm going over to pick up some control meds at the hospital. When I return, I'd like to talk to you and Jeff if you aren't on a call."

"Sure. What about?" Maya asked.

"I'll talk more when I return."

Roy left them to finish up shift change. Maya handed off the dogs, who reluctantly jumped into Em's car. Maya could tell that they thought they were going to spend the day at work with her, their disappointment reflected in their eyes. She knew that soon, once their paws hit the trail, they would forget about this.

After Em and Doug left, Maya and Jeff looked at each other.

"What do you think is up?" Jeff asked.

"You know as much as I do. We have seen far too much management during the last few rotations."

"Do you think the pastor filed a formal complaint?"

"It's possible."

Roy returned a half hour later. He walked in, poured himself a cup of coffee, and sat at the table. Maya and Jeff waited expectantly.

"So, I've received complaints about how the truck was left a couple of weeks ago. Seems that some equipment wasn't restocked, and the back of the medic unit was dirty."

"Really?" Jeff asked.

"Yes. Apparently, whoever complained was angry enough that they wrote a formal complaint and sent it directly to the chief."

"That's ridiculous. We always leave everything ready for the next crew. You know that, Roy," Jeff said.

"Look, I'm just the one who has to bring it up with you. I've never received complaints about you two in the past, so I headed off any kind of disciplinary action, but I need you to sign this form acknowledging that I brought this to your attention."

Maya looked at Jeff. She had a hard time believing Jeff would have missed a beat, and she knew she didn't. Something else was up.

"Well, just for the record, I disagree with this because we have no way to verify what was or wasn't done," Jeff said. "Can you be more specific?"

Roy opened his notebook and turned some pages. "It says here that there was blood under the stretcher cushion, and the suction was dirty."

"Can you give us a specific date?" Maya asked.

"The date of the complaint was last Friday. It doesn't say what day the incident occurred."

Maya thought back to the last few shifts. She and Jeff had a few calls and intubated a gunshot victim, but they had cleaned everything up. She was sure of it.

"Roy, look, I don't think either of us recall an incident where we would have forgotten to clean up. We will double-check our work so we can vouch for each other," Jeff said.

"Okay, that's all I'm really looking for. Just be aware that there was a complaint and make sure you keep your side of the street clean."

"Got it," Maya said.

After Roy left, Maya and Jeff discussed the situation.

Jeff leaned toward Maya. "You and I didn't leave that kind of a mess."

"Isn't it a little strange that the week after Alden visits me with a complaint from the pastor, suddenly we aren't doing our job well enough?"

Jeff nodded. "The timing is suspect. Something is up. Whether it has anything to do with the pastor, who knows? We should just make sure we watch each other's backs. There is more going on here than complaints."

"Definitely."

Maya and Jeff walked up through a maze of old clunkers to the muddy entrance of the house. As they walked through the doorway, the smell of stale cigarette smoke mixed with the thick haze of newer smoke assaulted Maya's senses. Her patient had probably gotten their last cigarette in before they arrived.

Sitting in the living room was an older woman in a dirty tan recliner. She was leaning forward with her hands gripping her knees. Maya watched as the woman's neck muscles contracted in a desperate effort to breathe. The firefighters were trying to put an oxygen mask on her, but she was vehemently pushing it away as she breathlessly exclaimed, "I can't breathe."

Maya reached into her kit and took out a breathing treatment as Jeff quickly confirmed her lung sounds were diminished along with the audible wheezing. He nodded to Maya.

"Ma'am, I know you feel like you can't breathe with a mask on, but this will deliver medicine through the mask and make it easier for you to breathe."

"No, no, I don't want," she said, then paused to catch her breath.

"Ma'am, trust me."

The woman waved her hand in halfhearted acceptance. Maya placed the mask on her face and watched as the mist of medicine was sucked in as deeply as the woman's lungs would allow.

"Her oxygen saturation is eighty-five percent," Jeff said.

"We'll see if this works. In the meantime, let's close that backdoor. We don't need more cigarette smoke coming in, making the situation worse." She'd seen a younger man, probably her son, standing in the doorway, sucking on his cigarette.

The woman seemed to respond to the treatment. Her face relaxed, and her breaths grew deeper. Maya looked and saw her oxygen saturation rising. *Good,* she thought. *Hopefully, we won't have to intubate her today.*

As she looked around, she saw the place was run down. The ceiling was coated in a dark yellow film from years of cigarette smoke. A glass ashtray on the coffee table overflowed with extinguished butts. The TV flashed behind Maya, at least muted while they treated the woman. Stacks of newspapers and magazines clung to tables. The floor was littered with layers of dirt and cat hair. The cat was sleeping on the chair next to the woman. She'd seen so many homes like this. People generally kept to themselves, except when their independence was confronted by a life-threatening medical emergency.

Two volunteer firefighters brought in the stretcher from

their medic unit. Glenn was always on the calls out here. She wondered if he worked a regular job.

"Hi, Maya. How are you today?" he said cheerfully. "Take care of Nancy here. She's a good friend of mine." He nodded toward Maya's patient.

"We will, Glenn. She's doing better already," Maya replied.

"How are your dogs doing? I was hiking earlier and saw Em. She said she was taking them hiking?"

"Well, they're having a good time today without me. Em's watching them while I'm on shift."

"Great looking dogs. I love Malinois. Great protection dogs. Gerald, one of the deputies, just got his new Mal for the K9 unit."

Maya was trying to interject as he rambled on. "Glenn, let's move Nancy onto the stretcher slowly."

"Oh, got it." He slid in next to Nancy.

"Just hold her steady while we have her stand and pivot."

Nancy transitioned easily to the lowered stretcher and then started breathing harder again. Maya grabbed some more medicine to replace the dose she had almost finished. They'd wait to move her until she recovered from the exertion. Sometimes slower was better when treating her lung patients.

Glenn placed his hand on Nancy's shoulder and had his head bent down and eyes closed.

Was he praying? Maya wondered.

He opened his eyes and looked up at Maya. "Hey, we need all the help we can get. Right, Nancy?"

Nancy quickly looked up at him as her hands gripped her knees and her arms held her upright.

When she recovered enough, they moved her legs onto the stretcher and rolled her to the medic unit. Maya noticed a flagpole she'd missed on the way in. On it was a large American flag and a Confederate flag entangled in the overhanging branches of a bigleaf maple. It struck her that the elections were next week. That could be why they'd had the uptick in complaints. Some of her coworkers, while nice guys, carried conservative ideas about politics and life choices. Maybe some of them were also friends of the pastor.

CHAPTER TWENTY

MAYA MET Em for a hike up Tiger Mountain with the dogs after work. Maya had gotten lucky and slept most of the night. Now a good hike would help relax her mind. The dogs bounded up the Cable Line Trail as Em and Maya scaled the steep incline behind them. The mud was slick from all the rain and required more care in placing their steps. The dogs, digging in with their four paws, left them behind, only stopping to make sure the two humans were following.

"Ugh, November." Maya sighed. "I need to remember to take a vacation and fly somewhere south of the equator to avoid this depressing weather."

"It's a little worse than December and January, but not by much," Em said.

"I think I'm just about done with this weather. Every year it gets harder to take. We had to hold our umbrella over our patients between the buildings and the medic unit to keep them dry."

"I guess you need lots of rain for this kind of green. I love how green it is here," Em said as she looked up at the towering

Douglas Fir and maple trees. Then her feet slipped backward, and her knees landed on a muddy shelf. "Okay, maybe a little less rain," she said as she regained her footing.

They crossed under some powerlines, and then the trail increased in steepness. They set their pace and concentrated on breathing and climbing. Maya always loved the focus of moving one foot in front of the other as her breath heaved from the exertion. Em led with a challenging pace. When they arrived at the section that gradually climbed along the ridge, they slowed down again, and Em started to talk.

"Charles isn't happy at Daniel's. He's not used to being taken care of by anyone, well, except his lady friends. The woman he was supposed to meet the night he was attacked has been driving up from Tacoma. She is quite a character. She's a blues singer and quite a bit younger than him. You should have seen the evil eye she gave me when she walked in. I think she thought I was competition."

"You, competition? You could be his granddaughter."

"I know, right. I just ignored her. She's nice enough. I wanted to let you know, Daniel's feeling depressed. He blames himself for his uncle's assault. He mentioned that maybe this was the wrong place for him. That maybe it would be better to move back to LA."

"Wow, everyone seems to be jumping ship. Randy, now Daniel's talking about leaving. I don't blame them, especially Daniel. I just don't want to lose such a great friend and coworker."

"I feel the same," Em said.

"I'll talk to him. We'll get through this tough time. We always do."

"Maya, can I confide in you?"

"Sure."

They slowed to a casual walk.

"You know I like Daniel, right?"

"I guessed as much."

"I've been hinting that I like him. I get the feeling he likes me too, but he backs off every time I try to get him to make a move."

"You do work together. That complicates things. You guys would be great together but having a relationship with someone you work with is tricky."

"I know, but who else? It's not easy to find someone with our schedule that I like spending time with."

"Don't ask me about relationships, Em. Nick and I are arguing more lately. Ever since I decided to go back to work with everything that has been going on.

"He'll be back tonight, but he'll be gone next week. Don't get me wrong. We're arguing. but it's been great when he's working from home. The dogs are taken care of. I see him during his breaks. We've grown a lot closer since Tahoe. Nothing like almost being murdered to put a good relationship into perspective. But I don't know. I guess I'm just not sure anymore."

Maya remembered their argument right before he left. Who was he to tell her she shouldn't be at work because it was too dangerous?

"I'm sorry. I got sidetracked. What I meant to say is, I get what you're saying. It would be nice to have someone on the same kind of schedule. But still, someone you work with? Are you sure that's a good idea?"

"If it's the right guy, then yes."

"You could tell him how you feel and see what he has to say."

"Maybe, but I thought it would happen naturally."

"You'll figure it out."

"Maya, really, that's the advice you have for me? I'll figure it out."

"Like I said, I'm not the best person to advise you on relationships. One minute I'm all in, and the next, I want to run."

They scaled the last steep pitch along the eastern edge to the summit, where clouds filled the space around them. They stood in a dirt clearing, packed down by thousands of boots, as waves of mist rolled in and out across the summit. The mist clung to Maya's face, and the wind chill sent a shiver through her body as she quickly started to cool down. They changed into dry shirts and put on their raincoats.

Maya dug around in her pack. Rio, smelling the emergence of treats, trotted over, followed by Kali. Their laser focus locked on to Maya's moving hand. Rio barely swallowed as he snatched the treat from her. Kali carried hers over to the side and took more time to inhale.

"Good thing they aren't slow eaters. I'm ready to head back down if you are."

"We should before this mist turns into rain. They're even talking about snow up here later today," Em replied.

They quickly descended the Cable Line Trail to the main Tiger Mountain Trail, a gentler descent on switchbacks that crisscrossed the ridgeline intersecting points along the Cable Line. Once they dropped off the summit, they were below the clouds and the mist with only the threat of rain.

"So, how are things with you now that you are back on the trucks full time? I've been meaning to ask you."

"Hit and miss. It's been tough. Now I'm dealing with these recent complaints leveraged against Jeff and me. I'm not taking it personally, because I suspect it has to do with a call we had.

"That is what Nick, and I were arguing about. He thinks I should have taken more time off, focused on myself. When he found out that Alden was threatening me about that call, he was even more upset that I'm working."

"Alden, threatening you? What's going on?"

With that, Maya told Em about Tamara and what had transpired.

"Maya, that's awful. What a creepy church. And Pastor Richter complaining about your intervention. You would think he'd be thanking you."

"I don't see that happening. My gut tells me he probably knows. If I hadn't promised Tamara that I wouldn't break her confidence, I would have reported it to the police."

"Local police?" Em asked. "They're probably friends with the Pastor too."

"Well, that's who I would have to report it to."

"Someone should talk to HS. Maybe the pastor has more going on than a youth pastor who is a sexual predator."

"Right, I'm sure that HS has more important things to worry about than the sexual assault of a young woman."

"Well, think about it this way. The pastor is openly supporting Titus. We have credible threats to our people that may be tied to right-wing militias. Titus may sympathize with them. He has the same talking points as the militias. The pastor, from what you described, sounds pretty radical. It's a possibility?"

"Possibly, but that's a reach. I mean, the relationship seems to be about politics and power. Titus wants power, and the pastor has a loyal following. You should have seen how entranced his parishioners were during his sermon. They kept echoing his words. The things I overheard him preaching about. It was cult-like. On second thought, you could be right. Politics and religion are powerful organizing tools.

"I wonder if that volunteer firefighter, Glenn, is a member of his church? Did I tell you he showed up on a call yesterday and prayed over my patient, his friend, while we treated her? There isn't anything wrong with that, but it just seemed weird. I had to remind him to get her loaded for transport. That even though God was helping out, she still needed a breathing treatment and a trip to the hospital."

"Did I tell you I ran into him yesterday while I was hiking? He's a weird one. He is one of those geeky 'Ricky Ranger' types compensating for something missing in his life. He is always responding to calls," Em said.

"He told me he ran into you on the trail. I wonder if he works. I always see him on calls, day or night."

"Who knows? He's just odd."

The dogs started barking wildly. Maya looked to see a frightened woman freeze as the dogs ran straight past her and landed their noses at the base of a tree.

"Ma'am, I'm sorry, they weren't coming for you. They saw a squirrel right behind you. See, they've chased it up a tree."

The woman half laughed and breathed out a sigh of relief. "I thought they were going to attack me."

"I'm so sorry. You must have been terrified. I wasn't paying attention. They do love chasing squirrels."

"I'm okay," she said before quickly passing them.

"You guys, come here."

The dogs hesitated, still focusing on the squirrel chattering in the tree above them. Raindrops dripped off the branches and pelted them on the head. They dutifully turned around and came running up to her. She had them sit. "You guys are going to get me in trouble."

Kali pushed her nose into Maya's hand, looking scorned. Rio turned his head back toward the squirrel tree.

"I mean, I want you guys to protect me, but please try not to scare innocent people on the trail." Maya gave them the command to stay with her.

"Let's jog the rest of the way, Em. I'm suddenly tired and ready to call it a day, but obviously, these guys still need to burn some more energy."

Maya arrived home and let the dogs out of the SUV. They immediately bolted towards the front door of the house. She guessed they didn't get enough of a workout. After grabbing her bags, she followed them. The front door was wide open. *Nick must have gotten home early*, she thought, as she walked through the door.

"Nick, are you here?"

Silence followed.

She hesitated and called out again. Nothing. *He must just be in his office*, she thought.

She walked down the hallway and set her keys on the entry table. "Hey, Nick, it's great that you were able to come home early." She said it to alert him, but also to make it seem that she wasn't alone as a feeling of danger started to creep into her mind.

She walked toward the living room. Where was he? As she entered the room she saw it. The couch was shredded, and the TV was missing. Every breakable item was in pieces strewn across the floor. The dogs were on high alert as their noses searched the room. She froze.

She immediately changed course. "Rio. Kali. Come!"

As she commanded the dogs, she slowly backed out the front door. She didn't want to take any chances after what had happened in Tahoe. She wasn't up for another life-and-death battle with a psycho. The dogs, sensing her alarm, followed right behind her.

She walked across the street and called 911, looking up and down the street for anyone that looked out of place. Other than the neighbors' familiar cars, the street was empty. Next, she called Nick. It went right to voice mail. Probably in meetings.

He wasn't due home until later that evening. She texted him as a follow-up, then waited and watched for anyone or anything that seemed out of the ordinary.

After the police looked around the house, they took her report. She decided to wait at a local brewery until Nick arrived home. Sitting at a table with the dogs tucked in around her feet, she felt her nerves settle as she drank her beer. Who had broken into their house? The question hung like a noose in her mind. She felt unsettled, every fiber in her body on high alert. Was she in danger? She texted Nick again. She wished he would respond. She felt on edge and just wanted to hear his voice reassuring her that this was just a random break-in.

A young man with short hair wearing a baseball cap entered the door of the brewery. He resembled the man at the Gold Trail Grange in Coloma whose piercing stare had sent her fleeing from the venue. Was she being followed again? She kept him in her sight and took another drink. Whoever had broken into their house was probably long gone, but she'd keep her eyes open, just in case. The question that kept circling through her mind was whether it was a random B&E or if they were targeted.

Nick caught an earlier flight home. Now they stood together, taking stock of the damage. Whoever had broken in had taken their television, Nick's desktop computer workstation, and some jewelry. In their wake, they left a mess of broken furnishings and decorations. Even their mattresses were shredded.

Nick walked over to his office wall and tapped a button on his phone. A door slid open, and inside, all his surveillance equipment, main computer, network, and documents were safely stored in "the vault," as he liked to call it.

"Good thing they didn't find this. I can live without the

desktop, but it would have taken some time to replace this setup."

"I completely forgot to tell the police about our security cameras. Well, at least you have it all backed up. That's why your clients trust you. Their information is secure," Maya said.

"It should be, they pay me enough."

He turned on his main computer in the vault. Up on the screen the high-tech security cameras he had set up were blank. They had been disabled.

He stood looking at the blank screen "This just doesn't make sense. This is a state-of-the-art system. Whoever broke in knew enough about my system to disable it. Without the house cameras, I don't have a visual record of the break-in. Except one."

He tied into a backup from the camera recording from his stolen desktop. He always left it to record motion when they weren't home just in case something like this happened. They reviewed the recording, and sure enough, there was the person who'd stolen Nick's desktop. Unfortunately, all it told them was that the guy was dressed like some two-bit black ops operative, wearing all black and a ski mask. He had a muscular build and dark brown eyes. Not a lot to go on. Behind the man, someone else was talking:

"Take anything that looks like it might have important information on it. We need to find anything that could tie the events to us."

"Events?" Maya asked.

"That doesn't give us much. It could be related to my business, but after what happened to Charles, it could be because of our surveillance of the militias. It's worth turning this incident and the police report over to HS. The fact that someone went to this level of interference tells me they are concerned with what we may have found out."

"But how'd they know we wouldn't be here. That the dogs weren't here?"

"Does the voice on the recording sound familiar?"

"No," Maya replied.

"Did you tell anyone I was out of town and the dogs were with Em?"

"No, the only time I said anything was at shift change when I handed off the dogs to Em."

"Who was there?"

"Just Jeff, Em, and Doug."

"So, do you trust them?"

"Well, we both know Jeff. I totally trust him. Em, I completely trust her as well. I was Doug's field training officer. He's a hometown kid from Maple Valley. Hard to read sometimes but kind of an innocent kid."

"So, the only unknown is Doug. I'll look at his background and anything that might tie him to right-wing groups. I'm worried about you. If a coworker is setting you up, that's an ominous development."

"It comes on the heels of the complaints the supervisor brought up yesterday." Maya sighed. "They were lies. Someone is either being petty, or we are being targeted. Roy even said he didn't agree that the complaints were valid. He just had to be the messenger and document that we were notified. It's so frustrating. You'd think after all these years I wouldn't even have to address complaints like that."

"Be careful, Maya."

"The election is next week. I'm concerned that if Titus doesn't win, we could see violence erupt on the streets."

"Like you said. You and Jeff better watch your backs."

CHAPTER TWENTY-ONE

MAYA WAS CATCHING up on her emails when her phone rang.

"Maya, have you seen the news?" Jeff asked.

"No, what happened?"

"The FBI brought Pastor Richter in for questioning. Local law enforcement arrested the youth pastor on suspicion of sexual assault. The FBI has also said Richter is under investigation for fraud. The stories broke this morning. It's all over the news. Even CNN is picking it up."

"How?"

"They didn't say. Maybe Tamara decided to turn in the youth pastor?"

Maya typed in "Pastor Richter arrested." The top search was from King 5 television. She clicked on the link.

"Local pastor questioned by law enforcement for fraud and covering up sexual assault at Evangelical church." Maya skimmed the article.

"That would explain why he sent Alden to intimidate me."

"Look for the interview with Titus. He is in full damage control right now."

Maya searched for Titus. She clicked on another King 5 link to a video.

Titus stood in front of a room of reporters. His jaw set defiantly as he waited for the press conference to begin. He wore his signature cowboy hat, a plaid shirt with a navy blazer, blue jeans, and cowboy boots. His wife, a petite blond, stood by his side. On the other side were his two grown sons.

"First of all, I've known Pastor Richter for years. He is an honorable pastor, family man, and friend. I will not stand by while our government attacks our religious freedoms and tries to pin these types of allegations on this dedicated man of God and his congregation. There are those who don't want to see us succeed in restoring our county and our country to the foundations it was built on. I stand by the pastor and his family during this difficult time. That is all I have to say."

He refused to take any questions, then turned and walked out of the room as reporters yelled out their questions.

Maya watched in horror as she realized that she may have stumbled into something much bigger than just the sexual assault of Tamara. Titus's election was built on support from the faith community. Pastor Richter commanded the respect and support of a large congregation. Members of that congregation also had their networks of political and local business support. Now she was worried that she would be blamed for the sexual accusations being lodged against him. But fraud. Where did that come into play?

"Well, that's just great. Now we're really caught in the middle," Maya said.

"Maya, you need to be careful. You don't want to mess with these people. We've already seen what they can do."

"Be careful. I didn't say anything to anyone but you, Melissa, Nick, and...Em."

"Em? When did you talk to her?"

"Two days ago. We went on a hike up Tiger Mountain. The whole sexual assault, Alden intimidating me, and then the complaints. It was wearing on me. It made me sick to think that the youth pastor was still out there potentially victimizing other young women in that church. I confided in her.

"God, I hope she didn't follow up on her thoughts to contact Homeland Security. She insinuated that she wasn't under the same responsibility I was when I promised Tamara I wouldn't turn her assault over to local law enforcement. Em and I agreed that local law enforcement would probably back the pastor. She casually said that someone should contact HS and that maybe there was more going on there than just the sexual assault."

"You need to get a hold of her and find out if we, the paramedics, can be linked to the leak. This puts us in a dangerous position if it gets out."

"I know. Damn. The break-in and now this. I'm going to call Em and find out what she did. I need to know what to do next."

Maya texted Em. "Call me ASAP."

Em called back later that day. "Em, what did you do?"

"You mean the news about the pastor?"

"Of course, I mean the news."

"I couldn't leave it alone. How could you tell her that you wouldn't say anything? She trusted you."

"But she asked me not to say anything. She wanted to deal with it in her own way. I honored that trust. Even though it's been bothering me ever since."

"Maya, I had to say something. I contacted Marcy from HS. I figured if I contacted the local police, nothing would happen. This happens more than you know." There was a long pause, and then Em dropped her truth. "I was sexually assaulted when I was thirteen. He was a well-respected colleague of my father. Impeccable reputation. Everyone loved him. I never said anything because I knew no one would ever believe me. But to this day, it still haunts me. I didn't want that to happen to another young girl. I can't change my silence then, but I can change it now. That youth pastor and Pastor Richter are in positions of power that demand a higher standard. They must be stopped so that the young women in that church are safe!" Em's voice sounded resolute and firm.

Maya understood better now. "Em, oh, I'm so sorry. I had no idea. That must have been life-changing for you. I can understand why you couldn't remain silent. That kind of experience never goes away.

"But the reason I held off is that she would likely be blamed and pay the consequences, and... other things are going on besides the sexual assault. She needed time."

"I'm sorry too, Maya. It was a secret I couldn't keep for you."

"I don't blame you, Em. If I had known, I never would have dumped that on you. I feel responsible for dragging you into this mess. Just tell me you didn't tell anyone else? We've got some coworkers with big mouths."

"No, I didn't tell anyone else. I didn't want it to get back to you."

"Well, the damage is done. Now we hope the fallout doesn't land on us, our coworkers, or Tamara."

Maya hung up, and a deep sense of foreboding engulfed her. She wasn't safe anywhere. Not Tahoe, not at work, and now not at home. Herding squirrels played through her mind. Her old chief had said that trying to get paramedics to work together as a group was like herding squirrels. Then she laughed, envisioning a herd of squirrels zigging and zagging up and down trees in separate directions, chattering at her from tree branches above.

A simple conversation with a coworker and friend had blown up in her face. That would be the last time she ever confided something confidential to anyone at work, even Jeff. She had to watch her back. Even good intentions could lead to unintended results. Even though she understood Em, she still felt betrayed.

She reached into the kitchen cabinet, pulled out a bottle of Merlot and filled a large wine glass. The red liquid looked, for a moment, like blood. At times like this, she felt a need for alcohol, like she needed the blood pumping through her veins. She'd seen the damage that alcohol left in its wake, but she didn't care. She just wanted to check out as the madness of what was happening threatened to derail her recovery.

Under siege on a scene was one thing. Being under siege, threatened by her coworkers, was something entirely different. She felt she wasn't safe within the station's walls or on the street. She could shore up her defenses to deal with the ugly things she saw on the streets, but it was too exhausting to maintain a wall of protection between her and her coworkers.

She brought the bottle with her and sat on the couch. The dogs jumped up on either side of her as she settled in to comfortably numb. Nick wasn't supposed to be home for a few hours. She'd be on her way to passing out if all went well.

She watched an old mob movie in the style of *The Godfather*. The code among gangsters led her to thoughts about her own gang. She always felt like the fire service was a brotherhood. She loved that comradery, but with it came the rules of solidarity. Step out of line, and the group could punish you severely. It was that brotherhood that both made her feel safe and also scared her to death. If they turned on her now, it could mean the end of her career and possibly even her life if the wrong people were notified. *Em, what did you do?*

CHAPTER TWENTY-TWO

"GET YOUR BIKE CLOTHES ON. We're going for a ride. You've been sitting there, drinking all weekend. Time to wake up and burn off some of that alcohol. What happened? You promised you wouldn't go down this rabbit hole again if you returned to work."

Nick looked irritated. He didn't lose his patience often, but she could tell he was not happy with her using alcohol to solve her problems.

"I don't want to go out. It's all blowing up out there. I need a break. Who knows what will happen on Tuesday when I return to work, now that Em got us involved?"

"We've been over this. How would they even know it was you? Anyone could have turned them in. You didn't know about any fraud."

"It doesn't matter if they know. Alden knows. Everyone will talk. It will come back to me. I'm already getting undermined with complaints. Now this. They'll blame me."

"Who'll blame you?"

"Anyone who sides with the pastor and Alden. It's just too much."

"Look, I know you're under pressure with the added danger and struggling to keep it together, but the only solution is to get up and get going. Lying around here in a deep depression and drinking isn't going to change anything. Let's just start with a bike ride and go from there. It will be good to get out. Look, it's sunny outside. Let's take advantage of it."

"Fine, but I'm only going because you won't leave me alone," she said and shot him a sly smile.

"A good enough reason. Let's go."

Maya stewed on her resentment at being tugged out of her pity party. Why couldn't he just let her check out?

The fog began to lift as they dropped off of Queen Anne and crossed over the Fremont Bridge. He was right. It was a beautiful day. Finally, some sunshine and left to her own decisions, she would have spent it indoors.

She followed Nick along the Interurban Trail as they wove around all the people outside on a sunny Sunday afternoon. Dog walkers, joggers with strollers, other cyclists, and people walking together blocking the trail. It was slow going, but it kept her alert and stopped her mind from sinking into her dark thoughts.

They passed by the University of Washington Medical Center, crossed over the ship canal, and exited the trail onto Lake Washington Boulevard in the Arboretum. The narrow roadway wove through the landmark park. Green and yellow maple leaves, with red accents, mixed with the autumn air. The tinge of cold hurried their pace now that their only competition was car traffic going in the same direction.

They sped up as the road narrowed under the archway of an old pedestrian bridge. Maya heard a sudden rev of an engine from behind them, and before she could register what was happening, a large black pickup truck barreled down on them. Maya quickly hopped the bike up the steep curb as Nick swerved into the oncoming lane and flipped up and over a compact car. The truck honked its horn, then sped away, leaving chaos behind. Maya jumped off her bike and tried to see the truck's license plate, but it was covered. She turned her attention toward Nick. He was lying on his back in the wet grass on the opposite side of the road.

The owner of the compact car yelled that he was on the phone with 911.

"Nick, are you okay?"

"I think so."

"Don't move." She reached down and felt his pulse. It raced beneath her fingers. She did a quick head-to-toe examination. He had some scrapes on his legs, but nothing appeared broken.

"I can't find any obvious fractures. Just abrasions. Does anything else hurt?"

"No, not yet, but I'm sure something will. I feel like I was hit by that truck, not a Tesla."

We were lucky it wasn't the truck that ran you over."

"I heard him speed off. Did you see who was driving?"

By then, cars were backed up on both sides of the road. People were walking over to see what was going on. Maya could hear sirens moving their way. She only hoped they could navigate the narrow roadway with everyone stopped.

"After I hopped the curb to keep from getting run over, I tried to get the license, but the plate was covered. I didn't see the driver."

"I caught a glimpse of that move before I hit the car. Pretty impressive maneuvering." Nick started to laugh before grimacing in pain. "I'm going to have some good bruises. My rib cage is already getting sore."

"Hold still. You'll need to go to the hospital to check for serious injuries. See, I knew we should have stayed home."

"You're probably right. Maya, I think we're being targeted."

"I told you things were blowing up!"

Maya brought Nick some tea as she listened to the news on the television. "A local pastor has been charged with money laundering, fraud, and embezzlement." The newest revelations about Pastor Richter. The FBI was set to formally charge him on Monday.

"I think this is about more than the sexual assault," Nick said. "Em may not have been the catalyst for the arrest and developments in this case. This sounds like something that was being investigated before you encountered Tamara."

"You may be right, but somebody thinks we are a danger to them. The break-in and now the truck nearly running us over."

"Have you heard anything about the truck and driver yet?"

"Nothing other than the news reporting that the truck was abandoned in the Arboretum parking lot."

"Anything from work?"

"Of course, the chief called me. He's very concerned about my safety. He tried to talk me out of returning to work. I refused. We are already down three medics."

"Are you sure it's safe to return to work after what happened? I wasn't sure what to think about your concern about the complaints at work, but now..."

"You believe me? I'm not crazy? Things like this have happened before. Years ago, another department ran a female medic out of the job because she turned one of her male coworkers in for sexual harassment. He kept his career, and she was set up and fired.

"If a few of the good old boys target me with complaints and set me up, I'll always be on edge, waiting for the next attack. It's not fair, but that's just the way it is. I'm well-liked, but sometimes that isn't enough."

"You don't think someone tipped them off about Tamara too?"

"As you know, there's the saying, 'Telephone, tell a medic.' As we found out with Em, nothing stays a secret for long."

"Ya, but she didn't mean anything malicious by it. She was just trying to help save Tamara and the other girls."

"I know, but what if someone else, who's less sympathetic, thinks I'm the one who turned in the pastor?"

"Well, did you tell the chief about your concerns?"

"I did. For what it's worth, he swears that none of the complaints have anything to do with retaliation."

"You should at least consider not going to work on Tuesday. You know it's Election Day."

"I've already made my decision. I'm not going to change my mind. I'm not going to be bullied out of a job I love by the pastor or any of my coworkers."

CHAPTER TWENTY-THREE

MAYA WALKED INTO THE STATION. Dag and Mike turned to look at her. She caught a look of irritation on Dag's face before he looked down at his paperwork. *I bet they are the ones that wrote us up,* Maya thought.

Dag lifted his head from his paperwork without looking at her. "Maya, are you and Nick okay? That's terrible what happened to you. It's not safe riding on the road."

Maya noted the insincerity in his voice and that he was avoiding looking at her. As far as he was concerned, everything was always her fault. Somehow, she caused this to happen because she was cycling on the road. *Right,* she thought.

"Well, Dag. It was a little more than just being in the wrong place at the wrong time. The driver tried to run us over."

"No way. Why would someone do that?" Mike asked.

"I don't know, but our house was also broken into last week. We are assuming both incidents are connected. Lots of crazy stuff going on. I don't think any of us should feel safe right now."

"Why you and Nick?" Dag asked.

"Your guess is as good as mine," Maya replied. She didn't want to give anything away.

"Maya, be safe out there today. We wouldn't want anything else to happen to you."

Maya wondered if she should consider that a veiled threat. Just in case, she said, "The FBI is taking these incidents very seriously. They are looking into them and working to determine who is involved." Maya wanted to let them know that going after her wasn't going to be that easy.

Perhaps Dag was just being Dag, but he could be more involved than just filing complaints. She wanted him to think twice before going after her again.

"Dag, thanks for your concern. If we're lucky, it will be just another typical day at work."

"That's what I'm afraid of," said Jeff as he came out of the bedroom.

"Come on, Jeff, you know I always get through my latest disaster or attempted assassinations just fine."

"Yes, but like Nick, it's the people around you who may not be so lucky."

"Hey, don't go there," Maya said.

"All I'm saying is we should just request SWAT on every call."

"I'm sure that will go over well with dispatch and the SWAT team," Dag said.

"So, Maya, did you know about the sexual assault by the youth pastor at the Resurrection Evangelical church?" Mike asked.

"Only what I've heard on the news that broke Friday."

"Well, someone from our organization apparently leaked confidential patient information without going through the formal channels. Didn't you transport a young woman from there a couple of weeks ago?"

"I did, but that didn't have anything to do with sexual assault. You know the rumor mill. Probably just someone trying to drum up drama."

"I guess, but I wouldn't want to be the medic responsible for the takedown of Pastor Richter's church. That guy has some important friends."

"Me neither. I know my place in the hierarchy of things."

"Sure you do." Dag stared at her.

"What?"

"Nothing."

"Dag, do you have something more to say? I've just about had it with the rumor mill and everything else going on. If you could do me a favor and shut down the rumors, I'd appreciate it." Maya surprised herself with the anger that erupted from her mouth.

"Hey, we're on your side. If I hear anyone blaming you for the leak, I'll let them know that you said you weren't involved."

"Thanks, Dag. I need all the support I can get."

"You have my support," Jeff countered.

"You have mine too," Dag quickly added.

"Mine too," Mike said as he walked out the door.

After they left, Maya turned to Jeff. "Thanks for backing me up there."

"Can you believe those guys? Do you think Dag was trying to blame you for what happened?"

"That's what it sounded like to me. I'm not entirely certain, but I think he threatened me."

"I heard that too. I hope today goes better than it started," Jeff said.

"It is Election Day," countered Maya, "things going well may be a relative thing."

"Sounds like a good reason to get some Starbucks coffee first thing."

"I agree."

They drove out of the garage into the pouring rain. It was so dark that Jeff flipped on the headlights.

They drove down Auburn Way after dropping a patient off at the hospital. They watched as a group of people were sprayed by the water churned up from the line of passing cars making their way home during rush hour. They held up umbrellas and signs wrapped in plastic. "Titus" in large letters and "Save your Country." Maya couldn't believe they were standing out in the torrential rain rooting for their team. Did sign-waving change anyone's mind? she wondered. Didn't they know that Titus and his cronies probably weren't as dedicated to them?

The same anger she'd felt earlier when she was talking to Dag bubbled up inside her. Why were these people supporting these tyrants? Tyrants that were likely connected with the attempts on her life as well as the deaths of six people she worked with.

"I'm so angry. When is this going to be over? Those guys are out there with signs. What if Titus loses? What then?"

"I hope that Titus's opponent, Sullivan, wins. Otherwise, we are in for a lot of unpleasant tactics. Titus will go after the County's unions. He has made no secret that he believes that bloated government pensions are an expense his constituents shouldn't have to pay for."

"That we pay for."

"I know, but all it takes is for someone to say something for the rumor mill to take over."

"Yes, but these politicians need to be held accountable when they spread lies that destroy lives."

The light turned green. The group waved at their medic unit, yelling, "We support you!"

"Right."

CHAPTER TWENTY-FOUR

THEY WENT to bed concerned by the report that said the election had been called. Sullivan had beaten Titus by a significant number of votes, a landslide, they reported. Surprisingly, they had slept through the night.

The quiet before the storm, Maya thought as she rolled over and looked at the time.

Maya walked out to make coffee as Jeff turned on the news. There in front of them was Titus. His face was red with rage as he spoke about the "rigged election."

"The democrats fabricated the charges against Pastor Richter and his congregation to damage my reputation. It was a hit job, a hoax. I will not concede until all the votes are counted. They're not going to get away with this."

This time he did take questions.

"Sir, were you aware that the pastor has been charged with money laundering and fraud as well? This is on top of the sexual assault allegations in his congregation."

"Those are lies. Lies meant to tarnish his name and, by association, mine. They'll stop at nothing to take us down."

"Sir, who are they?" one reporter asked.

"The people that hate us, the liberal elite, the socialists running our country into the ground! They are targeting us because we are good Christians trying to save this country. We are hard-working people trying to make a living and being taxed into poverty. We are fighting to protect our property rights and, goddammit, the Second Amendment. They'll stop at nothing until they've taken away all our rights and made Christianity illegal."

"Sir, weren't your supporters able to vote? Yet the votes counted thus far show that you are losing by a wide margin."

"That's yet to be determined. I wouldn't put it past them to tamper with the voting machines. They'll stop at nothing. We'll demand accountability."

Then he stormed off out of the room. A group of men, who'd stood next to him, followed him.

"Look out. Things are about to get worse," Maya said.

CHAPTER TWENTY-FIVE

MAYA SAT in Dr. Harrington's office. She felt able to keep her emotions in check. Even though the storm was coming, at least she'd slept through the night.

"Maya, so things are not going well from what I've heard."

"What did you hear?"

"Chief Anderson called me to let me know you're struggling at work. He thinks you are distracted and...making mistakes. Also, I heard about the bicycling accident."

Maya sat quietly. Could she trust Dr. Harrington? Should she talk openly about what was going on? She decided not to downplay the events. If anything, there needed to be documentation that she voiced her concerns about what was happening. She looked Dr. Harrington in the eye.

"I'm being targeted at work! The bicycling 'accident' was not an accident. It was an attempt on our lives!"

"You're sure about this?"

"Absolutely, and now I'm sure that the chief is supporting these complaints and the intimidation leveraged against me at work. Why would he say those things if he wasn't?"

"Out of concern for you."

"No, this is a hit job in more ways than one." Maya recounted to Dr. Harrington the events, Tamara, the pastor being arrested, the complaints, and the intimidation by Alden.

She did lie about one thing, telling Em about Tamara. "I didn't say anything to anyone about Tamara and the pastor. Yet now I'm being blamed and targeted because he was arrested by the FBI."

Dr. Harrington sat quietly for a minute. "If what you are saying is true, then you shouldn't be working on the trucks."

Did she make a mistake telling Dr. Harrington almost everything? She felt she couldn't trust anyone anymore.

"No, that's not how this is going to go. I'm not backing down. I've fought to get back to work, and these threats will not derail that," Maya said with more confidence than she felt. "I have every right to be there. If I let them win, they'll never stop. They'll do it to others. If a few coworkers sympathize with Titus and his cronies, that doesn't mean they should be allowed to interfere with our ability to save lives or run me out of my job."

"Maya, I'm concerned for you. They aren't out to get you. The chief is looking out for you. He knows that some of the medics complain a lot. You know as well as I do that sometimes that is their coping mechanism to deal with stress and fatigue. Know that the chief and I are aware of those issues, and they are being addressed. However, he is extremely concerned.

"Are you willing to consider that you are not being targeted, but that you aren't performing as well as you normally have in the past?"

"Dr. Harrington, I know I'm being targeted with complaints and rumors. Maybe their sympathy lies with the pastor based on their religious beliefs. Maybe they're targeting me because they think I'm the cause of the pastor's arrest."

Dr. Harrington sighed. "If what you say is true and if some of your coworkers are involved that makes it even more dangerous for you to be working. I hope none of your coworkers were involved in the ambush and bombing. I haven't heard anything to indicate that your coworkers are capable of that level of malice. My experience working with you and others is that all of you are exceptionally caring and dedicated to your work."

Maya felt her trust in Dr. Harrington evaporating as she realized that she'd probably side with management on this assessment of her ability to do the job.

"You've brought up a lot of concerning issues today. I see it from your perspective, Maya, but I'm concerned about your mental health and your safety."

"If you're concerned about my safety then please address these issues with the County directly. I'll give you permission to address my concerns with the County's Human Resources department. Don't go to the chief. Go directly to the head of HR. I know our department contracts with you, but if you feel strongly that I am in danger, go above them. I need to continue to hold my line and do my job. Just because I'm facing threats doesn't mean my patients have to suffer."

"I admire your strength and resilience, Maya, but how long can you continue to hold it together? It's just a matter of time before it all becomes too much. We are making progress, but you're not there yet, and now these new events are just compounding the trauma."

"I can keep it together but dealing with being targeted just makes it that much harder. I need to know you are on my side," Maya replied.

Maya left with a reprieve from Dr. Harrington, but she wasn't so sure she could live up to her determination to get through the next week, let alone the following year.

CHAPTER TWENTY-SIX

MAYA AND JEFF watched as newly elected County councilwoman Parnum accepted her victory from her living room. She was still recovering from her assault but emphasized she was engaged in the next steps as their newly elected representative. They knew her to be a go-getter, and she wasn't letting this assault derail her victory. Maya admired that about her. *That's what I'm trying to do by continuing to work,* she thought.

They turned when they heard the door opening. Maya's mind sank when she saw that it was the chief. She looked pleadingly at Jeff. "Help me," she said with her eyes.

Jeff jumped up. "Hey, Chief, what brings you here?"

"I wanted to check in with Maya and see how she's doing. I heard she's having some trouble, and I wanted to talk to her myself."

"I don't know what you heard, but I've been working with Maya since she returned, and she is her old self. We've even had some pretty intense calls, and she's held her own on all of them."

Maya looked over at Jeff. It was such a relief to have his support. She didn't feel like she was alone in defending herself.

"Jeff, that's good to hear. As you know, the rumor mill takes on a life of its own, which is why I wanted to come to talk to Maya myself and get her side of the story."

"Maya, can we go somewhere and talk?"

"We can talk here. As Jeff said, he's been working with me, so he knows what's going on."

"Are you sure?"

"Absolutely." Maya felt that having Jeff there was protection against more accusations.

The chief sat down at the table. "Well, it's probably just as well. I have three complaints that came in regarding your conduct on calls. Jeff isn't named in the complaints, but he is your partner, so he's part of the decision-making."

"What complaints?"

"The first two complaints come from one of the fire departments. They said that you were rude to a patient. They said you yelled at her when she wouldn't allow you to give her a breathing treatment. That you lacked empathy."

Maya rolled her eyes. "Chief, you do know who this came from, right? It was Glenn. I had to be firm with the patient because she was extremely short of breath and panicking. I was supportive and worked to calm her down. Glenn was unhappy because I had to remind him to quit talking and help move the patient to the stretcher."

"You know, Glenn is one of their best volunteers and is extremely dedicated to the department. You'd do well to make sure to stay on his good side."

"Of course, but I can't defend myself against accusations that are simply not true."

Jeff interjected, "Chief, I was the officer on that call. I take full responsibility for everything that occurred, but I will say that Maya was not rude to the patient, and she certainly doesn't lack empathy.

"Glenn is a dedicated volunteer, but he also lacks solid experience. Maybe his opinion that Maya was rude was because the patient was his friend, and he didn't understand the gravity of the situation. She had to take the medicine, or we would need to intubate her."

"Well, that is quite different from the information I was given. I can see where you are coming from. I'll make a note of it and talk to their chief before deciding what to do."

"Chief, if you are going to write Maya up, you'll need to write me up too."

"Jeff, the complaint wasn't directed at you."

"Yes, but it was my patient. I'm responsible for what happens as the officer on the scene. I think that you should talk to Glenn's chief. We can't have volunteers Monday night quarterbacking us on our calls. We can't be looking over our shoulders while a patient is dying and wondering if we need to watch our backs. Don't add to our stress. Support our decisions."

Maya was relieved to hear him defending her. She knew that what was going on had nothing to do with her performance, but without defenders, she'd be cornered and separated from the herd. Yet, she watched as the chief backpedaled when challenged by Jeff.

"Well, I wouldn't have taken this complaint as seriously if I hadn't received another complaint as well. The other complaint is directly from Pastor Richter. He says you broke patient confidentiality and accused him of covering up the alleged sexual assault by his youth pastor. Apparently, the young woman has a history of mental illness. He said she told Maya that the youth pastor sexually assaulted her when she was transported from the scene by you two."

Maya knew this was going to happen. She'd said as much to Nick. Alden wasn't content with just bringing it to her attention, especially after the pastor was arrested and the story broke in the news.

"Chief, we're done here," Maya said. "I won't continue this conversation until we schedule an official meeting with my union representative. I know you mean well, but there is more going on here than simple complaints."

"I support Maya's decision," Jeff said. "I also feel like there is more going on here. To continue puts all of us in a precarious situation. I think from this point on, we all need to follow formal procedures in case there are lawsuits."

The chief seemed unhappy that Jeff was supporting Maya. Maya couldn't tell if he was in on the attacks or simply caught in the middle. She hoped that he was caught in the middle. He'd been so supportive of her up until this point, but now she was questioning his position. Tears touched the edge of her eyes, and her feelings of betrayal threatened to overpower her. How could they turn on her so quickly? She was friends with him, or so she'd thought.

"I'm unhappy to hear this. I had hoped we could get this cleared up without elevating it to a more serious discussion, but if that is what you want, I'm happy to start a formal investigation.

"Maya, I want you to know that I support you. I just have concerns with you continuing to work on the trucks. Maybe we wouldn't be having this discussion if you had taken more time to work through the issues surrounding the ambush."

"Chief, I will say one thing more. This has nothing to do with the ambush on the streets. My performance is the same as it's ever been. I hope you will continue supporting me as you have in the past."

"I support you, but we have to have discipline in our ranks, and these problems need to be addressed."

She felt her tears turn to anger as she watched him leave.

How dare he support her attackers. She'd given everything to this organization and profession, and now they were trying to discredit her. Not if she had her way.

CHAPTER TWENTY-SEVEN

"UNITS RESPOND to a multi-casualty incident at the Kent Regional Justice Center. Large explosion confirmed. Units stage at North 7th and West Meeker Street. Await further instructions."

Maya noticed the dispatcher's voice sounded urgent. Not the usual measured tone. Maya could feel tension through the radio of the medic unit as more and more units were added to the dispatch.

Was this it? Another terrorist attack, the big one? A feeling of impending doom settled into her mind. They knew it was coming but still...

Maya and Jeff parked next to Roy in the command vehicle and another medic unit in the staging area. They watched as dark black smoke billowed into the gray sky. Sirens could be heard coming from every direction. Police, fire, and paramedics. From the safe vantage of the staging area, they listened to reports of people spilling out onto the sidewalks of the Kent Regional Justice Center. From where they staged, they watched as cars stopped in the middle of the street, their occupants looking upward at the smoke.

They waited for what seemed like hours for the scene to be secured. Was it just one bomb or more? That was the question on everyone's mind. Would they drive in to save lives or lose their own when the trap was unleashed with a second bomb?

Roy walked up to their window. "We are going to be first in after SWAT secures the scene. I want you to team up with these engine companies. Start triage. Keep it simple. Colored ribbon. This is too big for details."

"Units, clear to go in. Entry via James Street. Clear ingress and egress," dispatch reported.

As they started to drive, they heard another explosion and watched as orange flame boiled into the sky, followed by black smoke.

Dispatch announced, "Hold your positions. We've had another bomb at James at the County Park and Ride. Hold for further."

They stopped moving forward. They'd been afraid of this, a second detonation just as they were going in. Maya hoped none of the other emergency vehicles in front of them had been in the bomb radius.

They waited. Still determining when they would be able to continue in. Were there more bombs? The bomb squad expanded their perimeter to clear more of the surroundings and evacuated everyone. The staging units held their position; moving would just create confusion as units tried to turn around and maneuver to a new location.

Finally, they were given the all-clear to proceed via 4th Avenue.

They followed Roy's command vehicle into the melee. People were still running from all exits of the building, and flames surged from behind the rubble of what was the foyer of the Regional Justice Center. Some ran on their own. Others were being carried. People lay on the sidewalks screaming. First responders were scrambling to organize the chaos. It seemed impossible to find a place to start.

It was hard not to feel the panic rising in her mind. Maya pushed down her horror and got to work, starting with the people farthest out from the danger. They triage-tagged the victims: red for emergent, yellow for serious, green for walking wounded, and black for deceased.

She walked by one woman who had strands of burning flesh hanging off the left side of her body. Her right eye stared upward, unmoving, lifeless. She tagged her black. The next, a man in his fifties crumpled over, half sitting and half lying.

"Can you hear me?" she asked.

He mumbled something incoherent. She could see that he was drooling. She tagged him red and moved on. More reds: burns, gashes, amputations, and broken bones. One after the other, she worked her way to the left side of the building. As she made her way to a doorway on the left, she saw a woman sitting on the ground, holding a man's head in her lap. Tears streamed down her soot-covered face. His eyes stared at her as if it was the last thing he saw. Maya crouched down. "Ma'am, are you okay?"

She looked up at Maya and didn't respond.

"Ma'am, are you okay?"

Still no response. Maya reached down and felt her pulse. Rapid but strong. She tagged her yellow and moved on. It was so hard for her to keep moving. She wanted to focus, save that one life, but she had to detach and work on tagging each patient so they could be moved to corresponding treatment areas. It was their only hope for survival. Rapid triage, treatment, and transport.

Her job became a function of organizing chaos into

manageable tasks that would make the best of an overwhelming situation. She was one part of the highly orchestrated movement of patients from the scene to the region's hospitals. There wasn't time for emotion or connection to her patients. Instead, she moved swiftly from one face to the next, making the weighted decisions of whether someone was viable for saving or not. Whether they needed immediate attention or whether their injuries could wait.

Then she was at the door. As people streamed out, she intercepted them, tagged them, and directed them toward a funnel point. She tied in with a firefighter wearing his breathing apparatus coming from the interior. He alerted her that they were still evacuating the walking wounded and would begin bringing people out on litters as soon as possible.

She stood by. Her triage stopped at the door. With the remnants of the fire still burning, the air inside the building was full of toxic smoke. It curled out the door, carried by currents of moving bodies from the interior.

A team of firefighters strung flagging from the doorway down to the funnel point, where patients would then be directed to growing treatment areas along the south end of the building along James Street.

Suddenly she heard breaking glass, followed by screams. A body landed on the pavement five feet from her. The thud caused her to jump for cover in the doorway. She looked over and saw a woman, crumpled and twisted by the impact with the concrete. Blood flowered from beneath her long dark hair. Maya looked up as people stared down from the window above.

The incident command came over a loudspeaker. "Stay in the building. The fire is under control. We will come to get you. I repeat..."

The heads above disappeared into the window. It looked like the woman had panicked and jumped, fearing she would burn alive in the building. Maya's heart raced faster with the sense of urgency escalating, but she stayed focus on her part in the orchestrated incident command system that would get this scene under control. There was nothing she could do for that woman or the people in the window right now.

It was all shifting chaos. More people came through the door, walking wounded, green. One man was being supported by two others—red. Over and over, she made the triage decisions.

Finally, the door remained empty. A pause until the fire-fighters started carrying out people on stretchers. The ones that couldn't walk out on their own were carried past her, red and yellow. They left the black-tagged people inside. They could wait.

Hours passed, and the mad chaos receded into the sound of fans and generators for the lights. Ambulances moved in and out of the transport area, removing patients and transporting them to hospitals throughout the region. As early dusk settled in, a firefighter relieved Maya from triage. She was redirected to the treatment area, where she assisted in treatment before more patients were carried off to waiting ambulances. She started IVs, intubated if necessary, and administered drugs. Anything that could be a stop-gap measure to get them to the hospital alive. Their faces became a blur. Humanity was recorded in injuries: head, fractured left arm, femur fracture, shortness of breath, and third-degree burns.

She stood with Jeff, Dag, and other medics that had responded from home. All were called to respond to the largest mass casualty event in the history of their area. Jeff's eyes glowed with focus. He thrived on this kind of chaos. His training for wartime was an asset like no other in this moment. Maya was exhausted. She didn't feel the wired adrenaline or the compounding defeat that can accompany overwhelming events. She felt numb. Numb to the cold, numb to the drizzle of rain falling from the sky, numb to every moment that had brought her here.

"Jeff."

"Yes?"

I'm really tired of being a shit magnet."

Jeff suddenly burst out laughing. "Of course, this had to happen on our shift. That's it. I'm putting in for a transfer. I think I'd like to work with Em for a while. She's your opposite, a pink cloud."

"I think we've earned a break after this. I don't know about you, but I'm wrecked," Maya said.

"The only way out is through!" Jeff replied.

Dag had been looking down at his phone when he suddenly looked over at them, his eyes wide with disbelief. "Jesus, someone just bombed the Federal Building in downtown Seattle, too."

CHAPTER TWENTY-EIGHT

MAYA HAD to take the long way home the following day. I-5 was shut down through downtown Seattle due to the Federal Building bombing. Their chaos had been tenfold. She wondered if Georgia was at ground zero of that mass casualty event.

She walked through the front door. Nick looked up and immediately came over and wrapped his arms around her. The dogs tightened in around her legs, supporting her too.

"Maya, I can't believe they did this. Are you okay? I couldn't sleep last night, worrying about whether you were safe."

She looked up into his warm eyes and felt all the tension she'd held in her body melt away. "I'm so glad you're here." She laid her head against his chest and let the warmth of his living body fill her with a sense of safety.

Maya looked up at Nick, dark circles shadowing her usually vibrant eyes and concern etched around her mouth. "I guess we poked the wasp's nest. The pastor, Titus losing. I'm assuming it was them. They weren't happy."

"I just didn't think they were capable of these large-scale events. But who knows who they are working with?"

"Terror, bullying, they'll make us all pay if they can't get what they want. It's nothing different than what's been happening, but now it's bigger and angrier because they're losing."

"Let's get you in the shower. You're a mess. Even the dogs can smell the death on you."

Rio and Kali were tightly wound around her legs, but their noses moved a mile a minute, smelling the leftover stench from hours of triage and treatment. She hadn't even bothered to change before leaving. She just wanted to get home, to her family, to safety. In a few hours, she'd have to go back, but for now, she was miles away with everyone in her life that mattered.

Maya and Jeff were notified to stand down and show up for their regular shift. For now, the site of the bombing was past treating casualties and was now part of the evidence that would convict the perpetrators when they were caught.

Maya and Nick sat glued to the television, watching the coverage of the bombings. The cameras showed the sudden explosion of concrete and glass flying outward, followed by the billowing smoke and flames. Then people started exiting the doorways screaming, looks of terror etched on their faces. The second blast sent more debris, flame, and smoke into the air. What she'd missed prior to her arrival was now playing out on primetime, and it was more horrifying than the aftermath. She felt a deep sadness as she thought about all the people who'd been killed or maimed just for being in the wrong place at the wrong time.

A reporter stationed outside the police station in Enumclaw was tracking the progress of the manhunt for those involved in the Regional Justice Center bombing. He reported that it was believed to be a local militia group. It was reported that Titus, the defeated councilmember, was one of those involved.

They switched back to the bombing in Seattle. The reporters showed a sea of emergency lights and the Federal Building from afar. The reporter looked anxious as he expressed concern about other targets in the downtown vicinity. The entire downtown corridor was shut down as sweeps continued to secure areas. The bombing was being claimed by the group "White Dawn Militia." The group had simultaneously released a written grievance against the federal government and their demands. The details of the grievance were not released to the public.

Maya's cell phone rang. It was Jeff.

"Have you been watching the news?" Jeff asked.

"It's all I've been doing. I can't believe there were two separate bombing locations."

"It looks like our local militia was involved in the Justice Center bombing. We've heard helicopters flying back and forth all day, looking for them. Apparently, the MSO and the medics are on standby at the fire station while the manhunt searches for members in the foothills. It sounds like a war zone out there. I've barely slept since I got home."

"I hope they get these guys. What was their point?"

"Enforce their power through violence. The thing that pisses me off is that many of these militia guys haven't seen a day of battle in their lifetimes. Maybe the younger recruits but not these old armchair warriors. Maybe they wouldn't be ready to blow up our society if they had. I'm just disappointed this is a reality in my own country."

"Let's hope they prosecute these guys and send a message for anyone who thinks this is the way to get heard."

"Are you going to try to sleep before we go back tomorrow?"

Maya laughed. "Try is the operative word. I've been nursing a bottle of Tatoosh Whiskey all day. Might be time to kick it up a notch and become comfortably numb."

"I may have to do the same. Melissa is so wound up with all that's going on. She doesn't want me to go to work tomorrow. I think she is having a harder time than I am."

"I can't blame her, it's easier to be involved in what's happening than watching from the sidelines."

"I know. Just hearing the helicopters and the news makes me want to return to work now. I hate sitting here out of the action."

"We'll get enough of it in the next few days. I just hope there aren't any more surprises waiting for us tomorrow.

CHAPTER TWENTY-NINE

"I'M sorry you guys have to be the ones on standby, but I thought it best to bring in fresh crews on your medic unit. If this wraps up early, I'm going to send you home," Roy said.

"No problem. I'd rather be here in case anyone needs us. They're still barricaded up there?" Maya asked.

"We know they have an underground bunker in the old mill building. It's making it harder for law enforcement to root them out. The whole place is booby-trapped.

"Homeland Security has been trying to negotiate their surrender, but they haven't made any progress. They're looking at other options. We'll get an update at 10 a.m. So be ready."

Maya stood at the command post with Roy, the incident commander, and the standby team of first responders. There was also another team of firefighters and another medic unit manned by Jay and Daniel on standby at the fire station in downtown Enumclaw. Staging with the SWAT team was Jake as the operation's tactical paramedic.

Who knew what kind of ammunition and bombs might be part of their arsenal? From the sound of things, one wrong move could end up maiming law enforcement SWAT team members tasked with arresting the militia members held up in the mill.

She looked out from their command post. Far enough away to be safe but close enough to go in quickly. The old mill was a series of large, paved lots scattered with rusted machinery. Old roads went to and from an abandoned mill building once the hub of a booming logging industry. Clearcuts and young tree farms now surrounded the relic of another time.

As they waited for something to happen, 10 a.m. came and went. The tension was palpable. Maya looked at her phone every few minutes.

"I guess it was better than running calls and not knowing what was going on," Jeff said.

The heightened sense of alert was temporarily alleviated only by checking news updates online. The anticipation was unrelenting as they waited. Finally, Roy walked over to update them.

"So, they're waiting until this evening to execute a night operation. The tentative plan is to go in under cover of darkness if the next round of negotiations fails, which I suspect they will. So, rest up and be ready."

"All right. We'll keep these seats warm," Jeff said. Maya and Jeff had settled into their seats hours ago.

Maya watched as Roy walked back toward the fire vehicles behind them. He looked tired. He should have retired long ago.

"It says here that they've apprehended some White Dawn Militia members in Priest River, Idaho," Jeff said. "They're saying it's unclear if they're the members responsible for the attack in Seattle. The news is speculating that they are part of a larger organization with nationwide ties."

"I'm looking at Faux News, and they're saying this is a

setup. That it's Antifa who targeted the Federal Building. Next, they'll say armed bovines are taking over McDonald's."

Jeff laughed. "You're funny."

"I try to keep it light," Maya said and rolled her eyes. "It just continually surprises me that they even say this stuff. Who believes it? Here we are in a standoff with a militia group, and they're spouting off like it's a bunch of 'snowflakes' from the left carrying out the attacks."

The speculation and updates were moment to moment, keeping them glued to their phones as they waited.

A tap on the window caught their attention. It was one of the firefighters. Maya rolled down the window.

"Hey, The Mint sent up pizza for everyone. I've got a veggie and a pepperoni. Which one do you want?"

"Veggie," Maya said.

Jeff shook his head. "Pepperoni."

"Okay, good thing you guys aren't married." He peeled back the covers. Half and half. He handed them one box with half pepperoni and half veggie.

"Who said we aren't married?" Maya asked.

"Yes, she knows me better than my wife," Jeff said.

"My wife says I'm married to the job," the firefighter said.

"Man, I'm hungry," Jeff said.

The pizza was cold, but hungry was hungry.

They'd eaten their lunch hours ago, hoping they'd be done by now. Maya watched as the firefighter carried the pizza to the aid car in front of them. She continued to watch as he suddenly dropped face down onto the ground. His chest landed on the pizza box. The surreal scene unfolded as she heard the ping, ping as bullets hit the side of their medic unit. They heard yells, "Take cover!"

"Shit, we're under fire!" Jeff shouted.

Maya and Jeff dove into the tight space between the cab

and the patient compartment, almost crawling over each other in their panic.

"Sorry, sorry," Maya said.

"Me too, that..."

They heard more pings.

"Was close," finished Jeff.

Maya and Jeff hunkered down as close to the floor as they could, using the bulk of the storage shelving on either side of the patient compartment as shielding.

"What do you think we should do? Should we move the medic unit?" Maya asked.

"No, we don't know where they're shooting from. It could be anywhere."

The armored SWAT vehicle sped by them toward the mill.

"I guess we wait." Jeff looked at Maya. "Let's think about what we'll do when they neutralize the threat. I'm assuming we'll have more casualties. We can stage patients near the medic unit. Treat them while we wait for transporting units, depending on how many there are."

"How many?" Jeff's words hung in the air.

"Good plan." Maya was glad for the focus. She heard groans from someone out there and wondered if Roy was okay. She was worried about Jake, who was going in with SWAT.

Now they heard louder gunfire. Maya hoped that it was the SWAT taking out the shooters. Where were they shooting from?

They heard flash bangs and an explosion, but they couldn't see anything. It was too risky to stick their heads up and look outside.

There was a barrage of gunfire, more flash bangs, a helicopter flew over them, and they could hear more gunfire from above.

They were pinned and helpless as they waited. Things weren't going as planned, but then, things never did.

It seemed like time slowed to a crawl as they waited. Finally, the gunfire ceased. The brief silence was broken by calls for medics. A SWAT officer banged on their door. "All clear. We need you guys ASAP."

Maya and Jeff ducked into the back, grabbed their med kits, and exited the side door. As they came around the front, Maya saw the firefighter, who had handed them their pizza just a short time ago, lying in a pool of blood. A bullet had disintegrated the side of his head. Bile rose up in her mouth, and she choked back the feeling. This was no time to be a rookie. She and Jeff followed the SWAT member as he guided them through the vehicles. She looked and saw Roy slumped over in his command vehicle.

"Wait, wait. We have to help him." Maya veered over to open the door. Roy had a bullet to his head. She put her fingers to check for a pulse. The silence echoed through her fingertips.

"Wait, pull him out and quick look him. I can't just leave."

The SWAT member helped them lower him to the ground. Jeff slapped on the patches, while Maya turned on the machine. There, echoing her pulse check, was the flat line as confirmation she didn't want to acknowledge.

"Okay, we gotta go. We've got more inside," the SWAT officer said. A look of impatience spurred them to move along.

Maya hesitated before turning away, and they moved toward the mill. Behind her, she could hear more sirens. She hoped it was Daniel and Jay with more help.

As they entered the building, she saw an officer lying on the ground. One of his teammates was applying pressure to a gunshot wound to his upper leg. His pants were crimson from the loss of blood. Smoke hung in the air as Maya told a firefighter to grab a stretcher to carry him to their medic unit.

Maya choked back disbelief as she saw that just past the wounded officer was Jake. He'd barely made it through the door before he was taken down. She saw bullets had pierced his right eye, neck, and shoulder. The only recognizable part of his face was the left side, his familiar eye open, the spark of life gone from his upward gaze.

"Jake." Her call faded into recognition that he was probably already gone too.

"We've got one of our guys down there," the SWAT officer said.

"I'll check Jake and the other patient, Maya. You go with the officer," Jeff said.

She was relieved that she had to move forward, following the SWAT to a stairway that led down into the bowels of the mill. Below the old, abandoned machinery was a newer operation. Lights illuminated a series of passageways leading to rooms filled with weapons. She was led deeper inward to an entry into another passage. There, lying at the entrance, was the SWAT team leader. Some sort of explosive had detonated upon their rapid entry. Below his right knee was ragged flesh where his calf used to be. His partner had secured a tourniquet and was dressing the wound with gauze. Both of their faces looked pale, but the man lying on the ground was losing too much blood.

"Let's get him out of here and up top. We need to get IVs started right away."

Two of the other SWAT members grabbed their leader and carried him up and out of the bunker. Maya followed.

Maya met up with Jeff as he followed two firefighters carrying the other officer on a stretcher.

"He's gone, Maya."

"I know."

As they exited the door, they saw Glenn, the volunteer firefighter. SWAT had him cuffed and was leading him toward a transport vehicle. Before Maya even knew what was happening, Jeff stomped over and punched him square in the jaw, dropping him to the ground.

"You mother fucker! How dare you attack us!"

Glenn looked up at him and spat out blood. "It had to be done. Praise God's country. Now and forever." A look of defiance set on his face.

"Whatever, you have no idea what you've done," spat Jeff as he backed off. "You're not worth my time." He turned back and focused on their patient.

"Damn, that felt good!"

Maya was surprised. She'd never seen Jeff like this. Usually, he was calm and steady, not volatile enough to punch someone. But then, he'd probably never seen a traitor in his midst.

They arrived at the medic unit to find Daniel and Jay setting up triage and treatment. So far, it was just the two SWAT members. The militia members, so far, had been found dead. The ones on the roof were taken out by the helicopter, and two more were shot in the tunnels by SWAT.

"We've got two med helicopters arriving soon. They'll land over in that parking lot. Let us know what you need," the incident commander said.

"Thanks, we'll fly these two out, and if needed, we can fly more."

Maya squatted down and started IVs on the man with the calf amputation. Jeff set up to intubate him. Maya gave him morphine for the pain and watched as the tension left his face, and he drifted off. Then they did the best they could to splint the disintegrated leg.

"Were you guys under fire too?" Daniel asked.

"Absolutely. Jeff and I almost killed each other to see who could dive in the back first." It almost struck her as humorous, a

Laurel and Hardy skit as they twisted around each other to fit into the small space. That was replaced by a more somber vision. "Did you see Roy?"

"No, is he dead?"

"Yes, we stopped on our way into the mill, but he was already gone. He'd been shot once in the head. Flatline."

"Jesus."

"Jake's dead too. He barely made it through the door. So much for tactical paramedics," Maya said.

"Was he shot?"

"Didn't stand a chance, head, neck, and shoulder shots. He was already dead when we got to him."

They focused on the two officers before them. They could mourn later. For now, they had lives to save. Maya had the firefighters put the men in their medic unit, one on the bench and the other on the stretcher.

"Jeff, you want to go with them to hand them off? We'll stay in case there are more."

"Got it." He jumped up in the back and had one of the firefighters drive.

Maya wanted to get him focused on the officers. Who knew if they'd be asked to care for some of the militia members who'd targeted them. Considering what she had just witnessed, she didn't want to ask that of Jeff. Maya watched as the medic unit drove to the landing zone in the next parking area where logs used to sit piled high, waiting to be milled.

She turned to Daniel and Jay. "How are you guys doing?

"As good as can be expected. I'm relieved that more of our people weren't killed," Jay said.

"What the hell happened?" Daniel asked. "We were on standby for a night raid, and we heard all the radio traffic. Then they called us up."

"It sounds like maybe they were ambushing us before we

could get to them?" Maya said. "I saw Glenn, the volunteer. He's been arrested."

"He was involved?"

"Apparently."

"Do you think they were tipped off about the raid?"

"Anything could be possible," Maya replied.

"This is unacceptable. How are we supposed to do our job when our operations are compromised?" Jay said.

One of the SWAT members came over and motioned for Maya. "We need you to confirm death up on the rooftop. We have three men. Two obvious. The other may be viable."

Maya grabbed her kit and followed them back into the mill and up a ladder to the rooftop. There she saw the obvious two DOA. Their bodies were riddled with bullets from the helicopter. Blood congealing around their empty bodies. Over behind an elevated vent was another man lying motionless on the ground. She immediately recognized him; it was Titus. A dark thought crossed her mind, *I hope he's dead.* As she reached down to grab his wrist, he suddenly opened his eyes and grabbed her arm. The SWAT officer standing next to him stepped on his arm, and he released Maya's.

"I knew you were just playing possum," the officer said. "Watch it, or I'll do more than stand on your arm."

"Fuck you!" Titus said.

"Didn't work out so well for you, did it?" Maya said.

"Fuck you too."

"You're lucky that I have an oath to treat anyone. Your actions today took the life of my shift supervisor and coworker. I hope you live to face the jury...and executioner," Maya said.

"This is just the beginning. You have no idea. A red tide is coming from above, and we're going to take this country back."

"Ya, right. An army of God. Glenn flew that idea by us

earlier. Not going to happen! You can't attack everyone and expect to keep your allies."

Maya reached into her bag and reluctantly started to treat his shoulder wound. He'd been luckier than the other two, or maybe they'd been luckier. She wished the ideology had died with them because as long as it survived, they would never feel safe again.

CHAPTER THIRTY

MAYA AND NICK sat in their living room with Daniel, Em, Jeff, and Melissa. So much had happened in the intervening days after the standoff that they hadn't had time to truly process what had happened. Mourning the loss of more coworkers and attending the funerals for Jake, Roy, and the young firefighter had left them spent. Realizing that the situation was far from over weighed heavily upon them.

While it appeared the local militia's leadership had been dismantled, there were still the undercurrents of danger from larger coalitions brewing a storm of discontent. It left all of them wondering if it was even worth it anymore. A job that once felt rewarding was now calling on them to work in a perpetual war zone. Lou had commented that not even during the period when they had lots of gang warfare did it rise to this level of personal risk.

"I've decided to return to LA with my uncle. I've got a few options to work as a paramedic down there. I wanted to tell you guys before I gave my official resignation," Daniel said.

"I understand this has been a hard time, Daniel, but it will pass. We'll see it through to the end," Jeff said.

"Look, I can manage the known dangers of working in LA. At least down there, I know what to expect. Here, I'm an outsider without an insider's knowledge of how the game is played. Except for you guys, I'm working with people I can't trust. It almost cost my uncle his life. Someone tipped them off that we would be there, and someone was tipped off at the standoff. I'm sorry to leave you guys, but I have to do what is best for myself."

"Me too," Em said.

"Em, you too?" Maya asked.

"I'm leaving too. I'm going with Daniel to LA. I'm planning to apply for the Physician's Assistant program there."

Maya looked down at her drink. "I get it. It's one thing to endure the things we see year after year. It is quite another to have to protect yourself from your coworkers. It's wearing me down too. When I came back, I thought I'd have the support of our administration, but then the chief and Alden turned on me because of the pastor. Sometimes it's so frustrating I want to cry. This job is hard enough without being undermined."

"That's it. I would rather just deal with what I know in my hometown than try to figure out what makes these guys tick."

"I've been sitting on the sidelines watching what has been happening to Maya. I've been trying to talk her into quitting too. The cost is just too high," Nick said.

Maya sighed. "I know quitting would be the easier way out, but if I quit, they win, and nothing will change."

"What are you willing to sacrifice for that change—your life?" Daniel asked. "Because that's starting to feel like a growing reality."

"This job has always had risks," Jeff said.

"At least you've been in combat. I imagine dealing with combat and also the bureaucracy has got to feel familiar."

"It is. The only thing that made it worth it was my buddies. We had each other's backs. I still miss that about my team. There wasn't one of them that I didn't trust with my life. I have to agree, it's the one thing that is missing from this job. You guys are the closest to that I've found here," Jeff said. "I don't want to see you give up and leave. It will be hard to replace any of you."

"Well, my mind is made up. Like I said, I wanted to let you guys know before I submit my resignation letter."

"I'm going to turn mine in too. Maybe if more of us leave, they'll have to take a look at why," Em said.

"Well, I'm going to stick it out. I've got too much invested in my career here. Besides, who would keep Jeff company?" Maya smiled.

Nick stared at her, worry etched around his intense brown eyes. She wondered if he would stick around if things continued the way they were going. Would she be willing to walk away from their future marriage if he asked her to quit?

She knew what she signed up for when she'd gotten the job. One of the world's most prestigious medic programs built by dedicated men. If she could hold out, she could help guide the future to include more women, and possibly, someday, one of them would be the chief of their program.

"You're braver than I am, Maya," Daniel said.

CHAPTER THIRTY-ONE

NICK LAID fresh tracks on the snow-covered trail as he pulled the sled. The dogs followed behind them. The added weight of dog packs filled with dog food caused them to sink further into the snow, compressed by Nick and Maya's backcountry skis and the sled.

Maya and Nick were carrying their own heavy backpacks, and Nick pulled a sled filled with five days' worth of supplies as they headed into a remote cabin in Snoqualmie Pass. As Maya looked out through light snow floating down from the steely sky, the magic of the snow-covered landscape was a warm embrace. The muted sound of their skis flowing along the white carpet made the world around them feel smaller. The snow-laden winter branches of the pine and fir trees enclosed their pathway. They were happy to be getting away to a place far away from sirens, rain, and grievance. They figured that skiing into a remote cabin was an excellent way to try and leave it all behind for a while.

They'd seen off Em and Daniel as they packed their belongings and headed down to L.A. Charles had left a few days earlier by airplane. They'd be in L.A. in time for Christmas. She had hoped they would change their minds, but she understood why they had left.

Em and Daniel left an open invitation to visit and even come down and work in L.A. Maya knew they'd visit, but she knew she could never leave a job that allowed her to perform such a high level of paramedicine. To do anything less seemed impossible. L.A. had a great system, but the County was a world-class workplace that she couldn't replace so easily.

Watching them leave, along with the loss of Jake and Roy at the standoff, was devastating. Maya momentarily lost her stride as she thought of all the loss. She slowed behind Nick, mourning her friends and coworkers again. They'd shared so many calls and survived some of the worst incidents of their careers. The hole left inside her grew as she considered her future and the loss of her key allies at work. At least Jeff was still there.

She returned to the present. Kali, feeling impatient, had bounded around her, sinking up to her chest in the light, fluffy snow. Her nose looked like a black cupcake with frosting speckled on top. She continued to struggle to pass Maya but was soon breaking through Nick's tracks. Rio whined behind her, unhappy that he was bringing up the rear.

"Rio, be happy you have extra tracks to hold you up."

Rio quieted down after she acknowledged him. She picked up speed again; before long, Kali pulled off to let her lead again. She loved her dogs. It was the only thing that kept her grounded in the beauty and love in the world. With them, life was lived in the moment. Their eyes lit up as they embarked on another adventure with Maya and Nick. They were oblivious to the dangers of politics and militias. Their worries were more immediate. If they were confronted with a predator, they reacted in the moment. She was pretty sure they didn't dwell on it. They insisted mealtime be on time, and they were impatient if Maya sat out a perfectly good day when they could be outside doing something fun, like making tracks in the snow-covered landscape.

Maya thought Nick must be lost in his own thoughts. He'd left her and the dogs behind when she slowed. He didn't seem to notice they were falling further behind. This had been hard on him too. He felt responsible for not finding more intel about the bombing that led to so many deaths. It was as if the local militia group had set up the Russians and, in the wake, had managed to go undetected as they laid out and executed their plans to bomb the courthouse in concert with the group that bombed the Federal Building. She knew the people responsible for the Federal Building bombing were still at large and had disappeared into the ether. Until they were caught, they all still felt under threat. She knew that even though they were getting away from it all, Nick would inevitably continue work on following any digital trails they had left in their wake.

A trail branched off to the left. Nick stopped and looked back, finally noticing they had fallen behind him. He waited.

"Let's go check out the pond."

"Sounds good to me. We only have a little bit further to go to the cabin. It's still early."

They turned off and followed the old ski tracks that had recently been covered with new snow. The tracks guided them toward the edge of Gold Pond. They arrived at a clearing that was the summer parking area before joining the trail that followed the west side of the pond between the pond and Gold Creek.

The wide-open pond was frozen and covered with snow. To their left was the faint sound of running water making its way down channels filled with ice and framed in snow. Rio heard the running water and immediately wanted to find a place to swim. Maya gave her command "with me" to them, and they stayed in her tracks. She wasn't sure the pond or the banks of the creek were frozen enough to keep them from falling through.

The white of the snow-covered pond contrasted against the steely gray sky. They knew a snowstorm was coming, but she hoped it would wait until later to dump on them. As they skied, they saw coyote tracks. Other tracks emerging from bushes bent over from the weight of the snow revealed the winter homes of mice, birds, and snowshoe hares.

Kali and Rio strained against their desire to follow their noses to the entrances of these winter havens, but when they started to sink into the deeper snow, they decided staying in the tracks was easier.

"Later." Maya smiled as she assured them there would be other trails to follow.

They met back up with the main trail to the cabin. They passed the first private cabin. The winter shutters secured the windows. Snow was piled up to the lower windows and blocked the doorway inside. No tracks led to it as they passed by.

They continued up to the end of the road. They passed two more cabins on either side of the trail. Both were closed up for the winter as far as they could tell. Maybe their owners would open them up for winter recreation after the holidays. For now, it seemed that they would spend Christmas on their own.

Maya was glad she'd talked to the chief about taking Christmas off. Usually, she worked holidays so her coworkers with children could spend the holidays with them. Since Maya didn't have kids, she didn't feel the need to take them off. This year was different, though. She just wanted to feel as far away from work as possible. Christmas this year represented some-thing different. She'd spent her entire childhood excited about everything Christmas represented: family, presents, and decorations. Her parents had taught her the meaning of the holiday. It was the celebration of the birth of baby Jesus. They had a display on their fireplace mantel of the manger with baby Jesus next to Santa Claus on Nordic skis.

Now she felt the weight of intolerance by way of a version of Christianity she no longer recognized. When had this celebration of the birth of Jesus and Christianity become so militant? Even in the aftermath of the bombing, the pastor's church had doubled down on support for the pastor, Titus, and the youth pastor as if they were blameless victims instead of instigators of coverups, sexual assault, fraud, and murder. She shook her head. What the hell was happening?

She looked ahead as they rounded a bend that led to their cabin at the end of the road. It looked just like the photos. A two-story log cabin with an overhanging roof and a stairway to a second-floor deck. If the snow covered the first floor, access would be through the second floor. The deck also sheltered the lower entrance from the snow. If the snow continued to fall, they might be leaving from the second floor, but the main door was still visible for now. A narrow depression from someone using it before their stay led to the doorway. A shovel hung next to the door on the left. Nick and Maya took off their skis and hung them on the hooks provided along the wall. A wooden shutter covered a small window to the left of the doorway.

"I'll start shoveling and take the storm shutters off if you want to get everything inside opened up."

"I'll start a fire and get the place warmed up."

Maya opened the door and brought in packs and the sled bag before leaving Nick, Kali, and Rio outside. Nick removed the shutter on the window next to the door. She watched as the dogs tried to venture off the beaten path and disappeared in drifts deposited in front of the cabin. Kali soon discovered she could tunnel through the snow from the porch and then leap like a deer upward out of the snow and then back in. Maya watched her nose and eyes breaking the surface.

She turned her attention to the inside of the cabin. There was firewood stacked against the wall to the right of the fireplace. She reached inside the fireplace and opened the flue. Cold air wafted down from above. She piled kindling and paper in the fireplace and soon had a fire radiating heat outward as the flames filled the cabin with warm light.

She looked around at their rustic abode. It was a time capsule. Oil lamps hung from the walls for light. There were electric lights that looked like they had been added on later. They were given directions on starting the generator near the back porch out the back of the cabin. She'd wait until dark and decide whether they needed it. On shelves were memorabilia. Old postcards of I-90 when it was a two-lane road with snow piled twenty feet high above it. Another showed a fisherman casting his line into a creek. Above the fireplace were two vintage wooden skis crossed over each other. The screen she'd removed from the fireplace was handmade with an elk silhouette cut out of metal. An old leather bellow hung from a metal nail embedded in the mortar between the natural stone of the fireplace.

She found the bathroom near the porch. A new composting toilet was a modern convenience that had been added. A tin tub sat in the corner with a bucket suspended above for a rinse if needed. The hot water would come from the wood stove in the kitchen, which was also home to the only sink.

This tiny kitchen was on the other side of the small living room. Shelves were stacked with dishes covered with dish rags. A plastic bin held an assortment of spices. A hand pump stood by the porcelain sink, as the water was pumped in from a well. The view from the window above the sink was covered, but Maya knew that behind it was only a wall of snow.

She climbed the stairs behind the bathroom. The old wooden stairs creaked under her feet. She emerged to find Nick had already removed the window and door shutters on the second floor and cleared a walkway from the stairs to the door. The fireplace stone continued up the wall, and two warming vents radiated warm air from the fire downstairs.

A queen bed with a thick down comforter was covered by a red Pendleton blanket with a native design. On the floor was a brown bearskin rug. *Rio is going to turn that white before we leave,* she thought.

She unpacked their packs and settled in. Next, she made lunch. The door opened, and Nick stepped in while corralling the dogs to towel them off. Maya sighed. It was the simple things in life that calmed her and put her on solid ground. Seeing Nick, Rio, and Kali entering the fire-warmed cabin set the stage for a perfect getaway. This was how life should be. Not the world she found herself living in back at home.

"We're shoveled out for now."

"I've unpacked our gear, and as you can see, the fire is already warming the place up."

Nick walked over and kissed Maya. "I'm glad you talked me into coming on this adventure. I can't think of a better way to spend Christmas than here with you."

Rio whined.

"And you too, Rio and Kali," Nick said.

They sat on the couch in front of the fireplace, enjoying the firelight as falling snow began covering the pathways Nick had cleared. The dogs were tucked in near their feet, Rio lightly snoring. Kali, always watchful, lifted her head from time to time to make sure that Nick and Maya were still present.

Maya was content to sink into the well-worn couch. She

held her glass of red wine as the moment's glow filled her mind with possibilities that would be gone by morning. If she was lucky, she'd wake up refreshed instead of hung over. I'll cut down on my drinking when all this craziness is over. She leaned her head on Nick's shoulder and closed her eyes.

She awoke to Rio licking her face as a muted light filtered through the upstairs windows. She felt confused. The last thing she remembered was sitting by the fire, but here she was, lying under the warm down comforter, looking out the window. She looked over and saw that Nick wasn't in bed. She called down. "Nick, did I fall asleep in front of the fire last night?"

There was a pause that tipped her off that he was probably working.

"You did. I had to grab your glass of wine before you spilled it. One minute you were awake, and then the next, your eyes were closed. Don't you remember walking upstairs with me?"

"No, I'm afraid not. I must have been tired. I don't remember anything but sitting with you in front of the fire."

"Come on down. I made coffee with our Jetboil rather than turn on the generator. You'll just need to reheat it."

Maya grabbed her fleece pants and jacket and headed downstairs. Rio and Kali were already sitting between Nick and the warmth of the fireplace. It was good to see them following Nick around too. They had been her dogs before she met him. Now they were their dogs. It had taken a while for them to warm up to him, especially Kali. Now both dogs thought Nick was as great as she did.

She shook her head. One minute she wanted to spend the rest of her life with him, and the next...well, she hoped he wouldn't ask her to choose between her career and him. She'd be a fool to give up this guy for a career that kept taking so much from her and giving so little in return. But she had invested so much in her career that turning away now seemed unfathomable.

She sat down next to him with her coffee in hand. "What are you working on?"

What do you think? I'm trying to locate any evidence leading to where the White Dawn Militia are hiding out, but there's nothing. They're smart. They know if they leave a digital trail, they'll be found. They've gone underground. Maybe even, literally, underground."

"Look, it's just a matter of time before HS finds them. They'll get them. At least, I hope they do. You're not responsible for finding them."

"That's the problem too. As we found out. If local law enforcement is working with the militias, it makes it more difficult to find them. After what happened to you guys at the standoff, it became more apparent that moles are tipping them off from inside the ranks.

"That's how coups succeed. They recruit police and military to help overthrow governments. It's happened in other countries all over the world."

"Yes, but this is the United States. I wanted our country to be smarter than that."

"But it is happening. I hope the FBI prosecutes all these criminals to the fullest extent of the law to set an example of what will happen if they orchestrate these deadly events. We'll see what happens. I'm done. I haven't made any progress, so let's eat breakfast and then head outside and enjoy the sunshine and all this fresh snow."

Maya knew Nick was worried about her, which drove him to want to dig further into finding out who the other members of the more prominent militias were. He had a hard time letting it go.

As they cut fresh tracks through a foot of new snow, the sun was reflected in a million sparkles of light off the surface. The shadows on the trees shrank as the sun arced overhead. Rio and Kali took turns jumping off the trail through deep snow and returning to shadow Nick and Maya, following in their ski tracks. They skied out toward Gold Creek from the cabin and headed back down the valley. Up above them, the peaks cut a soft edge against the blue. The air was crisp and stung the tip of Maya's nose.

They passed by one of the cabins near theirs that sat in a clearing. Snowmobiles were parked along the side. The windows were clear of shutters. Smoke curled up from a chimney.

"Looks like we've got company," Nick said.

"It does. Who wouldn't want to spend Christmas in this beautiful snowy valley?"

They made their way down along the trees paralleling Gold Creek. Their route wound in and out of stands of trees, passing several more cabins. They stopped at a wide, shallow section of braided creek. Maya and Nick scouted for the best route to cross the creek, solid enough to prevent the dogs from dropping into the water below. They found a large log over the deepest section of the water, and they made tracks across its wide surface as the dogs followed them to the other side. From there, they skied over a couple of shallow channels that just touched over the tops of their skis.

As they skied down the valley, they skirted the bottom of the ridge to the Kendall Knob trailhead. From there, they followed a well-established depression up an old logging road. Someone had set early morning tracks, so they followed the easy path as it wound upward through a young forest laden with snow.

They crossed over to an open meadow as they crested the western slope. Following the previous tracks, they entered a valley between the two knobs of Kendall Peak. Below they skied along a frozen stream to Kendall Peak Lakes. They stopped at the second lake before the terrain rose steeply upward. Ahead of them was jagged rock blown bare by the wind. The tracks continued up the west side of the valley.

"We should probably turn around here," Nick said. "We won't be able to ski from the knob down into the steep chute today. Too much potential for an avalanche."

"How about we ski the trees from that first open spot we came to?"

"We'll have lunch there and take a closer look."

They returned to an opening above Gold Creek Valley with expansive open views up the valley and south towards Mount Rainier and the I-90 corridor. The sound of traffic was barely audible from their lofty perch. As they ate their lunch, a pair of gray jays landed on a short fir tree a few feet away, hesitating as the dogs moved in to investigate. Rio sat down and stared at the birds as Kali circled around the tree, looking for a way to catch her new prey. She gave a quick bark and sent the pair flying farther afield, but rather than leaving, they watched Maya and Nick eat their lunch.

Once they finished eating, they stood up and walked along the eastern edge. Nick pulled up the GPS on his phone and looked at possible routes downward through the trees.

"If we follow this line, we can stay in the trees along this fall line, then drop back into the valley between these two steeper areas here." He pointed to the area where the topo lines looked less dramatic.

"It's going to be challenging for Rio and Kali, but I think they can make it."

They reached the edge of the clearing and dropped into a space between trees. They traversed north before skiing down the trackless snow. In some areas, they circumnavigated tight clusters of young firs and cut tele-turns in the broader spaces between trees. The dogs followed their tracks and, at times, tried to cut the turns, disappearing into deeper snow, only to explode back into their tracks. Maya lost her sense of time as she directed her focus to the movement of her skis. Nick followed off to the side, also cutting his fresh tracks.

Halfway down, at a small opening in the forest, they stopped to catch their breaths and waited for the dogs to catch up. Maya watched as they bounded down her tracks. Their tongues hung out, and their breath sent curls of mist pumping from their open jaws.

A crack erupted above them, and then they heard it. It sounded like a grumbling freight train. To the north, they saw snow billow up like smoke from a forest fire. White clouds reached skyward as an avalanche let loose down an avalanche shoot. They could feel the ground under them rumble, an echo of the event to the north. Kali shook, and Rio whined before diving between Maya's skis.

It happened so fast they didn't have time to react. Maya took a deep breath and stroked Rio's head as the sound settled down, and she realized that they were safe. They'd made a good decision skiing the trees. With so much snow coming down, it was inevitable that there would be avalanches. With any hope, the snow would settle before they left, and they could ski some wide-open bowls in the high country.

Maya and Nick looked at each other.

"That was close," Nick said.

"A little too close."

"Rio, we're okay. You'll live to run another day."

He looked up at Nick with a look of terror. Maya could feel him shaking between her legs too.

"I know, Rio. I got ya," Maya assured him.

She loved the backcountry in the wintertime, but, as with

everything, they had to mitigate the risks with knowledge. Maya had learned a lot from Nick and his experience as a NOLS instructor. In these environs, she followed his lead. In others, he followed hers.

After Rio recovered from the shock of the trembling snow, they continued down the mountain. It was getting later than expected. Shadows started filling the valley below them. The last of the descent dropped them just upstream of where they had crossed Gold Creek earlier. They followed their previous tracks back to the cabin. As they passed the neighboring cabin, they saw that the snowmobiles were still parked on the side, but the smoke from the chimney was gone. They crossed snowmobile tracks that went up the valley and followed those back before breaking off and entering the forest to their cabin.

The fire was smoldering, and the air was cold when they came inside. They quickly added wood to build up the heat again, then set to work cooking dinner. Maya felt a deep tired sink into her body as she finished heating up chili and cornbread she'd made at home. Nick fed the dogs, and then they settled onto the couch, enjoying the reward of a good meal, wine, and firelight as the sky glowed a muted peach and then golden blue before settling into a star-filled midnight blue. The wood crackled, and both dogs were snoring away before Maya and Nick had finished eating.

"So what should we do tomorrow?" Nick asked.

"We could head up the valley and check out the avalanche chute. Then see if it looks safe enough to venture farther up the valley."

"Yeah and maybe we could explore the east side of the valley on our way back down, maybe get a few turns in on some of the forested side slopes."

"I like that idea. A few more turns would be nice." Maya always enjoyed their back-and-forth sharing of ideas and collaboration. It's what had drawn her to Nick. He always seemed to really hear what she had to say. She'd had boyfriends in the past who were adventurous, but they always seemed to discount her ideas, and she felt they never really gave her credit for her experience.

She often felt that way at work too. She'd held her own and often went above and beyond what was expected, but when it came time to listen to someone with expertise, she was often left watching as one of her male coworkers was asked his opinion instead of her.

She could live with that at work but couldn't live with that kind of dynamic with someone she was engaged to. Luckily, she didn't have to. She knew that Nick would listen and hear what she had to say.

"Do you want some more wine?" Nick asked.

"Sure."

Nick poured the last of the bottle into her glass.

"I was just lost in thoughts, thinking about how I really like talking with you and how lucky I am to have you in my life." She reached over and kissed him on the cheek. "I'd go anywhere with you."

He returned the kiss, and she forgot all about the wine in her glass as they headed upstairs.

She woke abruptly at the sound of gunfire. Rio jumped up and started barking wildly. There was silence, and then pop, pop, pop.

"Nick, did you hear that?"

"Oh, ya. Who's shooting their guns off at...," Nick looked at his phone, "2 a.m."

"Maybe it's avalanche control at the ski area?"

"No, that's gunfire."

Suddenly, they heard glass break at the back of the cabin. Rio shot down the stairs, barking wildly. Kali was glued to something outside the window where the deck was. She let out a low growl.

Nick and Maya grabbed their clothes, quickly putting them on just as the window in front of them shattered. Nick suddenly fell onto the bed as Kali leaped out the window and took off after something or someone.

"Nick, what happened?"

"I'm shot. My leg."

"Hold on."

She heard Rio tearing into someone at the back of the cabin. Then she saw another man standing on the deck. There was another gunshot, and she watched the man pitch forward, falling through the broken glass.

More growling and screaming could be heard off to the side of the cabin. A man screamed as Kali tore into his flesh. Maya crouched down as she waited to see if more bullets would fly through the broken window and hit her too.

"Nick, can you move back here with me out of sight?"

"I'll stay low and crawl around."

When he made it behind the bed, Maya carefully took the low light of her headlamp and illuminated his leg before shutting it off. She saw that he was bleeding from a wound in his right thigh. Luckily, he hadn't managed to get his pants all the way on.

"Hold still." She took a pillowcase from her pillow and applied pressure to the wound. She felt the rag quickly become soaked in blood. She grabbed another pillowcase, adding it to the other one, and pressed hard.

She heard more gunfire and yelling. A voice yelled orders that she couldn't quite make out. Following a commotion on the stairs, Rio bounded into the room.

"Nick, keep pressure on your leg."

"Down," she whispered as she grabbed Rio's collar. She didn't want him to get shot by whoever was out there.

Downstairs, Kali started growling again.

"Maya, call your dog off. It's me, your chief. I'm here with Homeland Security. We intercepted militia members who came here to murder you and Nick."

Maya felt momentarily relieved at the sound of his voice, but then an overwhelming sense of fear paralyzed her and kept her from responding to him.

"Maya, you're safe now. We staged at the cabin just up the road. You must have seen our smoke?"

Still, she hesitated. *Something isn't right*, she thought. Then she heard Kali growl again. "Kali, come," Maya commanded. Kali ran up the stairs.

"Good. I'll be up to help you." This was followed by foot-steps. Rio and Kali growled.

Maya whispered for them to stay down. "Chief, stay where you are. Send the FBI up first."

Before she knew it, he was standing at the top of the stairs. "I can't do that. Don't move, or I'll shoot both of your dogs. I know how much you love them."

That stung. Maya froze as she realized that she'd let the one person know where she had gone that she shouldn't have, and now she was trapped with Nick lying beside her, bleeding to death.

"You're the traitor?" she spat out.

"Not a traitor. A patriot. You just had to go out on your own and fuck things up. You and your fiancé. I'm disappointed in you, but then you shouldn't even be a paramedic. Affirmative action hire. If I had my way, you wouldn't have been hired."

"Chief, I'm confused. Why are you here?" She'd been here before. God, when was she going to be free of misplaced revenge?

"To finish what we started."

She heard a commotion and another gunshot outside.

"Chief, this is the FBI. We have you surrounded. Surrender!"

The chief yelled, "Don't come in, or I'll shoot Maya and Nick."

Maya realized that his entry into the house was more out of desperation than part of their original plan to murder Maya and Nick. She tried to think of a way to get them out of this that didn't include being murdered.

Rio growled as Maya tightly held onto his collar. She knew they'd die trying to protect her if she let go of either of them. "Stay down," she whispered.

"Chief, I don't know what I did to you. I've always had the greatest respect for you. You've been so supportive of me the last few months. Why this? It's not who you are!"

"Not who I am? Who am I, Maya? Do you even know? You, sniveling about how hard this job is? We never had to "take time off" because of a tough call. You really worked that, didn't you?"

Maya felt the betrayal in that statement. Instead of being supportive of her, he thought she was weak.

"Do you know what has happened since they let you Birkenstock-wearing college kids take over our profession? It means that hardworking men, qualified men like myself, aren't getting jobs as paramedics and firefighters. Instead, I was told by the Executive's office to make sure I meet quotas and priori-tize a college education over who's qualified. We're done playing games, Maya. We're taking this country back."

"Maya was devasted by that police officer's death, and you're berating her for it," Nick said. "I can't believe you guys. Maya dedicated herself to this job; still, you discount her contributions. I've told her this isn't worth it for her to continue.

Look, let us live, and she'll quit. I'll make her quit." His last sentence sounded strained. She was losing him.

She felt a searing anger rise inside her as it sank in that the chief was responsible for the deaths of her coworkers. "What did Kelly, Brian, Roy, and Jake do to deserve to be executed? They were just doing their job."

"Collateral damage. There must be sacrifices in any war."

"Sacrifices, they were your employees, people that you...you attended their funerals. You consoled us and said you were there to support us. Was that all for show?"

A male voice called up. "Chief, you have no choice. You can shoot them, but we're still coming in for you. Surrender now."

"Stay out, or I'll shoot Nick first, then the dogs, before I leave here with Maya as my hostage."

Maya shuddered. Her heart sank as she realized she had put them in danger.

"Chief, take me. Leave Nick and the dogs. You can take me as a hostage. Leave them. This is between you and me."

"You hear that?" the chief asked. "Maya is going with me. I want a snowmobile brought out front."

"We can't do that. You know we don't negotiate with terrorists."

"Just let him take me. Nick's been shot. He needs medical aid. Please save Nick."

There was silence, and then they responded. "Okay, we'll bring the snowmobile up."

"Then you're going to stay put until we clear the area. Got it?" the chief yelled.

"Okay. You're calling the shots."

They waited for what seemed like an hour before they were finally cleared to leave.

"Get up," the chief said.

Maya quickly tied Nick's bootlaces through the dog's collars and handed them to Nick.

"Don't let them go no matter what. I don't want them to get shot." She looked at Nick; he was still with it but barely. She wished she could see him better, to know how bad it was. She hoped he could hang on to the dogs and hang on until help could get to him.

"I'll be okay. I love you!"

Surprised by his words, Maya stood up. "Can I grab my coat on the way out? I don't think I'll survive long in what I'm wearing."

"No, grab that blanket. You go out that door first."

Maya grabbed the Pendleton blanket and wrapped it across her shoulders. She knew she would only survive a short time without her cold-weather gear. Dressed in fleece sweatpants, a fleece jacket, and her socks, she was doomed to be dependent on the chief or die of exposure if she tried to escape.

He grabbed her around the neck, shouldered his rifle, and took out a handgun. As he pointed it at her head, they stepped forward. "Don't try anything, or I'll pull the trigger. You and I know I have nothing to lose at this point."

She heard a snowmobile motor growing louder as the driver made his way to the cabin. Time moved in slow motion as she ran through her options. If he left with her on that snowmobile, she was sure that she wouldn't survive the night, either because he would kill her, or she would die of exposure.

The FBI agent tried to get the chief to stand down. "Chief, I'll give you one more chance. Surrender now and we'll work this out. You don't want any more blood on your hands, do you?"

"You don't know what I want. Sacrifices are to be made in the service of the greater good. Do me a favor and just have your man move back away from the snowmobile."

"If you're sure." There was silence and when the chief didn't respond, the agent followed with, "Okay. My man will step back, and we'll give you the all-clear to proceed. Just know, this isn't over."

"Leave the engine running," the chief said. Maya could hear just a hint of uncertainty in his response.

The chief whispered in her ear. "Don't make any sudden moves. We're going to take this nice and slow down the stairs."

They exited the doorway onto the deck. The chief kept her in front of him as they sidestepped down the stairs. At the bottom step, he moved her forward toward the snowmobile. She felt the cold snow seep through her socks.

Then he told her to sit on the snowmobile seat while positioning himself between her and where the voice of the FBI agent had come from. She doubted they were only in one location, but he didn't have too many options for getting out of there alive.

She pulled the folds of the blanket as tightly around her as she could. She turned toward the chief and saw a dark figure leap toward the chief from behind. Kali's jaws latched onto his arm holding the gun, yanking him off balance. The gun dropped from his hand. Maya dove to the ground behind the snowmobile to avoid the trajectory of the gun. Rio was right behind Kali and launched onto the chief's back, ripping into the flesh below his helmet. As Kali pulled him to the side, Rio pulled him backward like they were playing tug-of-war with a chew toy. The chief screamed in agony as the dogs buried their teeth into his flesh. Both dogs bore down on him again and again. Kali repositioned and sank her jaws into his stomach as he flailed about. Before they could finish the job, the FBI agent who'd delivered the snowmobile trained his headlamp and gun on the chief.

"Rio, Kali, release," Maya commanded.

They reluctantly released him and backed away.

"Sit." They obeyed without taking their eyes off the chief.

Maya looked up at the face of the FBI agent and couldn't believe what she saw. It was Randy.

"Randy, what are you doing here?"

"Cleaning up my mess," he replied.

"What?"

"I'll tell you later."

The other members of the FBI team emerged from the forest. A spotlight came on, illuminating the area around the front of the cabin. The FBI spread out and secured the perimeter. Randy and another member hauled the chief to his feet and carried him toward a sled behind a snowmobile.

Maya ran up the stairs to Nick. He was still lying on the floor, putting pressure on the pillowcases with his hands.

"It sounded like the dogs took care of the chief?" Nick sounded relieved.

"That they did."

"Good! I think the bleeding has stopped, but I don't feel so great. I couldn't keep ahold of the dogs. They were not going to let you leave without them."

"Don't worry about it. Rio and Kali saved my life. Now I need to save you."

"Hey, can I get some help to get Nick to a hospital?" Maya shouted.

"We have a helicopter inbound. ETA twenty minutes in the clearing at the Gold Creek parking area."

Maya was relieved. That would speed things up. She was worried that Nick's condition could deteriorate if they couldn't get to the hospital soon.

"Okay, did you hear that, Nick?"

"Yes. I just want you to know I didn't sign up to take a bullet or be run over by a truck when I asked you to marry me."

"I know you didn't, Nick. I'm so sorry. Hang in there. Hold on while I grab my med kit from downstairs."

"You brought a med kit. Is that why that sled was so heavy?"

"Did you think I would come up into the mountains unprepared?"

She quickly went downstairs and retrieved her kit. She started two IVs to give him fluid to replace the blood loss from his wound. "We need to get you to Harborview."

She looked up and saw Jeff looking down at her.

"Maya, I got him from here. You take care of your dogs, and I'll get Nick on that helicopter and off to Harborview."

"You too?"

"I wasn't going to let them set you up without solid backup."

"Set me up?"

"Well, you set the perfect trap when you told the chief you and Nick were going up to this cabin. Luckily, Nick let me know what you had planned, and the FBI did the rest."

"Can you believe it was the chief?"

"Unfortunately, I can."

Maya watched from Nick's side, inside the snowcat, as the helicopter touched down. The blades whipped snow in all directions before they slowed as the pilots turned the engine off.

Maya had taken back care of Nick. Jeff was asked to treat the chief in another snowcat. His injuries were severe enough that he was sedated and intubated. Maya was relieved that he was incapacitated.

Maya hopped out of the snowcat and crunched across the ground with Jeff to greet the helicopter.

"Jeff, I want to fly too. We'll need both of us to take care of Nick and the chief. But we need to get Rio, Kali, and our gear back home..."

The pilot overheard them. "Hey, we can take the dogs if they'll stay calm. We fly our K9 soldiers all the time."

"They're solid. Kali's a search and rescue dog who's flown for missions, and Rio, he'll just lie where I put him."

"Okay, bring them on board."

Jeff ran over and opened the snowcat door. Rio and Kali jumped out and bounded toward Maya. She commanded them to jump into the helicopter and sit on the floor. Rio put himself between her and the chief. He let out a low growl but stayed put.

"Rio, your job is to make sure the chief doesn't move," Jeff said.

Rio's eyes were glued to the chief as Jeff closed the helicopter door and sat next to the chief to monitor the ventilator and the chief's vital signs. Maya and Jeff fell into the familiar routine of working together.

They had a duty to treat everyone but watching as the man who had tried to murder her and her family lay there, Maya had this sudden urge to yank out his breathing tube, but she didn't. Instead, she turned her attention to Nick.

He was lying quietly on the stretcher connected to the monitor that informed her of his vital signs. She reached over and touched his arm. A relaxed smile spread across his face.

Maya made sure she was buckled in and put on her headphones as the pilots prepared for takeoff. The engine engaged as the hum of the blades grew faster and faster. Lights illuminated the darkness, and the snow whipped violently around them.

The familiar bup, bup, bup of the blades vibrated inside as they slowly lifted straight up from the ground. Then the helicopter turned to the south, climbing gradually upward along the creek drainage.

The darkness enveloped the ground again as the helicopter

lights illuminated the route in front of them. As the valley widened, they turned down the I-90 corridor, following the ribbon of freeway toward Puget Sound. Rural lights that dotted the forest landscape gave way to the city lights of Issaquah. Then Bellevue. Christmas lights intertwined with strip malls and housing tracks passed by. They followed the freeway over Lake Washington. Lights reflected off the water in reds, blues, and whites. A line of Christmas boats made their way along the lake between Mercer Island and Seattle.

"Nick, look out the window." He lay on the stretcher with a window to his left.

"It's beautiful." His words slowly drifted to a finish as his eyes closed again.

"This is one of the perks of the job, looking out the window of a helicopter at the city lights below."

Nick didn't respond. In his sedated stupor, he was somewhere else.

As she checked his vital signs, she heard Rio growl. She looked over to see the chief's arm straining upward to reach toward the tube. Jeff quickly gave him more medicine.

"I guess it wore off. This last dose should last until we get to Harborview."

"I wish he had spent more time in the field. Maybe he wouldn't be so ready to sacrifice us for his cause if he had. I knew our office politics could be toxic, but this has taken it to a whole new level."

"Well, there are going to be some changes coming," Jeff replied.

"It's about time!"

As they approached the landing zone at Harborview, the lights from downtown Seattle reflected on the water of Puget Sound. In the distance, she could see the Space Needle.

The pilots set the helicopter down on the landing zone on

top of the parking garage. Two Seattle Aid Units waited to transfer the patients to the ED. As they loaded Nick and the chief, one of the HMC social workers met them and took the dogs from Maya. "I'll put them in the family room until you're ready to get them."

Maya was relieved. She could turn her focus to Nick and their entry into the ED. As Jeff and Maya walked through the doors, the head of the ED, who ran his ED with military discipline, directed his trauma teams to take over. Maya took a deep breath and let them take her fiancé into Trauma room 1.

She followed the attendant to the family room. There, glued to the door, were Kali and Rio. When they saw her, they nearly knocked her over. She backed up and looked in horror as she realized their muzzles were covered in drying blood from their attack.

"Can I get some towels and water to clean these dogs?" Maya asked. "They're going to scare everyone in the ED."

"Sure thing. We all wondered what was going on when these two came through the doors."

As she directed her attention to cleaning up the dogs, Maya thought about the betrayal that had been harder than anything she had experienced. She couldn't believe that the chief, of all her coworkers, was their traitor. He seemed so concerned when Kelly, Brian, Roy, and Jake were murdered. He'd been so supportive of her and everyone, asking if they needed anything. She shook her head. Rio tilted his head sideways as if he was listening for words that would follow her motion.

"Oh, Rio. It's not about you. Thank you so much for rescuing me. Without you two, I'd have been doomed many times over."

Typically, she would give them a big hug, but she withheld that for later when they were clean and dry.

There was a knock at the door. Maya looked up and saw Jay. She motioned him in.

"Jay, are you here as a friend or as the new acting medical services officer?"

"Both. How are you doing, and how is Nick?"

"I'm surviving. Nick is with the trauma team. I'll check in soon, but I had to get these guys cleaned up."

"What happened to them?"

"It's a long story, but let's just say they saved my life."

"Hmm, the chief?"

"Yes!"

"You know, I've worked with him for a long time, and I didn't see this coming. There has got to be more to this."

"It seems that he didn't like the fact that he had to hire women and minorities. At least that is what he hinted at earlier."

"That doesn't justify murder of so many of our people. Besides, I always thought he supported integrating more diversity into our teams."

"I don't know what to believe anymore. I trusted the chief. I even told him where Nick and I were staying just in case something happened to us."

"You can't blame yourself. People hide their intentions. The chief has always been ambitious. He was always focused on attaining the position of chief from the time he walked through our doors as a new paramedic."

There was another knock on the door. Maya looked over and saw Randy standing there.

"Hey, Jay, good to see you again." Randy shook Jay's hand. "Maya, how are you and the dogs doing?"

"Surviving. What are you doing here?"

"Well, if Jay could give us a minute, I'd like to talk to you about what I said earlier. Jay?"

"Sure, no problem. I'll check in on Nick and get an update for you, Maya."

"Jay, thanks. That would be great."

Jay left. Randy sat down on the couch along the back wall. Rio and Kali lay down around Maya's feet as she sat in a chair next to the door. She felt slightly on edge, wondering about Randy after seeing him at the cabin.

"Randy, you have some explaining to do. What happened? One minute you were working with Em on the medic unit, and the next, you resigned and went MIA."

"Maya, I'm so sorry about everything that happened and my part in it. This is for your ears only. I'm responsible for supplying weapons to the militia group that attacked you and our other coworkers."

Maya's vision narrowed as fear surged inside her. Was he about to murder her? Rio sensing her anxiety, let out a low growl.

"No, it's not what you think. I, well, I've been working undercover with the FBI to take down my business partner. He was involved in many shady business dealings, including human trafficking. That raid you were on was due to months of our investigation.

"What I wasn't aware of until then was that he was funneling weapons from our company to Russian organized crime networks. That local network was reselling weapons to the local militia involved in your ambush. His interest in supplying weapons to this group wasn't just about the money.

"The ambush of the police officer was an execution, but it wasn't supposed to be an ambush. He was a member of the militia and was going to turn them in over their business with organized Russian crime involved in human trafficking. His own people, other cops in the militia, executed him, but Glenn shifted the operation to ambush the first responders. He blamed you and other 'minorities' as his reason for not getting hired.

"What a dick! We didn't hire that guy because he wasn't a good candidate. Maya, our weapons were used in your ambush and in the bombing that killed Kelly and Brian."

Maya was stunned as she realized there was so much more to these events than she'd ever imagined. "Randy, I want to understand how you could have allowed this to go on for so long?"

"Big picture, Maya. Our goal was to take down my partner's organized crime syndicate, which was bigger than one local militia. We believe these Russian connections are part of a larger plot to destabilize our country. Glenn, the chief, and some of our local law enforcement are part of this larger plot orchestrated by Russia. My partner was just one pawn in the endgame.

"I want to say I'm truly sorry that this has impacted you directly. Rest assured; we won't stop until we've arrested everyone responsible for all these acts of terrorism."

Maya suddenly felt very small. Being a paramedic helped her feel that she was making a difference in the world. But there were powerful forces moving chess pieces that she couldn't see. She thought of what the chief said about hiring women and minorities. Had all this grievance been exploited in an attempt to destabilize her country?

That one event, the ambush, had destabilized her life. It tore apart everything she had believed in. She'd become a para-medic to make the world a better place, but the cost to her personally was too much. How could she continue to save the public when she wasn't sure she could save herself and the ones she loved?

She looked up at Randy, and before stopping herself, she said, "Fuck you, Randy!"

With that, she picked up the dog leashes and headed out of the ED, walking away without a clue as to where she was going.

EPILOGUE

NICK AND MAYA sat on a deck overlooking the Pacific Ocean at Daniel's favorite ocean side bar. Across from them, Em and Daniel looked relaxed as they sipped their beer in the evening light.

"Maya, now that you're here, I want to know what really happened after we left." Daniel leaned forward on his chair. "The official report is that the chief was put on leave while investigations are underway. How does that even happen after he attempted to murder you and gave inside information that led to attacks on us in the streets?"

Maya looked out over the water, soaking in the sun and warmth of Southern California.

"Well, it seems that the chief wasn't necessarily on board with what the militia had planned, but he made some mistakes that made him easy to manipulate. Apparently, he had a gambling problem and accumulated considerable debt owed to a certain Russian bookie. A debt that the militia agreed to pay if he gave them information so they could conduct their attacks and avoid detection.

"Nick found out that not only was he in debt, but he was also underwater on his mortgage and was teetering on the verge of foreclosure and bankruptcy. Quite a motivation for cooperating with his friends in the militia.

"Now, he is cooperating with the FBI to build a case against the militia and the local players, including Titus and Pastor Richter. So, he may avoid prosecution."

"How do you feel about that, Maya?" Em asked.

"Like everything else about this situation, I feel I'm being sacrificed for the greater good. There are agendas far above my pay grade that have put me in harm's way."

Em's concern for Maya was reflected in her eyes. "Is that why you took a leave of absence? Last time we talked, I remember you telling me you were going to stick it out."

"I can't stay there right now. Jeff will do a great job as acting chief, but there is still work to do to root out the rot that has settled into our organization. I'm sure there will be more firings and prosecutions before this is over.

Maya filled them in on what they'd discovered. Daniel and Em had been out of the loop as the details of what happened reverberated through their organization.

"On that note, did you know they arrested Doug for aiding the militia in carrying out the bombings of Highline Community College and the Kent Regional Justice Center? I guess the bombing of the Environmental Climate Science building was a statement about all the environmental regulations the County has put into place in the rural areas. Apparently, his family owned a bunch of land out in the foothills that they wanted to develop and couldn't because it was all wetlands and steep slopes."

Daniel shook his head.

"Bob, you know the homeless guy who was carrying the bomb? Well, apparently, he was recruited by Pastor Richter.

Not long before the bombing he'd started attending the pastor's church. The militia told him if he didn't cooperate, they'd kill his dog. I guess that dog was all he had in the world. A dog he was willing to die for.

"Anyone who'd event threaten to kill a dog..." Daniel's voice trailed off as he thought of Maya's dogs.

"Mike is on leave following an investigation of his comments in right-wing online forums. Two County sheriff's deputies have been arrested for participating in human trafficking, illegal weapons sales, domestic terrorism, and the execution of Officer Petrov.

"I don't know who to trust anymore. Did you know that Glenn took the opportunity during the execution of Petrov to target us? Apparently, he felt he wasn't hired because of quotas instead of the fact that he just wasn't a good EMT. He was just a below-average volunteer who thought he was entitled to the job. And don't get me started on Randy."

"What about Randy?" Em asked.

"Well, Randy had been working with the FBI on investigating his business partner."

"Randy was working with the FBI?" Em raised her eyebrows in disbelief.

"It seems I wasn't the only one who had questions about Randy's business associate, Sergei Volkov, and his other businesses." Nick took a sip of his beer. "It went further than that, though. Randy told Maya that Volkov was part of a larger plot to destabilize our country by stoking the grievance of the right-wing militias and funneling weapons to them."

"Holy shit," Daniel said. "This goes deep."

"That's what I'm saying," Maya said. "I have no confidence in our organization anymore. I will not continue to risk my life while they sort out who is and isn't involved in this criminal conspiracy."

"The right-wing militia was not only dealing in weapons but also making and selling meth to fund their operations," Nick said. "Pastor Richter was helping them launder the money through the church through donations and creative accounting."

"Who knows how long they could have gotten away with fraud and money laundering in the name of Jesus," Maya said. "It makes me wonder if Alden knew about that or if he was just a faithful member of the church. He certainly came after me when they thought I turned in the pastor. But that's the problem, I don't know who to trust there anymore."

"I know I made the right decision to leave. From the sound of it, you might want to extend that leave," Em said.

"Yeah. I can't believe Jeff decided to take the acting chief's job, but if anyone can turn things around, it will be him. However, that is going to take time.

"The other thing I wanted to let you know is that I'm on the waiting list to check into the IAFF Center for Excellence. In hindsight, I should have done that instead of returning to work, but I thought I needed to be there.

"I have moments when I feel great, but I still can't sleep through the night. I guess I want to blame the recent events, but I think it's all of it. I've got to get some relief."

Daniel looked directly at Maya with his kind brown eyes. "It's about time. I was concerned when you came back, but I didn't want to say anything. As always, you surprised me with how well you kept it together."

"Thanks, Daniel."

"Besides, I'm going to convince you to work with us here so I can get some good calls! Here I am working in LA, and all I'm going on are chest pain and respiratory."

Maya laughed. She was never going to live down her reputation as a shit magnet.

"I love you guys, and I'm so glad I have friends like you. I don't think I could have survived this without you."

AFTERWORD

I found out in June of this year, that my paramedic coworker, April, had taken her life, I was shocked and devasted. A year prior I had tried to reach out to her, plant any seed that might take hold in her mind to help her find her way out of the dark place she was living. Others; friends; coworkers; and family tried, but no one could reach her.

April was strong. She was a professional and caring paramedic. She served in the military in Iraq. She was a devoted mother and a wife. She cared for her aging parents and provided love and support for her two kids and husband. On the surface, she didn't look like someone who would take her life.

Over the years, as a paramedic, I have known firefighters and paramedics who have taken their own lives. Often, there didn't seem to be any warning signs on the surface, but maybe if we had known what to look for, we might have seen something that would have let us know that the person working next to us was in trouble.

Times are changing. What was seen as stigmatizing is now being recognized as something that can be talked about, and it's okay to ask for help. If you or someone you know is struggling with mental health issues, seek help.

ABOUT THE AUTHOR

Lisa Parsons is an adventurer, writer, photographer, paramedic, conservationist, world traveler, and dog companion. She crafts stories with depth and creativity that are enhanced by real-world experience.

Her writing and photographs have been published in books, newspapers, magazines, and blogs in the Pacific Northwest and across the globe.

She has published the first two murder mystery books in her Emergence Series and is working on the third book, scheduled for release in 2025.

Lisa lives in Lake Tahoe, California, the perfect base camp for her next adventure.

For more information visit
www.lisaparsonsauthor.net

Aftermath: Murder • Adventure • Revenge in Lake Tahoe, Emergence Series Book I

Ambush: On the Streets of the Pacific Northwest, Emergence Series Book II

* 9 7 9 8 9 8 6 1 9 8 6 3 7 *